HIGH PRAISE FOR
THE CONTRARY BLUES

"Billheimer seasons his debut with quiet humor, warmly appealing characters, and enough inventive plot twists to make a Contrarian out of straighter arrows than Owen."
—*Kirkus Reviews*

"John Billheimer has written a mystery with a difference—it's got humor, sweetness, humanity. *The Contrary Blues* is terrific entertainment."
—John L'Heureux, author of *The Handmaid of Desire*

"This is a funny book, and, in Billheimer's hands, West Virginia may become a favorite destination."
—*San Jose Mercury News*

"John Billheimer's ear for dialogue and knowledge of his 'Contrary' folk make this an entertaining, powerful, and satisfying read. It's an outstanding first mystery—the first of many, I hope."
—Michael Z. Lewin, author of *Underdog*

"With humor as dark as the coal dust that clings to the buses that the town actually runs through the hills and hollows around Contrary, Billheimer sketches a sympathetic portrait of the town and its resources. . . . I hope to see Owen Allison in action again."
—*Gazette-Mail* (Charleston, W.V.)

"John Billheimer has a perfect ear for dialogue and Owen Allison is an unpredictable yet engaging hero. I genuinely enjoyed spending time with the West Virginia characters and setting in this impressive debut."
—Jeremiah Healy, author of *The Only Good Lawyer*

THE CONTRARY BLUES

BLUES

JOHN BILLHEIMER

To Cleise and David —
I hope you enjoy
the Contrary folk.

Thanks for
your support.

John Bill...

QUARRIER PRESS
Charleston, WV

Quarrier Press
Charleston, WV 25301

Original hardback published by St. Martin's Press
Original paperback published by Dell Publishing
Reprinted with permission by Quarrier Press

ISBN: 1-891852-25-6
(Formerly ISBN 0-440-23504-9)

Library of Congress Number: 2002094051

10   9   8 7 6 5 4 3 2 1

Printed in USA

Distributed by:
Pictorial Histories Distribution
1416 Quarrier Street
Charleston, WV 25301

For Carolyn, who still laughs a lot

THE CONTRARY CORPSE

"I DIDN'T RECKON on no killing."

Hollis Atkins stood in rolled-up bib overalls and a soaked T-shirt hosing water over the side of a shiny new minibus. He kept his eyes on the stream of water, not looking at the man in the checkered vest standing free of the spray.

Purvis Jenkins, the man in the vest, mopped the back of his neck with a handkerchief and said, "What killing? Weren't no killing."

Hollis directed the spray against the soapy windows of the bus. "Man's dead, ain't he?"

"Man got liquored up and tried to sleep it off next to the bone pile. Slag fumes got him. Used to happen quite a bit."

The spraying water rinsed soap down the side of the

bus, where it puddled in an oily film around Hollis's bare feet and exposed the name painted under the tinted windows: *The Contrary Comet,* written in a bright yellow script riding on the orange tail of a shooting star. Hollis rinsed the rear fender where it touched the tip of the star. "Don't happen no more. Local folks know not to go near the bone pile."

"Man wasn't local, Hollis. He didn't know."

Still not looking at his companion, Hollis bent to direct a jet of water at a gleaming yellow hubcap. "We got him liquored up. We knew."

"City fellow. Just wasn't used to corn liquor."

"Dammit, Purvis. You knew." Hollis directed the spray toward the puddle at his feet, splattering the oily film over the black asphalt.

Purvis Jenkins mopped his brow and stuffed his handkerchief halfway into the pocket of his open vest. "Hollis, that bus is already as bright as a baby's behind. Stop spraying that water and pay me some mind here."

Hollis picked up a bucket of soapy water and tugged the hose away from Purvis toward the rear of the bus.

Purvis twisted the valve controlling the flow of water to the hose. Spray spritzed and the hose went limp in Hollis's hands. "Let's review the bidding, Hollis. How many buses do you see here?"

Hollis pointed the dripping hose across the asphalt at the Quonset hut wedged between a stream and a jagged tree-covered slope. "Counting the one in the barn there?"

"Counting that one."

"There's two."

"And how many did we . . ." Purvis stopped and shook

his head. "No, let's be clear about this." He took a manila folder from under his arm and pointed it at Hollis. "How many did *you* charge the federal government for?"

"Twenty. But that was a mistake. Nobody caught the extra zero."

"Be that as it may, how many did the federal government pay for?"

Hollis shook the drips from the lip of the hose and began coiling it up. "Twenty."

"And are you personally prepared to give the feds back the nine-hundred grand they paid for the extra buses?"

Hollis coiled the hose tighter. "You're the mayor, Purvis. It was you and Mary Beth that decided to charge them for running twenty buses."

"Well now, Hollis, how'd it look if we charged them for buying twenty buses and then told them we were only running two?"

"They'd probably want their nine-hundred grand back."

"Along with the extra five-hundred grand they give us every year for drivers and maintenance."

"That wasn't my mistake. It was you and Mary Beth dreamed that up."

"Hollis, let's stop talking mistakes. That money is keeping Contrary on the map."

"But the buses don't exist."

Purvis tapped the manila folder in his hand. "They exist on paper. Which is all the federal government cares about."

"Then why'd they send that Mr. Armitrage?"

"He came down to audit our books once a year. Once a year, that's all. He just had to make sure everything added up so he could approve our invoices." Purvis waived his folder at Hollis. "First three years, all he did was complain about the drive down from D.C., sneak a few peeks down Mary Beth's dress, and add up the numbers."

"And they all added up."

"Slicker than snot on a doorknob."

"But not this year."

"This year's numbers added up just fine. Mary Beth knows her way around a computer. This year, though, Armitrage decided he should inspect the system. Ride the rubber. Feed the fare box. Count the change. We both know what happened then."

"I thought we weren't going to talk about no mistakes."

Purvis put his arm around Hollis and steered him out of the puddles. "It's important we learn from the experience, Hollis. Now, the fed's Mr. Armitrage was a man who couldn't find shit in a one-hole privy. It shouldn't have been too hard to show him as many buses as he needed to see."

"But we only had two to show."

"Hollis, a man gets on a bus, he don't know how many buses he missed or how many are coming later. He just sees the one he's on. All you got to do is follow the route and make sure one or two people get off and on. The feds don't expect full buses in a town the size of Contrary."

Hollis ducked out of Purvis's grasp and bent to roll

down his pantlegs. "He didn't get on no bus. Just stood there at the stop with his damn clipboard."

"I thought we'd gone over that." Purvis pointed his folder at the Quonset hut. "The bus you've got in the barn looks just like the one you've been washing. You just have to run a bus by the stop he's at every fifteen minutes like the schedule says until he gets on or gives up. Unless he's on board, it don't matter where the bus goes after it passes his stop. Send it around the block if you want. Just make sure it passes him on schedule and that there's a few passengers on board."

"And the driver," Hollis said.

"A driver, yes. Well now, Hollis, I'd say that's where the pig squeezed out of the poke."

"You told me somebody down from D.C. would expect to see niggra drivers."

"Black, Hollis. In D.C. they also expect you to call them black."

"There wasn't a lot to pick from. We got three, maybe four black families in the whole county."

Purvis shook his head. "Slim pickings don't excuse shit-stupid selection."

"I thought they'd all look alike to him."

"Hollis, you let Bobby Joe Buford drive the lead bus. Bobby Joe Buford don't look like any black man you're ever going to see outside an Action comic. He weighs three hundred pounds, has WVU shaved into his hair, and wears a gold ring in his left nostril. You couldn't find a driver's uniform to fit him, and if you could have, you would have had to slit the sleeve to fit it over the cast on his forearm that says *Fuck Penn State*."

"We taped over the *Fuck*."

"Well, that little disguise didn't fool nobody. The third time Bobby Joe wheeled his bus past the fed and his clipboard even Mr. Armitage's dim bulb flashed on."

Hollis mimicked the auditor's high-pitched squeal of discovery. " 'I've see that driver before,' he said, 'not more than half an hour ago.' "

"That's when he asked to count the day's passenger receipts and inspect all the buses."

"And that's when you invited him to stop by Pokey Joe's for some corn liquor. You told him Mary Beth would likely be there."

"Man just couldn't hold his liquor."

"It wasn't the liquor that killed him, Purvis."

"Let's not mine that seam again, Hollis. It was the fumes. Man picked the wrong place to sleep off his drunk."

"When I left, the man wasn't in shape to pick his nose, let alone a place to sleep a half mile away."

"Hollis, what's done is done. We got ourselves another problem today." Purvis took a letter from the manila folder. "The feds are sending somebody to finish Armitage's job."

"Thought his job was pretty much finished."

"He didn't have time to report back."

"Lucky for you."

"Lucky for you, too, Hollis. Lucky for all of us. Lucky for Contrary."

Hollis turned the water back on. "We gonna have visitors, guess I better wash down the other bus."

Purvis crimped the hose to stop the flow of water. "And Hollis. Listen now. This is important."

"I know. I'll find a few riders, too."

"I don't care about riders. If you use Bobby Joe Buford again, though, get at least one other driver. Just for contrast."

1

THE RETURN OF THE NATIVE

CONTRARY WASN'T EXACTLY what Owen Allison was expecting. The other mining towns he'd passed through on the drive down from D.C. had boarded-up store fronts and streets covered with thin layers of coal dust that shifted as he roared past. Here in Contrary, the main street glistened cleanly in the afternoon sun and the small shops all seemed open for business. Parked cars surrounded a creamy white Dairy Queen.

He spotted the red brick courthouse and pulled his convertible into a parking place across the street, in front of a lazily rotating barber pole and a window that advertised BARBER SHOP in block capital letters. Barber shop, he thought. Not a "styling emporium" with a cutesy name like "Shear Indulgence" or "Mane Attraction." He scratched at his shaggy beard. He'd give the barber shop a try if he finished his audit quickly enough. Everything he ate was beginning to taste like his moustache.

As he waited to cross the street, a gleaming minibus with a *Contrary Comet* logo passed in front of him. The driver, an enormous black man with a nose ring and a splotchy haircut, glared at Owen as the bus slowed, turned into a small traffic circle, and wheezed to a stop in front of the courthouse flagpole. A thin man with sandy hair and an ill-fitting tan suit got off the bus and walked across the manicured lawn and up the white courthouse steps.

Owen crossed the street and tried to close in on the bus to get a passenger count, but the tinted rear windows kept him from seeing inside. Owen swore under his breath. Four years with the department and he was back counting heads on a rural bus route. Fucking bureaucrats. He should have told them what they wanted to hear. But if he could do that, tell people what they wanted to hear, he wouldn't be with the department. He'd still be in California, still married to Judith.

The bus pulled away, expelling a smelly stream of black diesel exhaust that dissipated before it reached the flags flying overhead. Owen read the inscription on the state flag: *Montani Semper Liberi.* He remember the translation from his childhood. "Mountaineers are always free." Not if they work for the Department of Transportation, he thought as he started across the courthouse lawn.

The courthouse looked like Hollywood's idea of an antebellum Southern plantation, with whitewashed steps and white colonnades leading to a two-storey building of red-orange bricks. Two massive oak doors were flanked by large windows with stenciled block letters identifying the offices of the mayor and the public works department. A hand-lettered sign inside the main doorway pointed up a white-banistered stairway to the office of the McDowell County Transportation Agency.

The banistered stairway took Owen through a time warp from a world of rolltop desks and oak chairs to a world of partitioned cubicles and computer work stations. The *Contrary Comet* logo he'd seen on the side of the bus hung in bas-relief over a marble receptionist's desk that held a computer, a rack of bus schedules, a push-button telephone, and a striking blonde woman who looked as if she belonged in a travel ad. Leaning over the desk was a tall, balding man with rolled-up shirtsleeves and an unbuttoned vest that couldn't cover the beginnings of a pot belly. Both the woman and the man looked as if they were expecting him.

The balding man straightened and extended his hand, which enveloped Owen's. "You must be Owen Allison. I'm Purvis Jenkins, mayor of this fair city, and this here's my sister Mary Beth. Mary Beth's the heart and soul of the Contrary Comet. She makes up the schedules, cuts the checks, and can tell you anything you want to know about this here operation."

Owen pulled his hand free of Jenkins's grip and extended it to Mary Beth. "I'm looking forward to hearing all about it."

Mary Beth took his hand and smiled tentatively. "I'm at your service."

"Somebody else you should meet," Jenkins said. "Where the hell's Hollis?" he asked his sister. Then, before she could answer, he turned toward the cubicles and shouted, "Hollis!"

A shock of sandy hair appeared above the nearest partition. Owen recognized the man in the ill-fitting suit who had gotten off the bus as he'd arrived.

"Hollis here is a board member and our general factotum," Jenkins said. "Hollis, Mr. Allison's here from D.C. to finish the job that Mr. Armitrage started." Jenkins put his hand on Owen's shoulder. "Damn shame about your man Armitrage."

He wasn't my man, Owen started to say. Far from it. Instead, he nodded silently, took his shoulder out of Jenkins's reach, and shook hands with Hollis Atkins.

Mary Beth turned pale blue eyes on him. "We're all so sorry about Mr. Armitrage. Did he have any people?"

"An ex-wife somewhere. She didn't show up for the funeral."

"That's something, anyhow," Mary Beth said. "At least he didn't leave anybody depending on him."

There was a short, uneasy silence as the subject of Armitrage hung dead in the air.

"I'm still not clear on what happened," Owen said. "How can a man suffocate out of doors?"

"Sulphur fumes got him" Jenkins said. "Out Route 10 there's a bone pile where the local mines dump their shale waste. Been dumping there for years, good times and bad. The waste smolders and burns deep down. Every so often a tanked-up wino lured by the heat suffocates in the fumes while sleeping off a toot."

"Provides local preachers with a strong object lesson on the evils of drink," Hollis said. "They call it the devil's bone pile."

"Armitrage was drunk, then?" Owen asked.

"That was the report," Jenkins said.

"Mr. Allison," Hollis Atkins interrupted, "you got kin-folk in Barkley?"

"My mother lives there."

"Thought so." Hollis beamed. "You the same Allison that pitched for the Wildcats in the state championships twenty-odd years ago?"

Owen nodded, sensing that they were all happy the conversation had left Armitrage.

"Thought so," Hollis said. To Purvis Jenkins he added, "Sucker struck me out twice." He turned to Owen. "Remember?"

"Slider low and away," Owen said.

"You do remember then."

"No, that's the only pitch I ever struck anybody out with." He looked at Mary Beth. "They used to clock my fastball with an egg timer."

Hollis tugged at his shirtcuffs, which poked a good two inches beyond the sleeves of his tan jacket. "That slow floaty stuff set us down all day. You still playing ball?"

"Softball is all," Owen said. "I played Industrial League baseball for a while after college, but the other teams kept getting younger and faster."

"Always glad to see a West Virginia boy make a success in the outside world," Purvis Jenkins said as he moved forward and recaptured Owen's shoulder. "We're going to get along just fine."

Owen didn't try to shake free of Jenkins's grasp. If he were really making a success in the world, Owen thought, he wouldn't be down here counting buses. "Maybe you could show me around," he said to Mary Beth.

Jenkins kept his arm around Owen's shoulder as they

followed Mary Beth through the maze of partitions. Owen notice that most of the cubicles were empty. Hollis started to join them, but turned back when Jenkins reminded him that he had tasks to see to. As they left Hollis behind, Jenkins said, "So you're from West-by-God-Virginia. Well now, don't that take the sting out of the nettle? I declare, if the world got any smaller you could smash it with a baseball bat."

OWEN BENT OVER Mary Beth's chair to get a closer look at the computer screen. She wasn't wearing perfume, but her hair smelled of fresh violets. "That's our route map," she explained. "We've got four regular routes, plus the school runs."

Owen recognized the main road he'd followed down from D.C. The rest of the bus routes extended like spider legs from the main road, following switchbacks into the hills or meandering beside creek beds. Small square blips appeared at irregular intervals along the route lines. One of the blips jumped forward across the screen.

"Those little squares show the positions of our buses," Mary Beth explained. "They radio in their positions automatically."

"I'm surprised transponders work that well in this hill country," Owen said.

"We put them at the highest points along the routes," Jenkins said. "There's a clear sight line between every transmitter and our receiver."

Owen counted the blips. "I only see eight buses. Don't you have twenty?"

"Two are spares," Jenkins explained. "We use the rest

for school buses in the morning and Meals on Wheels during the afternoon. Those that don't have fixed routes don't show up on the screen. We send buses all over the county."

"Maybe Mr. Allison would like to see our monthly reports," Mary Beth said.

"Armitrage had the latest ones in his office," Owen said. "They all seem to add up just fine."

"My sister here knows her way around a computer," Jenkins said.

"I can see that."

Mary Beth turned her head from the computer screen, wet her lips, and asked, "Is there anything else I can show you?"

Owen was still leaning over her chair and their faces were inches apart. He considered the obvious answers to her question, censored them, and drew away. "Not right now, thanks. Is there someplace I can go to watch the buses operate?"

Mary Beth blinked and seemed to lose her composure for the barest moment, as if she'd expected some other answer. Maybe her question really was a come-on. Had he missed something?

"I can help you with that," Purvis said. He took Owen's elbow and started to lead him back through the maze of empty cubicles.

Owen turned back and held out his hand to Mary Beth. "Thank you for your help, Miss Jenkins."

"It's Hobbs, actually."

"Excuse me?" Her hand was cool in his.

"Hobbs is my married name."

"Oh, I didn't see a ring." Owen released her hand.

"I'm divorced."

"I'm sorry." He wasn't, but there was something in the way she said *divorced* that made him want to commiserate.

"So am I. Will you be staying long in Contrary?"

"He'll have to if we don't show him some buses soon," Purvis said, still trying to lead him out.

"I was going on to Barkley to visit my mother. Maybe I could stop on my way back if I have any more questions."

"You do that," she said.

"Yes, you do that," Purvis echoed, taking Owen's elbow again and pulling him away.

PURVIS JENKINS LED Owen Allison across the courthouse lawn to the traffic circle where Allison had seen the bus stop earlier. Jenkins crossed to the small island in the center of the circle and examined the BUS STOP sign affixed to the island's flagpole. "Number four bus should be along any minute," he announced to Owen.

As if on cue, a minibus with the *Contrary Comet* logo pulled into the traffic circle and chugged to a stop. As its doors wheezed open, Owen recognized the driver as the same burly black man who'd driven by earlier. With the bus door open, he could see that the design cut into the driver's hair spelled out WVU, and that he was wearing a massive forearm cast with a message printed on it.

Jenkins stood beside the open door. "Shall we get on?"

Owen took another look at the driver. "Something *Penn State*" was the message on the cast, but he couldn't make out what "something" was. "Let's wait for the next bus if you don't mind," he said to Jenkins.

The driver glared at him, levered the door shut, and the bus pulled away, trailing a dark stream of diesel exhaust.

"How much longer to the next bus?" he asked Jenkins.

"Shouldn't be too long this time of day."

A battered blue van filled with children followed the bus into the traffic circle, and a middle-aged woman wearing a flowered print dress got out of the passenger seat. "Afternoon, Purvis," she said. "Looks like we just missed the bus."

"Be another one along directly."

"This is where Hollis wanted us to bring the children to catch the bus, isn't it?"

Purvis looked up at the flags overhead, avoiding Owen's eyes. "You'll have to talk to Hollis about that, Millie."

"I'm sure this is where he said to come." She turned and called inside the van. "Missy, Wayne Evan, Susie, and Little Joe. Y'all get out here."

Four backpack-laden children scrambled out of the van. Owen judged that they were each about ten years old.

The woman lined the children up in front of the flag-pole. "Now I want y'all to wait right here for the next bus. You've got the money Mr. Hollis gave you?"

Each of the children held up a quarter. Missy's was knotted inside a soiled lace handkerchief.

"That's fine," the woman said. "You'll have to give those to the driver or he won't let you on his bus."

The woman got back in the van and smiled at Purvis. "We'll take the rest of the kids on up to the Piggly Wiggly. Like as not we can catch up with the bus that just left by that time. Won't do for it to be riding around empty."

As the van pulled away, a freckle-faced boy in the backseat waved his upraised middle finger at Purvis. Missy and Susie giggled and watched for Purvis's reaction.

Purvis studied the two flags overhead as if he wanted to redesign them. He cleared his throat loudly and addressed

Owen. "Millie's our third-grade teacher. Must be doing some sort of school project."

"Looks like some sort of project, all right."

Wayne Evan started to chase Little Joe around the flagpole. Missy squealed and tried to hit them with her knotted handkerchief as they passed.

Purvis signed. "Maybe you'd like to see the bus barn."

"Sounds like a good idea."

"I'll get my car and drive us out there. Won't be much activity. The buses are all out on the road." He watched Owen carefully. "The barn's out by Pokey Joe's. Bet it's been a long time since you've had real corn liquor."

When Owen failed to react, Purvis added, "Maybe I'll get Mary Beth to join us. We can show you the bone pile on the way."

2

THE LEAKY BUCKET BLUES

"You want to tell me what's going on?" Owen asked as Purvis backed his ten-year-old Dodge away from the curb.

"Got some stops to make first." Purvis drove in silence down Contrary's main street, passed two blocks of shops, and parked in front of a small frame house with a glassed-in front porch. A sign on the door read CONTRARY CLINIC.

"Might want to see this." Purvis took three pay envelopes from the glove compartment.

Owen followed Purvis inside. The glassed-in porch had been converted into a waiting room that was jammed with patients, most of whom seemed to be over sixty or under ten. A grizzled miner wearing a grimy Consolidated Coal cap spit into a handkerchief, while the woman beside him, probably his daughter and at least sixty herself, stared impassively ahead. A pregnant woman clamped a baby stroller between her knees while she held the arm of a thumb-sucking toddler. A young boy with his leg in a much-autographed cast propped it on a round hassock, impaling several well-thumbed magazines on the cast's metal heel. The antiseptic smell reminded Owen of waiting rooms where he had held his mother's hand in Barkley.

A woman wearing a worn gray cardigan over a white nurse's uniform came from the main house into the waiting room, greeted Purvis, and said, "Something ailing you today?"

"I'm fine, thank you, Rosie." Purvis held out the three pay envelopes. "Mary Beth sent these over."

Rosie pushed the envelopes deep into the pocket of her cardigan. "High time, I'd say."

"Looks like Doc Pritchard's got his hands full today."

"Yesterday, today, and tomorrow, too, most likely."

"This here's Owen Allison, out of Barkley by way of D.C. He's down here looking around."

"Pleased to meet you. I've been to D.C. They've got some good-size hospitals there."

"Looks as if you could use a little more room here."

"We make do."

Purvis took a wrinkled scrap of paper out of his pocket. "Wonder if Doc Pritchard could re-up this prescription for me, Rosie. I went through it powerful fast."

Rosie stuffed the scrap of paper in her pocket alongside the envelopes. "We'll see." She opened the door to the interior of the house and called to the pregnant woman, "Mrs. Straub, Doctor's ready for Dougie now."

The pregnant woman leveraged herself out of her chair

and pushed her stroller toward the door with one hand, dragging the thumb-sucker with the other.

Purvis patted the glass door of the porch/waiting room. "Got this here house for the back taxes when the owner died. Glassing in the porch was my idea."

When Owen didn't respond, he continued. "We help pay Rosie and Doc Pritchard out of the town funds to keep them around. Only town in the county with its own clinic."

Rosie returned with a fresh prescription and handed it to Purvis. "Take it easy on that stuff. There's enough there to kill you and the horse you rode in on." She smiled at Owen. "Nice meeting you, Mr. Allison. Enjoy your stay in Contrary."

PURVIS TURNED HIS Dodge around and made another trip down Contrary's main street. This time he made two stops, one at the red-brick police station to deliver more pay envelopes, and another at the corner pharmacy to fill the prescription he'd picked up at the clinic. He came out of the pharmacy, tucked the plastic pill bottle into his vest pocket, squeezed behind the wheel of his car, and said, "How about we call it a day and go out to Pokey Joe's?"

"How about we go to your garage and look at some buses?"

Purvis turned the key in the ignition. "Why bother? Seen one bus, seen 'em all."

"It's pretty clear that's what you'd like me to think."

Purvis turned off the ignition. The engine sputtered and died. "What's that supposed to mean?"

"What was that little show back there with the third-graders?"

"Oh, that. Hollis thought you might have a better opinion of us if we beefed up the ridership stats."

"Hollis doesn't strike me as a man who does a lot of thinking on his own."

"All right. We both thought the buses would look better with a few riders. We've been running a little shy lately."

"I know. I've been reviewing your records."

Purvis restarted the car and pulled away from the curb. "Well then, I don't have to tell you about it. Let's head on out to Pokey Joe's."

"What about the buses?"

Purvis stopped to wait as a coal train rumbled by, trailing plumes of sooty dust. "Truth to tell, riders aren't the only thing we're shy of."

"What's that supposed to mean?"

"We're a little light on buses, too."

Owen braced himself against the passenger door. "How light?"

"Two."

"So you've been running without two spares?"

The caboose passed and the crossing gate rose, sounding a series of warning bells. Purvis shook his head. "Fifteen coal tenders. Time was when the N & W had fifty cars on that run."

"We're talking buses here, Purvis, not trains. You're saying you're only running eighteen buses?"

"Not exactly. We're light eighteen. We're only running two."

"My God, man. The Department of Transportation is paying you to run twenty buses. What happened to the rest of them?"

"You might say there's been a clerical error."

"Clerical error?"

"Hollis slipped a digit in the invoice and you paid it. It was an honest mistake."

"You've been running four years. That's way past the statute of limitations on honest mistakes. One year might be an honest mistake. Four is out-and-out fraud."

Purvis bounced the car across the railroad tracks. "Let's not rush to judgment. A slipped digit don't amount to fraud. Nobody's lining their pockets here. The money goes right into the town's general fund."

"And where's it go from there?"

"You seen some of it this afternoon. We run the clinic, pay the police chief, keep the town going. Takes cash to run a town like Contrary. We lost our tax base when big coal pulled out. You drove down on Route 10. You seen what's happened to the other coal town around here. Picked over and boarded up. Nothing more than piss holes by the pavement."

Purvis turned off the main highway onto a narrow road that followed a creek bed. "But it's not going to happen to Contrary. Not while I'm mayor."

Owen did the arithmetic. "That's five-hundred grand a year. Plus whatever the buses cost in the first place. You must pay yourself a hell of a salary."

"Same salary for the past ten years. Twenty-five grand a year. Hard to tell who's cheating who. Time was when being a mayor meant something. I mind the first election I ever voted in. Kennedy was running for president against Humphrey in the Democratic primary. His folks scoured the hills buying up votes. Sold mine for two bits. Know what I got for my vote for mayor?"

"You sold that, too?"

"Hell, yes. To Short-Deck Riordan for two dollars and fifty cents. See, a vote for Contrary's mayor was worth ten times what a vote for president went for, 'cause the mayor handed out so many local jobs. County sheriff handed out even more. That was the real plum. Votes for sheriff got up as high as five bucks apiece when the race was close. But that was when we still had a tax base to support the jobs."

"You've still got the tax base. It just comes from farther away."

"It don't go so far, though. Costs a lot more to run a town now than it did then."

They'd left Contrary well behind. Purvis ground his car's gears as the narrow road forked upward past a yellow BUS STOP sign. "Whole damn state's built on a slant," he said.

Purvis was taking it slow, feeling his way along, not driving like somebody who really knew the roads. Finally, he said, "Two buses is all we really need. They take the kids to school in the morning and ship the old folks around in the middle of the day. You're willing to pay for lots of buses we don't need. I don't see you've got any call to complain if we put the money toward things we do need."

Purvis pulled the Dodge over to the side of the road. "This here's the bone pile where your man Armitrage died."

Owen stepped out of the car onto a path of matted broom grass. The shale waste dumped by the local mines fell away from the path to the creek bed far below. The smell of burning sulphur prickled Owens's nostrils. "What the hell was Armitrage doing here in the middle of nowhere?"

"Nobody knows for sure. Pokey Joe's is just around the

bend yonder." Purvis waved his hand toward the bend. "Sheriff thinks he was trying to clear his head, walk off a drunk."

Owen scaled a flat piece of shale into the void. "Long walk for a drunk. Did Armitrage know what you've been up to?"

Purvis moved up behind Owen and nudged him toward the edge of the bone pile. "Meaning no disrespect, but your man Armitrage couldn't find his pecker with a magnifying glass and both hands free. He just checked our addition and went on approving our invoices."

Owen felt Purvis crowding him toward the steep slate slope. His shoes slipped on the grass and he stuck out his arms, looking for support. When he found none, he sat down hard and dug in his heels, stopping himself just before he hit the shale.

"Watch it there," Purvis said. "Slope's a little slippery." He offered Owen his hand. "You wouldn't want to end up like your man Armitrage."

Owen ignore the extended hand. He wasn't sure whether Purvis had pushed him, but he certainly hadn't helped when he was off balance and flailing. He got to one knee and stood up. "Armitrage wasn't my man."

"I meant no offense. Damn shame he had to die, is all."

"Damn shame for your little scheme, you mean."

"There's that, too," Purvis said. He opened the door on the driver's side of the Dodge. "Still want to drive out to the garage?"

"Not much point. Seen two buses, you've seen them all."

Purvis slammed the door. "You got that right."

★   ★   ★

THE ONLY LIGHT in Pokey Joe's roadhouse came from a fluorescent lamp over the bar, neon signs advertising Budweiser and Miller Lite, and the thin slits of late afternoon sun that forced their way through louvered blinds and past black lunch buckets sitting on windowsills under the neon signs. Four smudge-faced miners crunched peanut shucks underfoot as they slid shuffleboard pucks along the polished table perpendicular to the bar.

In a dark corner booth, Owen nursed a beer silently while Purvis sipped corn liquor from a jelly glass and described the medical, police, refuse, and street-cleaning services Contrary was buying with their bus money. Owen had nearly finished his beer when Mary Beth Hobbs and Hollis Atkins squeezed into the booth. Hollis had shed his ill-fitting suit for khakis and a plaid workshirt, while Mary Beth had changed into jeans and a denim jacket that covered a white cotton blouse.

"He knows about the buses," Purvis said as soon as Mary Beth and Hollis were seated.

Mary Beth smiled tentatively with what Owen took to be relief.

"It wasn't Bobby Joe Buford again, was it?" Hollis asked.

"No, Hollis, it wasn't Bobby Joe. It was Millie Stauder and her third-graders."

"I gave them all the right change," Hollis said.

"Did you tell him where the money is going?" Mary Beth asked.

"I showed him the clinic and the police station. I was starting to tell him the rest when you two came." He turned to Owen. "None of the money is lining our pockets. It all stays right here in Contrary. Mary Beth keeps the books. She can show you exactly where all the money goes."

"I'm sure she can," Owen said. "Just this afternoon she showed me twenty buses on her computer."

Mary Beth fiddled with the top button of her blouse. "I'm sorry," she said.

"No need to apologize," Purvis said. "Lemme explain how all this works." Purvis went to the bar and returned with four empty jelly glasses and a Chivas Regal bottle filled with a suspicious-looking clear liquid. "Don't be fooled by the fancy label," he said, pointing to the bottle. "This here's genuine white lightning."

He lined the four empty jelly glasses up in front of Hollis and stood behind him, holding the bottle. "Now, Hollis's uncle made the batch of liquor that filled this bottle. Been moon-shining for forty-odd years. Hollis here helps with the production. Before he can enjoy it, though, there's some has to be doled out." Purvis leaned over Hollis's shoulder and filled one of the jelly glasses. "First off, some goes to the local law to pay them for looking the other way." He shoved the filled glass in Owen's direction, well out of Hollis's reach.

" 'Course, some's going to get lost in the delivery process." Purvis sloshed a little of the clear liquor onto the table, soaking the cigarette butts in the shallow ashtray.

"And then the runners keep a little for their risk." Purvis poured another glassful, reached across Hollis's shoulder, and shoved it toward his own seat.

"Finally, Pokey Joe buys a case to sell and keeps a little for himself." Purvis filled the third glass and shoved it out of Hollis's reach toward Mary Beth. "You get your fill," he said to Owen and Mary Beth, "but there's precious little left for Hollis." He splashed about an inch of liquor into the last jelly glass and left it sitting in front of Hollis. "But it was Hollis here put all the effort into it in the first place."

Purvis returned to his seat, picked up the glass he'd poured, and offered a toast. "To your wives and sweethearts. May they never meet." He tilted his head back and took a long gulp of moonshine.

Owen sipped from his glass. The liquid burned in his throat. Mary Beth, who had barely lifted her glass during Purvis's toast, shoved the liquor away untouched.

"Reba, honey," Purvis shouted at the barmaid. "Bring Mary Beth here a Coke."

Purvis surveyed the table. "Now our town's a little like Hollis's moonshine route. We work hard here and collect a lot of money in taxes, but we got to pour it into a bucket and ship it to Washington before we can get any use out of it. And the bucket it goes in leaks like a sieve. And everybody wants a ladleful before it gets back to us."

Purvis held up the empty Chivas Regal bottle. "Congress takes some for their salaries. Some they ship to old folks in Florida. Some they give to folks like Owen here to follow the bucket around and make sure nobody without a proper ladle gets any."

He reached across the table and used his handkerchief to mop up the liquor he'd spilled around the ashtray. "And half of it leaks out God knows where."

Purvis stuffed the damp handkerchief back into his vest pocket. "By the time the bucket gets back to us, there's not enough left to wet a red ant's whistle. And if there was, sure as shit there'd be some regulation that said we had to wet a black ant's whistle first."

"Amen to that," Hollis said.

Purvis turned to Owen. "Now I've never been able to figure out why we have to ship our money all the way to Washington, take their leavings, and follow their say-so in spending it. Seems like we ought to be able to spend our own money any way we want. To take care of our own with it. That's all we're doing with the bus money."

"It's fraud," Owen said. "Out-and-out fraud."

"Fraud's an ugly word, Owen," Purvis said. "We're just taking care of our own."

"You're misusing funds clearly earmarked for buses. How do you know what's really best for your people? What gives you the right to play God?"

"Hell, Owen," Purvis said, "I'm not playing God. God doesn't give a shit about Contrary. He's an absentee landlord here, just like the big coal companies. God's willing to let Contrary starve. Let it go under like the rest of the coal towns on Route 10."

"It's got to stop."

"If we stop now, we go to jail and Contrary goes down the tubes. And your department stands to get a very public black eye."

"I can't let it go on."

"All you got to do is sign off on our invoices," Purvis said. "Pretend you're Armitrage and don't know any better."

"Armitrage is dead."

"So maybe he's not your best role model. Look, Owen. It's not your money. It's not your worry."

"You're talking to the wrong guy."

"Aren't you the guy that approves our invoices now?"

Owen picked at the label of an empty beer bottle. "No offense, but this job counting your buses isn't exactly a plum assignment. My bosses gave it to me as punishment because I refused to put a pretty face on research results they didn't like. If I wouldn't roll over for them, what makes you think I'll sign off on something I know is wrong?"

"Look here, Owen. We won't insult you by offering you money." Purvis paused, leaving an opening for Owen in case he didn't find a bribe all that insulting. When Owen didn't respond, Purvis added, "Besides, the money's pretty much spoken for already, what with the clinic, police, and all. But you'd be doing your fellow West Virginians here in Contrary a real big favor, and we'd be awful grateful."

Purvis placed both hands palms down on the table. "That right, Hollis?"

"Powerful grateful."

"That right, Mary Beth?"

Mary Beth stared at the glass between Purvis's palms.

Purvis rose and held up the empty Chivas bottle. "Hollis, let's you and me see if Reba's got any more from this same batch. Leave these young folks alone for a minute."

"What do you mean, young folks?" Hollis said. "I'm the same age as them."

"We'll be right back." Purvis led Hollis to the bar.

Owen nodded toward Mary Beth's Coke. "You're not drinking?"

"I'm a recovering alcoholic."

"I'm sorry. This probably isn't the best place to recover."

"Pokey Joe's doesn't tempt me, if that's what you mean. I never liked liquor much. I drank mostly to keep up with my husband."

"It didn't work?"

"If it had worked, I'd still be drinking." She looked at his glass. "You're not drinking much yourself."

"Low tolerance for moonshine."

"Had lots of it?"

"A couple of sips from a concoction my dad kept in a Seagram's bottle tucked in the back of a kitchen cabinet. I was a college freshman who thought he was mixing Seven and Sevens. My folks found me passed out on the kitchen floor the next morning."

"Sounds like low tolerance to me."

She was silent. He couldn't think of anything to say, but he wanted to say something, to keep the connection going. "That was a long time ago," he said. He waited for a response. When she still said nothing, he added, "Beer's okay. I mean, I can drink it okay. But I still steer clear of this other stuff."

Purvis and Hollis returned with another bottle of clear liquor. This one was labeled J & B Scotch.

"You'd think they'd store it in vodka bottles," Owen said. "At least that's the right color."

"That's the first place the revenooers look," Purvis said, offering to top off Owen's glass.

"No more for me. I'm still working my first glass."

Purvis raised his own glass in a short salute. "Work a little harder. We need to convince you what we're doing is good for Contrary."

"Oh, I don't doubt that."

"That's something, at least," Purvis said.

Hollis drained his glass. "That's something all right. Armitage didn't even believe that."

Owen took a sip from his glass. "I thought you said Armitrage hadn't found out about your shenanigans."

Purvis glared at Hollis, then looked kindly at Owen. "No, I believe I said Armitrage couldn't find his pecker and a magnifying glass and both hands free."

Hollis made a sound somewhere between a laugh and a hiccup. "Not even if a bulldog was biting the end of it."

The word *bulldog* echoed in Owen's head. He wasn't sure whether Hollis had said it twice or if he had heard it twice. Hollis's lips were moving, but Owen couldn't make out what he was saying. It was as if he were talking underwater.

He turned in panic toward Mary Beth. She frowned, looking worried. Concerned, he thought muzzily. She's concerned for me.

He reached out to Mary Beth with an oddly disconnected arm, spilling his glass. Then he pitched forward, blacking out before his head hit the table.

3

HIGHWAY ROBBERY

OWEN'S VISION SWAM in and out of focus. He could make out close-up objects, but anything more than an arm's length away was a blur. He was jack-knifed into a too-short couch, wrapped in a frayed quilt covered with dull orange suns whose triangular yellow rays stabbed at his stomach. From his position on the couch, he could make out a varnished wooden floor and the fringed edge of a striped throw rug.

Beyond the throw rug, a filmy figure in white seemed to be sending semaphore signals with a dim mirror from the far corner of the room. He blinked once, closed his eyes, and thought about filmy figures in white, considering the possibilities. Angels, mummies, Casper the Friendly Ghost, and his ex-wife on their wedding day. To the best of his knowledge, none of them knew or needed Morse code.

He opened his eyes and willed them to focus. The

filmy vision was Mary Beth Hobbs. She was curled up in an armchair, wearing a white terrycloth robe and reading a hardback book with a glassine cover that reflected light from the lamp at her side as she turned the pages.

Owen lay still, watching her. She turned a page and adjusted her reading glasses. He moved his hand under the quilt, taking a quick inventory. He was wearing pants and a shirt, but his belt and tie were gone.

She sensed his movement, looked up, smiled, and asked, "How are you feeling?"

"Not good." His larnyx felt fuzzy, but it seemed to work. "Like the entire Russian army marched across my tongue in its stocking feet."

She set aside her book and reading glasses. "That's a good one. I hear it a lot at my AA meetings."

"I think W. C. Fields said it first."

"He probably heard it at an AA meeting."

Mary Beth padded barefoot to a small kitchen alcove, rummaged in her refrigerator, and began mixing a drink. Owen heard an egg crack and the clink of glassware as she put away a small bottle of Tabasco sauce. She returned with a tall glass of murky red liquid and two small round tablets. "Take this. It'll help."

His hand trembled as he reached out and returned it to the quilt. "What was in that drink Purvis gave me?"

"Moonshine. You said you couldn't handle it."

"Just moonshine?"

"What else would you expect?" When he still didn't take the glass, she said, "Oh, for heaven's sake," lifted the liquid to her lips, swallowed, and offered him the glass again. "It's safe. Satisfied?"

He sipped gingerly from the glass, feeling the thick liquid coat his throat with a tangy film.

She held out the two tablets. "Take these with it."

"What are those?"

"Aspirin."

He remembered the prescription Purvis had picked up earlier and hesitated again.

Mary Beth closed her fist and jammed the tablets into the pocket of her terrycloth robe. "Don't take the aspirin then." The action loosened her robe and Owen could see a wisp of slip.

She stood over the couch, staring down at him. "If we were really the kind of people you think we are, you wouldn't be alive to think it."

"I'm sorry. I'm not processing things very well. I'll just get on the road to Barkley." He swung his legs to the floor and tried to sit straight up. The room tilted. "Whoa."

"It's nearly midnight. There's no point in going anywhere tonight. Even if you could." Mary Beth took his empty glass back to the kitchen and returned with two cold, damp washcloths. She knelt beside him, pressed one washcloth against the nape of his neck, leaned his head back, and smoothed the other against his forehead.

"Umm," Owen murmured. "Where'd you learn to do that?"

"Lots of practice with my husband." She massaged his forehead through the damp cloth.

"Why'd he ever leave?"

"I left him. The government you work for took him to Vietnam and taught him to do drugs, crawl through tunnels, and kill people. When he got back to Contrary, there wasn't much killing to be done. He could still drop acid, drink, and crawl around in holes, though."

She turned the washcloth over and placed it back on his forehead, continuing her massage. "He'd pick coal out of the local mines by day and drink away the profits by night. I was going down that hole with him until I found AA."

She removed the washcloth from his forehead, folded it in quarters, and laid it on her lap. "What about you? Ever been married?"

"Divorced."

"Any kids?"

"None. My wife wanted to wait until we were both what she called established. She got herself established. I didn't."

"What happened?"

"I had a little consulting firm out in California. It went belly up." Owen tried to straighten himself and the washcloth on his neck fell between his back and the couch. He fished the cloth out and handed it to Mary Beth, catching another glimpse of her slip.

"My firm was planning transportation up and down the state. Little jobs, mostly. Signal timing, route layout, stuff like that. People in Santa Clarita came to me with a big job. They wanted to get federal money to build a light rail system. Hired me to put together a plan and predict ridership. I laid it out on paper and figured it would attract about twenty-thousand riders a day. They thought they'd need at least forty-thousand riders to get federal funding and asked me to bump up my forecast. I said no way. They cut me off at the pockets and gave the job to another consultant who predicted the system would carry, big surprise, forty-thousand riders."

Owen shrugged. "When they jerked the contract I had to lay off people. Then the state went into hock, so there wasn't much money around for consultants. I moved to Washington to work for the feds, my wife stayed in California to climb the corporate law ladder. We thought the separation would be temporary. Turned out to be permanent."

"What happened to the light rail system?"

"Santa Clarita got the federal money it needed and built the system. Carries twenty-thousand people a day, about what I predicted. County taxes and the highway fund took a big hit to cover what the fare box couldn't."

"How much?"

"Costs about twenty million a year."

"And you're worried about a measly five-hundred grand for Contrary?"

"My signature wasn't on the Santa Clarita report."

Mary Beth puffed out her lower lip in a half frown. "Sounds like highway robbery to me."

"How'd you get mixed up in this?"

"When my marriage broke up I had to find some way to make a living. I moved to Huntington, waitressed during the day, and took night school courses in accounting and computers at Marshall. Learned to balance ledgers, found out I was good at it. Never got a degree, but got what I needed to do what I do. Came back to Contrary and went to work for Purvis."

"You are good at it, you know."

"At first it bothered me, backing and filling to cover

Hollis's mistake. Keeping two sets of books. Moving all that money around." Mary Beth leveled her eyes on Owen's face. "Then I figured, what the hell, it's a payback for Stony. For what the federal government did to my husband. And, like Purvis said, it's our tax money anyhow. Isn't it?"

"Comes from gasoline taxes in the highway trust. It's exactly what you said. Highway robbery."

If she found his remark funny, she didn't show it. "We're putting the money to good use," she said.

The last thing Owen wanted to do was argue with her. "What happened when Armitrage caught on?"

"He wanted money. Lots of it." She spread her hands apart as if she were relating a fish story and her robe pulled open at the neck. "Purvis took him to Pokey Joe's. To negotiate."

"Same as me."

"Not the same as you. You didn't even nibble when Purvis mentioned money. Armitrage jumped right in. Wanted half of what we were getting."

"But you wouldn't give it to him."

"We didn't have it to give. It's mostly all spoken for already. Purvis explained all that. But the drunker Armitrage got, the more money he wanted."

Owen waited for more.

"When Armitrage saw he wasn't going to get what he wanted, he shifted his sights. Suggested we expand the system. Add ten buses. He'd approve it so long as we funneled him the extra money."

"What did Purvis say to that?"

"I think he would have worked it out."

"Don't you know?"

"It never came to that. Armitrage kept upping the ante. Asked for money up front." Mary Beth shuddered slightly. "He even wanted me thrown into the bargain."

"Jesus Christ."

"I walked out at that point."

"I'm sorry."

"Don't be. It had nothing to do with you."

"He worked for the same people I work for."

"Any fool can see you're not like Armitrage."

"That's the nicest thing anybody's said about me today." She traced a finger gently along his eyebrows. "Anybody ever tell you you have hickory eyes?"

He kissed her fingertip. "That's even nicer."

She kissed him. Her tongue tasted like Tabasco.

Owen fumbled at the belt of her robe. The Tabasco reminded him of pills in her pocket and he pulled away.

"What's the matter?" she asked.

"I know why I'm doing this," he said. "I'm not sure why you're doing it."

She gathered her robe around her and backed away from him. "Then we're not doing anything."

"I'm sorry," he said. "I can't promise you everything you want."

"You don't have the faintest idea what I want."

He knew better than to say what he was thinking, but he said it anyway. "I wanted to be sure we weren't bargaining for buses."

"You're seventeen different kinds of a fool. This isn't about buses."

"I'm sorry."

"So am I." She stood up. "Purvis will come by in

the morning to take you to your car." She turned off the reading lamp and went out through a door behind the couch.

Owen tried to find a position on the small couch that wouldn't leave a permanent crick in his neck. She'd called him seventeen different kinds of a fool. He counted twice that many before he fell asleep.

OWEN AWOKE TO find a hulking figure looming over him. The figure blocked out the morning sun and carried some kind of club. Owen swung his feet to the floor and shoved himself to a sitting position out of range of the club. Startled, the figure took a step backward, dropped the club to his side, and shrank in Owen's eyes to the size of a teenage boy wearing blue jeans, a gray sweatshirt, and a baseball cap with its bill twisted backward. He was carrying an aluminum baseball bat.

They stared at each other for five seconds before the boy asked, "What're you doing here?"

"I got a little drunk last night."

The boy raised the bat level with his waist. "My daddy gets drunk. But he don't sleep here no more."

Owen pulled gently at the barrel of the bat. "Let me see that."

The boy let go.

"I can't get used to aluminum bats," Owen said.

"That's what my daddy says."

Owen returned the bat and held out his hand. "My name's Owen Allison."

"Mine's Stuart Hobbs. Actually it's Jeb Stuart, but Jeb is kind of a hillbilly name."

"Jeb Stuart's not a name to be ashamed of," Owen said.

The boy smiled, glad to have his namesake recognized. "Not many people know that anymore."

"I see you've met Stuart." Mary Beth was balancing herself against the back of the couch as she put on a pair of flats. "I'm taking Stuart to baseball practice. Purvis will come by for you shortly."

"You practice before school?" Owen asked Stuart.

"Some of us work the mines after school. I help out my dad from time to time."

"What position do you play?"

"Catcher. But I'm only a sophomore. Coach says he might let me pitch next year."

"Mr. Allison pitched for Barkley," Mary Beth said.

"Maybe you can show me some stuff," Stuart said.

"I'd like that."

Mary Beth told Stuart to wait in the car. When he had gone, she turned to Owen. "You'll do what you think best about the buses. I just want you to know I'm not ashamed of anything I've done."

"I want to see you again."

She stopped with her hand on the doorknob. "Then you probably will."

OWEN WAS STILL sitting on the couch when Purvis came through the door without knocking. Purvis surveyed the rumpled quilt and said, "That couch don't look like the most comfortable place in the house to sleep."

"Where'd you expect me to sleep?"

"No need to be hostile, son. I'm here to deliver you from temptation."

Owen followed Purvis to his battered Dodge. Hollis

was leaning against it, smoking a cigarette. He opened the passenger door for Owen and climbed into the backseat.

They drove in silence past the bone pile. When they passed Pokey Joe's, Owen said, "Mary Beth tells me Armitrage tried to negotiate a deal."

Purvis snorted. "Man had the negotiating skills of a blind mule that knows 'Gee,' but hasn't learned 'Haw.' I'd try a little give and take, but he only knew take and take. When we wouldn't meet his price, he wanted Mary Beth thrown into the bargain."

"Followed her out to the parking lot and tried to rape her," Hollis said.

"She didn't tell me that," Owen said.

"She wouldn't," Purvis said. "She likes to think she can take care of herself. Hollis and I had to pull him off her."

"He wasn't so tough after that," Hollis said.

"We had him dead to rights," Purvis said. "Assault with a friendly weapon. I let on my cousin was sheriff, and Armitrage came to terms pretty quick. It's tough to drive a hard bargain with your dick dangling in the breeze and a woman ready to yell rape."

"So you came to an agreement with Armitrage," Owen said.

"Let's just say he was willing to cooperate," Purvis said. " 'Course, that's all pus out of the pimple now he's dead."

Owen wondered if Mary Beth had been setting him up for a rape charge the night before. He imagined Purvis bursting through the door, flashbulbs popping, the minute her robe opened. Maybe he wasn't seventeen different kinds of a fool after all. Maybe only sixteen.

"Armitrage couldn't believe we weren't pocketing the money," Hollis said.

"I can't imagine why," Owen said.

"No need to take that tone with us, son," Purvis said. "We showed you where the money's going."

"You showed me phony buses on a computer screen, phony riders at a bus stop, and phony numbers on your Reg 15 reports. For all I know, you showed me phony patients at a phony clinic. It looks just like any other house on the street."

Purvis bumped his Dodge over the railroad crossing, turned onto Contrary's main street, and drove past the courthouse and Owen's parked car. He pulled to a stop in front of the glassed-in porch of the Contrary Clinic, reached over Owen, and shoved his car door open.

"You think the clinic's a fake?" Purvis said. "Just march on up there and tell Rosie you want to watch Doc Pritchard handle the patients. Tell her I said it was okay. Ask Doc some college-boy questions. Get him to write you a prescription in that scribbly hand of his."

Owen got out and stood beside the door. He could see patients sitting in the glassed-in waiting room.

"Go on," Purvis said. "What are you waiting for?"

"It's all right," Owen said. He got back in the car and closed the passenger door.

"Son," Purvis said, "you got to decide where you're going to put your trust. You going to trust your eyes, or some fool federal regulation that says we ought to be running empty buses from here to hell and gone?"

Purvis pulled away from the curb. "You want to help people, you help them direct. Cut out the middle man. You give to United Fund, the chairman takes his cut and flies off to Bora Bora with his secretary. Half your money goes up her skirt. You got a hundred dollars to help the poor, best thing to do is go out in the street and give ten dollars to the first ten panhandlers you see."

"Ain't no panhandlers in Contrary," Hollis said.

"Damn straight," Purvis said. "Won't be so long as I'm mayor."

Nobody said anything as they drove the four blocks back to the center of town. Purvis pulled his car up in front of the courthouse, parked beside a fire hydrant, and turned toward Owen, asking, "Well, what do you think?"

"It's dishonest."

"Son, you were honest in Santa Clarita and they fired you. You were honest with the DOT brass, and they sent you down here to count buses. Appears to me you should have figured out by now that honesty isn't your best policy."

Owen didn't answer. Mary Beth must have told Purvis about Santa Clarita. Either they'd talked this morning or Purvis was listening last night. Maybe he was only fifteen kinds of a fool. He opened the passenger door.

"At least do this," Purvis said. "At least think on it. Take some time. Give us a week to get all our peckers pointed in the same direction. Maybe I can find us some cut-rate buses. Deal?"

What the hell, Owen thought. How many different kinds of fool could there be? "I'll give you a week." He edged out of the car. "But no more."

Owen walked toward the barber shop where he'd left his car a day earlier. He remembered promising himself a haircut and beard trim before he left Contrary, and he was beginning to feel like Rip Van Winkle. He watched the barber pole beckon lazily as he lowered his convertible top. Then he got in his car, slammed the door shut, and backed out of his parking place. The haircut could wait until he got home. He didn't want anyone in Contrary holding a razor near his neck.

4

THE PINK EDGE

STONY HOBBS HAD RECOGNIZED the bearded man in Purvis Jenkin's car as the same one he'd seen drinking with Mary Beth and Hollis the night before at Pokey Joe's. He'd watched from the porch of the Contrary Clinic as the man got out of the parked car, stared at the clinic, turned, and sat back down in the passenger seat.

"Now there's a man who must have heard about Doc Pritchard's bedside manner," Stony rasped to Pritchard's nurse Rosie.

Rosie looked up from the bill she was preparing. "How's that?"

Stony described the way the man had gotten out of Purvis's car, taken a step toward the clinic, changed his mind, and returned to the car. It was an effort to talk and his voice sounded like sandpaper scratching. "Tall, bearded fellow. You seen him before?"

"Sounds like the man who was in here yesterday with Purvis. Down from D.C."

"Fixing to move in?"

"Don't think so. Something to do with buses, according to Purvis."

"Umm." Stony said, saving his voice. If it had to do with buses, he could find out more about the man from Hollis.

Rosie finished the bill. "That'll be forty-five dollars."

"Good Christ," Stony said. "All Doc did was look down my throat and put a price on an operation. He didn't even give me no medicine."

"That's what an office visit costs nowadays. Been a while since you seen us."

"At those prices, it'll be a while before I see you again." Stony took a twenty and two tens from his wallet, then fished five crumpled one-dollar bills from his overall pockets and smoothed them on the counter. He glanced around the full waiting room. "Prices don't seem to be hurting your business none."

"Insurance, mostly. All the company miners have it."

Stony snapped his wallet shut. "You know I ain't no company miner."

"Wouldn't hurt you to think on it, what with your throat problem."

"Ain't got insurance. Ain't going to get it. Not if it means picking coal for somebody else. I got my own coal to mine."

"It's too bad, is all. The operation won't be cheap."

"This visit wasn't cheap."

"You'll do what the doctor says, though, won't you? Have it cut out, I mean."

"Doc said he didn't think it was serious."

Rosie came out from behind the counter so that she stood beside Stony, facing away from the patients in the waiting room. "Doc said he didn't think it was malignant. But it's in your windpipe. It's the size of a quarter. If it grows to the size of a half-dollar, where it is, it won't matter whether it's malignant or not. If it's the money, maybe Mary Beth could help."

Stony grabbed her wrist. "Don't you go telling Mary Beth about this."

"I just thought . . ."

"You hear me, Rosie, I don't want you telling nobody. Especially not Mary Beth."

"You got to do something, Stony. You can't handle this all by yourself."

"Don't need nobody's help. Not now. Not ever." He turned loose Rosie's wrist and went through the glass door into the street. Purvis's car had taken the stranger away.

STONY DROVE HIS truck to his mine and lost himself in the routine of hacking and heaving. Coal gleamed in the light of his miner's cap as he picked it free from the seam, loaded the half-ton cart and let it roll toward the hazy patch of light at the mouth of the mine. Then he'd follow the cart out, hunkering on his haunches until the mine throat widened to give him standing room. Outside, he'd load the cart's coal into the dusty blue dump truck. Finally he'd take a break, smoking Camels and swigging a Strohs until it was time to shove the cart back into the cool blackness.

He had enough room at the mine face to work the seam from a kneeling position. As he swung his spade, the seam began to narrow. Goddamn, Stony thought. That'll mean more shoring for less coal. You never know what you're gonna find when you start picking. He wondered how doctors knew.

By lunchtime, he'd filled the back of the blue truck with coal. Then he jounced the truck down the narrow winding road to the rail line, grinding its gears as he passed the bone pile where the nearby mines dumped their shale waste. Between the bone pile and the rail line, he speeded up and the truck whipped the layers of coal dust sheeting the roadway into different designs. The grimy black outlines of chuckholes were the only constants in the swirling patterns.

Stony pulled off the coal-streaked blacktop at a wooden ramp buttressed by railroad ties. Faded red paint on the funnellike tipple at the end of the ramp spelled out

HOBBS MINE #1
MARY BETH

The fifty-ton Norfolk & Western hopper car below the rusting tipple was half full of coal. A full car sat on the track spur beyond the tipple. Standing in the truck bed, Stony could see the spur merge with the main Norfolk & Western line before it disappeared around the creek bed. A third hopper car sat empty on the track above the tipple. Only three cars. Time was when the N & W spotted fifteen cars a week on this spur. But the few miners that had stuck through the hard times had left to work for the big company miners farther up the creek.

Stony spaded the last of his truck's coal into the tipple. He couldn't come close to loading the volume moved by machines in the company mines. So long as the N & W kept spotting cars under his grandfather's tipple, though, he could go on sending his scrapings to market. He'd have to hump it just to get the three cars on the tipple loaded by the end of next week, when the N & W would bring three more empties. He'd never make it if he took time off to let doctors pick at his throat.

On the return trip up the winding blacktop road, Stony stopped at the bone pile. The smoldering shale waste dumped by the local mines fell away sharply to the creek bed far below. A half-hidden path of matted broom grass skirted the edge of the shale. As children, Stony and Hollis had dared each other to walk the path on their way home from school. The devil's dare, they'd called it. The steepness of the drop hadn't frightened them half so much as the hellfires simmering deep within the bone pile.

Standing on the path, with just a little buzz from his break-time beers, Stony could still feel the pull of the sloping shale. He'd felt the same pull when he and Hollis had "dared the devil" on their walks home from school. The first one across the path would wait, shouting encouragement, until the other was close enough to grab his hands. "Cheated death one more time," they'd yell, scrambling uphill against the pull of gravity and the bone pile.

Stony wondered whether Stuart and his friends ever dared walk the bone pile path. Teenagers think they'll live forever. He remembered feeling that way. He was sure he had. He could usually trust his pre-Vietnam memories. It was his later memories he couldn't be sure of. Dreams of tunnels and hand grenades. Even dreams of the bone pile. Sober, he thought he could remember driving a rusted-out pickup over the matted path and letting it bounce down the bone-pile slope to the creek bed. He remembered it, but it didn't make any sense.

A pickup drove by and honked. On its way to Pokey

Joe's most likely. Let them go. Time enough for Pokey Joe's after he got another truckload to the hopper. He scaled a piece of shale into the void and turned his back on the bone pile.

THE MINING SHED where Stony slept smelled of axle grease and sawdust. He sat on the edge of his cot and poured himself a Jack Daniel's, stirring the ice with his finger. He fished a cube out of the glass and sucked it to the back of his throat, holding it there, hoping the cold might shrink the lump lodged against his vocal cords. He waited until the cube melted, then tried his voice. "Cheated death," he said aloud. Then, "Goddammit all to hell." The rasp was still there. Maybe it wasn't what Doc Pritchard thought, though. Maybe his throat was just a little sore. Maybe if he gargled with saltwater. Maybe. Maybe. Maybe ice cubes could cure cancer. What did Doc Pritchard know, anyhow? After all, Pritchard hadn't spotted his father's problem in time.

He remembered his father, blood and spit caking in his beard, as the white-coated attendants loaded him onto the stretcher. He had lifted his trembling hand straight into the air before disappearing inside the ambulance. At the time, Stony had thought he was waving. Now he thought he must have been reaching out for help.

Stony poured himself another Jack Daniel's, waiting for the world to get the pink edge that told him he could go to sleep. Sober, without the pink edge, he confused dreams with reality, reality with dreams. When he drank enough, though, nothing was real. The world had a pink edge to it, and his dreams announced themselves as dreams, as if they were labeled with those little tag lines that run along the bottom of the TV screen to advertise "News at Eleven," or "Stay Tuned for David Letterman." His drunk dreams didn't exactly have subtitles saying "Disregard This, It's Only a Nightmare," but there was always something in them to let him know he wasn't awake, that what was happening wasn't real. The Vietcong would be riding pink lizards, or Mary Beth would be tricked out like a Saigon whore, or the Dundee twins would be alive beside him.

Drunk dreams didn't pass themselves off as reality. Sober dreams were different. Sober dreams took him to dark booby-trapped tunnels with scuttling noises that could be fleeing rats, a scavenging child, or a crawling enemy. In sober dreams he had to use his grenade before he knew whether he was dealing with rats, children, or Charlie. Sober dreams left him biting his pillow and wringing the sweat out of his sheets. Even the good ones, the ones where he made love to Mary Beth, left him damp with loss and regret.

The third Jack Daniel's brought his pink edge, and he stripped to his skivvies and lay back on the cot. With nothing to fear from his dreams, he closed his eyes and thought about Mary Beth. Who was that man she was drinking with, and what would he look like without his beard? Wouldn't he look a lot like the guy he'd caught screwing her? Or had that been a dream, too?

5

WHAT'S IN A NAME?

The Department of Transportation covers a city block in Southwest Washington with a twelve-storey fortress of corridors surrounding a square concrete courtyard. Back in his ninth-floor office, Owen Allison set aside his Contrary Comet file and tried to catch up with the research he'd ignored during his field trip. He'd give Purvis Jenkins the week he'd promised and then reopen the file. Maybe it would look different to him in a week, or maybe Purvis would find a loophole to wriggle through.

He logged onto his computer and tried to retrieve the safety report he'd refused to revise, the report that had gotten him banished to the backwoods in the first place. Each time he punched the OPEN FILE command, the slate gray screen blinked back FILE EMPTY. Had he inadvertently purged the file the last time he'd worked on the report?

He punched the keyboard hard, as if to punish the

computer for losing his report, and a series of dates and times appeared on the screen. The missing report had last been altered two days ago, while he was visiting Contrary. Somebody else must have purged his report. But that didn't make any sense.

He rummaged through his desk drawer looking for the backup files he kept on floppy discs. He found the report disc; labeled PICKUP ACCIDENTS, and checked to make sure it hadn't been altered. Whoever had purged the report in his computer hadn't known how compulsive he was about keeping duplicate copies. But who would have wanted to erase his report in the first place?

He stormed into the suite next door, passed his group secretary without acknowledging her greeting, and barged into Walker Bashford's office. His supervisor, a Southerner with sandy hair and a salt-and-pepper moustache, looked up, nodded, and went on with his phone conversation. Bashford's office on the ninth floor of the Department of Transportation had a view of the Virginia Northern Railroad tracks and one corner of the Air and Space Museum. Owen stared at the converging tracks and tried to calm himself as his supervisor murmured concerns about "policy implications," "swing votes," and "the other side of the aisle" into the phone.

"What the hell's going on, Walker?" he asked as soon as Bashford hung up.

"Apropos of what, exactly?"

"Somebody's been erasing my computer files."

Bashford smoothed his moustache. "That's very strange. Are you sure you didn't erase them yourself by mistake? I do it all the time on my computer at home."

"It wasn't me. I wasn't even around when it happened."

"How do you know?"

"The computer. It says the files were purged two days ago. I wasn't in the office two days ago."

"Oh. Well. Those computer clocks never work right. Leap years and daylight savings time mess them all up."

"Mine's working just fine."

Bashford swiveled his chair so he was looking out the window. "Which files are missing?"

"My report on pickup trucks."

"Well, then, it doesn't really matter. I told you we'd never release that report."

"It's six months' worth of work."

Bashford made a church steeple of his fingers. "The secretary has decided to recall those pickups. It would be very embarrassing if any part of your report were leaked to the press."

"Those pickups aren't dangerous."

"Owen, we've been through this. People died in those trucks. Horrible, fiery deaths. There are several prominent lawsuits. 'Sixty Minutes' has called us."

"Mile for mile, just as many people died in other makes and models. More, in fact."

"Owen, it's a political decision."

"And you're a political appointee."

"And I outrank you. And that's the end of it."

"It's a goddamn grandstand play. It'll wind up costing billions. And you won't save a single life."

"Owen, I said that's the end of it." Bashford walked to the side of his desk and put his foot on top of a cardboard file box. "I'm glad you came, actually. I've been meaning to give you this." He inched the box toward Owen.

"What is it?"

"Dwight Armitrage's working files. We didn't have the budget to replace him, so I'm splitting his duties among a few of our staff members. This is your share."

"I'm a researcher. Armitrage was a bean counter."

"It's all number crunching to us political appointees," Bashford smiled, drawling out the word *appointees*. "You've got the experience, what with your little trip to West Virginia. And you should have some free time, now that you've finished counting truck accidents."

"It was more than just counting . . ."

"I'm sure it was. You'll have to excuse my ignorance in these matters. After all, you have all those degrees in statistics, and I'm only a poor political appointee."

Bashford watched as Owen lifted the cardboard box and started back out of the office. "I'm afraid there's something else, Owen."

Owen stopped in the doorway.

"Since you'll be taking over some of poor Dwight's duties, I thought it would be appropriate if you took over his office as well."

"Armitrage's office? It's just a goddamn cubicle."

"Well, yes. Technically you're right, of course. It is a cubicle. But it does have all the square footage you're entitled to at your GS level."

"I'm happy with the office I have, Walker. It's got a door I can shut and a window I can look out of."

"I'm afraid I have other uses for it."

"If we're not hiring, what other uses could you possibly have?"

"At your level, you are, of course, entitled to more furniture than Dwight had in his old office. At least one more file cabinet, I believe. You'll be happy to know we can fit all of your file cabinets into Dwight's old space. You can use his desk and chairs."

"Know what I think, Walker? I think somebody who isn't too shy about sneaking into my office and measuring my furniture might not be too shy about erasing a few computer files while he's there."

"I advise you not to say any more, Owen. I've arranged to have maintenance move your file cabinets next Wednesday. It was the earliest they could send somebody up."

The cardboard box was heavy in Owen's arms. "Well, have maintenance leave the file cabinets on casters. You'll be gone after the next election, and I'll still be around to move back in."

Bashford crossed his arms. "You seem to think I'm the villian here, Owen. I've read your personnel file. You've had this problem with all your superiors. I hate to say it, but you're just not a team player."

"You're right, Walker. At least not on your team."

OWEN DUMPED ARMITRAGE'S cardboard box on the desk in his soon-to-be-ex-office. Not a team player, Bashford had said. Screw that. The guards at Belsen were team players. That's what he should have told Bashford. It wouldn't have done any good, though. The starched asshole's so wrapped up in politics and sports metaphors he'd probably think the guards at Belsen were football linemen.

Owen opened the cardboard box and riffled the tops of the files. Each one was labeled with the name of a small town written in Armitrage's tight, crabbed hand. Inside, fastened to either side of the manila file folders, were detailed descriptions of each town's bus system, along with quarterly statistical reports, neatly organized on Form Fifteens. Not much to show for Armitrage's twenty-five years in the federal government. Who was he to judge, though? At the rate he was going, they'd be able to fit his own contribution in a shoebox. In a shoebox in a god-damn cubicle.

A single manila folder lay crosswise on top of the other files in the box. Owen flipped through its contents, which included several staff memos issued after Armitrage's death, a paper-clipped sheaf of invoices, and a loose batch of pink phone message slips. Some of the phone slips were dated just last week; the most recent were from somebody named Craig Young, who had an internal phone number.

Owen called the number. A deep voice on the other end of the line answered, "Accounting. Young speaking."

"I'm calling for Dwight Armitrage," Owen began.

"It's about time. I sent fifteen invoices over there for his signature a month ago. I need his approval before I can cut the checks. There's towns out there waiting for their money and the secretary's on my ass. What's with that guy Armitrage, anyhow? He's been late before, but never this late."

Owen picked up the paper-clipped sheaf of invoices from Armitrage's file folder. They were payment requests from the bus companies he'd been monitoring. Owen leafed through the batch and found one from Contrary signed by Mary Beth Hobbs, with a blank space for the signature of the DOT representative approving the release of federal funds. Accounting had typed Dwight Armitrage's name under the signature space, but it was Owen's responsibility now.

A faint "hello?" came from the earpiece.

Owen decided to be a good team player. He said, "I'll take care of it," and hung up.

EVIDENTLY BASHFORD HADN'T bothered to inform Accounting of Armitrage's death and have the approval protocol changed. It was typical of Bashford. He liked talking policy with the secretary and issuing quotes to the press, but the day-to-day details of running his branch didn't interest him.

Owen took the unsigned invoices into Bashford's office. "Walker, we've got a little problem with Armitrage's files."

"Whatever it is, take care of it. That's why I gave them to you."

"Accounting needs Armitrage's signature to release DOT funds to the properties he was monitoring. They're a month overdue, the bus companies are crying, and the secretary's steaming."

Bashford straightened when Owen mentioned the secretary. "Well, sign the invoices. You have the authority. I gave you Armitrage's job."

"I can't sign them, Walker. My signature's not on the approval list. Nobody even told Accounting Armitrage died."

"Marge must have slipped up there. I'll speak to her about it. We'll get the approvals you need."

"That'll take some time, Walker. You need three levels of signatures, including the secretary's . . . and the bus companies need their money now."

"Why three levels of signatures?"

"There are sizable sums of money involved, Walker. Some of these properties draw ten to twenty million a year."

"But you're sure the secretary needs to sign off on it?"

Owen wasn't sure, but he knew Bashford wouldn't want the secretary to know he'd screwed up the approval process, and he enjoyed watching his boss squirm. "It's a lot of money, Walker."

Bashford pursed his lips as if he were sucking on a lemon. "Well then, you'll just have to sign Armitrage's name to those invoices. It'll keep the money flowing."

"You want me to forge Armitrage's signature?"

"I gave you the authority to do his job. It's no big deal. I endorse my wife's checks all the time."

"Then maybe you should sign these invoices."

"It's your job Owen, not mine."

"Don't you think you should at least initial the signatures?"

"For Christ's sake, Owen. If you can sign Armitrage's name, you can sign my initials. You've got a Ph.D., after all. I expect you to do your job without pestering me with these petty details."

Back in his office, Owen closed the door and spread the fifteen invoices out on his desk. What Bashford said was true, in a way. Theoretically, he had the authority to sign, and signing Armitrage's name would keep the money flowing. It would also buy Contrary three months more of operating time, much more than the week he'd promised Purvis. Let Purvis and Mary Beth keep their buses a while longer. If he was going to be a team player, he'd rather suit up with the West Virginians than with Walker Bashford.

He took the top invoice and copied Dwight Armitrage's crabbed signature into the approval space. It didn't look too bad. Barely legible, just like Armitrage's scrawl. He signed thirteen more invoices the same way, saving

Contrary's for last. By that time he had it down. Without pausing, he scribbled Armitrage's name next to Mary Beth's signature on the Contrary invoice. It was actually easier signing someone else's name, anyone else's name, rather than his own to that invoice.

Owen compared each of his signatures with a copy of Armitrage's original. Then, for good measure, he initialed them all with a florid WJB, for Walker J. Bashford.

6

NOT THE REAL MCCOY

"OWEN, HELP ME OUT HERE." Walker Bashford peered through bifocals at four or five sheets of paper. "You're familiar with this Contrary bus system, aren't you?"

Owen shifted his weight from one foot to the other. "I wouldn't say familiar, exactly." Had Bashford found out about the Contrary's bus scam?

"You visited them, didn't you?"

"Visited them? Yes, I visited them." Owen tried to keep his voice calm. If Bashford knew about the scam, Owen would look like a fool or a coconspirator for approving Mary Beth's invoice.

"And you grew up around there, didn't you?"

"In Barkley. About forty miles down the road." What did that have to do with anything, Owen wondered.

"So you understand these people."

"I wouldn't say all that. What's your point, Walker?"

Bashford hadn't expected a response and proceeded as if he hadn't heard Owen's question. "So you're the man to handle this." He reached across his desk and handed the sheets of paper he'd been reading to Owen.

They were letters addressed to the Secretary of Transportation, badly typed on a machine with a faded ribbon. Owen started to read the first letter, but stumbled over a stream of X's that masked several false starts at spelling the word disabled. "What's all this?"

"Complaints from a Contrary citizen."

Owen read the scrawled signature. "Hatfield McCoy?"

"The name's a bit schizoid, isn't it? It seems Mr. McCoy is confined to a wheelchair and feels that Contrary isn't providing him with the bus service he's entitled to."

"What service is that?"

"His letters aren't clear. But he cites the ADA repeatedly and claims the Contrary buses won't take him where he wants to go."

Hardly surprising, Owen thought. Two buses don't buy much in the way of personal service.

Bashford tapped the letters with his spectacles. "You know the department's position on this, Owen. The ADA says bus systems have to supply fully accessible service to meet the needs of the disabled. Essentially, they have to take the disabled anywhere their regular systems run."

"Maybe this McCoy wants to go somewhere the buses don't run."

"Then the matter's easily settled. I expect you to get down there and rectify the situation one way or another.

We can't have letters like this popping up in the middle of an election year."

"This isn't an election year."

"It's always an election year somewhere."

Owen called Purvis Jenkins as soon as he got back to his office. "Who the hell is Hatfield McCoy? It can't be a real name. It's an oxymoron, for Christ's sake."

"That's Hatfield, all right. Stubborn as an ox, brains of a moron. And it is his real name. Though he'll be the first to tell you he's not a real McCoy."

"I thought not," Owen said. "No real McCoy would name a kid Hatfield."

"He's a real Hatfield, though. His momma's three generations down from Devil Anse. Had a falling out with her daddy and married a drummer named McCoy just to spite him. Wasn't one of the feuding Kentucky McCoys, but it riled her daddy just the same. He put two loads of buckshot into the trunk of the groom's car as a wedding send-off. Marriage lasted just long enough to produce Hatfield."

There was a pause as Owen digested McCoy's genealogy.

"How come you want to know about Hatfield?" Purvis asked.

"He's been writing the Secretary of Transportation complaining about your service."

"The hell you say. He's been hanging around here for months claiming we've got to cart him wherever he wants to go just because he's in a wheelchair."

"He could be right."

"You've got to be shitting me. First you tell me I've got to run empty buses from here to hell and gone. Now you're telling me I've got to provide a private limo service for a scumsucker like Hatfield McCoy?"

"Maybe. Maybe not. The department's sending someone down to investigate."

"You know who they're sending?"

"Me."

"Well, then. That's all right."

"It's not all right. I might not be able to help. And it won't always be me they send."

"But they're sending you this time."

"This time, yes. But you've got to run a tighter ship. Loose cannons like this McCoy will just bring more people nosing around. And you can't afford that."

"Don't I know it."

"How many people know what's really going on down there?"

"Just me, Hollis, and Mary Beth. Doc Pritchard suspects the deck ain't being shuffled and cut, but as long as his checks clear, he don't much care where the money comes from."

"What about the rest of Contrary? Don't they suspect anything?"

"They all think what anybody'd think. They imagine their good fortune's all due to their own hard work, perseverance, and the smiling face of God."

"See they go on thinking that," Owen said. "And set up a meeting between me and this McCoy character later this week."

"You've got a real treat in store for you," Purvis told him.

"HATFIELD WAS NEVER on time when he had two good legs," Purvis said. "It's some kind of power thing with him."

Owen and Purvis were standing in the Contrary Comet's reception area on the second floor of the courthouse building. Mary Beth had come out of her office to greet Owen, but she'd left the two of them alone to deal with Hatfield McCoy.

"McCoy hasn't always been in a wheelchair, then?"

"Hell no. He was our deputy sheriff for ten years. Snake mean and coon ornery. Way too quick with his pistol and his pecker. A powerful persuader, though. Never seen the like for finding what a person holds dear and setting a match to it."

Purvis checked his watch. "One time Hatfield lowered a four-month-old baby down a well in a bucket to get the baby's daddy to tell where he'd relocated his still."

"Good Christ."

"When the daddy told, Hatfield hauled the bucket up and carried the baby in it while they rode out to the site to make sure the man was telling the truth."

"Was he?"

"Hell yes. Wouldn't you? When he found the still, Hatfield set up a monthly payment schedule to let the man stay in business. Now that he's no longer a deputy, he gets the same kick-back for going out every so often and sitting around with his shotgun to guard the site. He thinks we ought to help him with his commute."

"How'd he lose his legs?"

"Actually, he wasn't careless enough to lose his legs. Only a foot. Claims he shot it off accidentally chasing a prowler out at the Widow Perkin's kennels."

"Sounds like you don't believe his story."

"Hatfield's never been on speaking terms with the truth. Fact of the matter is, he was stirring his shotgun in a litter of prize hunting pups to convince the widow she should perform a uniquely personal service for him." Purvis made a zipping motion near his fly to indicate the general location of the personal service Hatfield had in mind. "The bitch that whelped the litter snuck up behind Hatfield and clamped her jaws on the shotgun barrel. Startled him so, he jerked the barrel back and the gun went off. Took the tail off the bitch, the leg off a rocker, and the left foot off Hatfield."

"Too bad he didn't aim higher."

"He was on duty at the time, so he dreamed up the prowler story and put in for disability."

A blaring symphony of auto horns sounded outside the courthouse window. Purvis checked his watch again. "That's likely Hatfield now."

Through the open window Owen could see a stringy man in a motorized black wheelchair putting slowly down the center of Contrary's main street. He was followed by a line of creeping cars, all with blaring horns. The lead car pulled within a few feet of the wheelchair, honked twice, crossed into the oncoming traffic lane, sped past the wheelchair, and screeched to a stop at the courthouse traffic light.

The man in the wheelchair putted alongside the stopped car, lifted a black cane from his lap, and raised it overhead. He brought the cane down sharply against the passenger's sideview mirror and rocketed away toward the curb at twice the speed he'd managed on the road itself.

By the time the driver emerged from the car, the wheelchair was over the curb cut and careening across the courthouse lawn. The traffic light turned green, and the line of cars began honking at the driver, who, staring helplessly after the wheelchair, climbed back into his vehicle, and drove away.

"You don't want to mess with Hatfield if you can help it," Purvis said. "He ran the local Klan for a while. Once he cold-cocked a black vagrant and dragged him out to the bone pile to let the fumes finish him off. We never could prove that, but when he come to us with his disability application, we fell all over ourselves to approve it. Figured it was better to have him on the county dole than on the sheriff's payroll with a gun and badge."

Purvis turned away from the window. "Losing his foot put an end to Hatfield's days with the KKK. Even if he could have found a sheet big enough to cover both him and his wheelchair, there was no way he could stay anonymous." He led Owen toward the stairwell. "We'd best go down to meet Hatfield. He'd play hob trying to get his wheelchair up these stairs."

JUST AS OWEN and Purvis reached the first floor, the courthouse doors swung open and Hatfield McCoy wheeled in. At close range McCoy reminded Owen of pictures he had seen of John Brown before his Harper's Ferry raid. They both had the same bony face, glinting eyes, and straggly white beard. McCoy's beard, though, was split into thirds by two long tobacco stains leading from the corners of his mouth.

As McCoy wheeled himself in, he was joined by a short man in a rumpled white linen suit who was carrying a battered briefcase. McCoy pointed at the briefcase with the ebony walking stick he'd just used to break the car mirror and introduced the newcomer as his lawyer, Brady Jackson. Up close, Owen could see that the slim, straight handle of the walking stick was shaped like a silver wolf's head.

Purvis led the way to an out-of-use courtroom, where he and Owen sat across from Hatfield and his lawyer at a long oak table. Purvis inquired about the health of the lawyer's wife, and the lawyer asked about Purvis's back pains.

"I ain't paying you to socialize," Hatfield told his lawyer. To Purvis, he added, "Can we get on with this? I got other shit to fry." Purvis made a quick phone call and they were joined by Mary Beth and an older woman with a court stenographer's machine.

Owen introduced himself and explained that he'd been sent by the Department of Transportation to hold an informal hearing regarding complaints of ADA violations by the Contrary Comet Transportation System. For the sake of the stenographer, he listed those present as Purvis Jenkins, ADA Compliance Officer for the Contrary Bus System; Mary Beth Hobb, System Comptroller; Hatfield McCoy, the complainant; and Brady Jackson, counsel for the complainant.

Jackson, the lawyer, stood, laid his white hat on the table, cleared his throat, and began. "*In re* the matter of my client Hatfield McCoy versus the Contrary Bus System, I wish to open these *intra parietes* hearings by saying my client's rights have been violated by the Contrary Bus Company's repeated refusal to provide him with the *in transitu* service he needs to satisfy his employer . . ."

He droned on in a twang that blended with the muted

whine of the overhead fan, using more Latin than Owen had heard since before the Catholic Church switched to an English Mass. The gist of McCoy's complaint seemed to be that the Contrary Bus Company refused to provide convenient daily service from his home to his place of employment, which was located outside the city limits at the end of the Comet's line four run to a place called Gobbler's Knob. The fan continued to whine after Jackson had sat down, so that for a moment Owen didn't realize that the lawyer had finished.

Then Owen rapped his knuckles sharply on the table. Purvis's eyes snapped open, and Owen asked to hear the Comet's answer to McCoy's complaint.

"Let's get right to the crotch of this complaint," Purvis began. "First place, our buses don't run regular out to Gobbler's Knob. Our route maps may look like they do, but we actually only make one round trip a week there to bring Eulie McCaffrey in for chemo and take her home again."

He stared at Hatfield. "Second place, it's a bad joke to say Hatfield's employed out at Gobbler's Knob. What he does out there ain't exactly work. He'd have you believe he spends his time there guarding a still. Hell, that's illegal right there. But he don't guard it so much as sit around swilling samples and taking pot shots at gophers and spare bottles. And the only reason they let him do that is because he's running a protection racket. What's he guarding the still against, I'd like to know? Everybody knows it's out there. The only threat to the still is Hatfield himself. And he's only a threat if they stop giving him free samples and paying him protection money. Saying Hatfield is employed out at Gobbler's Knob is like saying a vulture is employed by the roadkill he's gorging on."

Hatfield drilled the tip of his ebony cane into the lawyer's side.

Brady Jackson jumped to his feet. "I object strenuously to your *ad hominem* characterization of my client as a lazy black-mailing layabout . . ."

"Just which of those terms do you object to?" Purvis asked. " 'Cause I'm perfectly willing to substitute several others."

"That's enough," Owen interrupted. "It doesn't matter why Mr. McCoy wants to go to Gobbler's Knob. As far as ADA compliance is concerned, even if he goes out there to get drunk, his trip is just as important as Mrs. McCaffrey's chemotherapy runs."

Hatfield McCoy glared at his lawyer. "You didn't tell me that, Brady."

"I didn't think it was relevant."

"The fuck it's not relevant. If I'd knowed I didn't have to lie, I never would have hired me a lawyer."

"And as far as ADA compliance is concerned," Owen told Purvis, "I have to assume your system runs where your route map says it goes."

"Yesiree Bob," McCoy said.

"The law is quite clear on that point," Owen continued. He didn't like to sound like a lawyer, and he didn't like the conclusion the law demanded. "So long as you have any routes running to Gobbler's Knob, you have to provide fully accessible service to Mr. McCoy here, assuming, of course, he gives you adequate lead time."

"I don't have enough buses to put a limo service at Hatfield's beck and call," Purvis said.

"Then I suggest you get an extra bus," Owen told him. "Or at least a van that can accommodate Mr. McCoy's wheelchair."

"Right quick, too," Hatfield said. "I'm losing my prime working years."

"It takes more than buses. It takes extra drivers, too," Purvis said.

"You had an extra driver last time I was here," Owen said. "The Penn State rooter with a cast on his arm."

Purvis grinned. "Bobby Joe Buford, you mean."

"That's the one, I believe."

Hatfield swiveled his wheelchair to face Purvis. "Ain't gonna ride with no dinge."

"I beg your pardon?" Owen said.

"I said, I ain't gonna ride with no dinge. I want a regular driver or I ain't budging."

"Then I'm afraid you're not budging, Mr. McCoy," Owen said. "Contrary isn't required to schedule its drivers to suit your ethnic preferences. They are, however, required to offer equal opportunities to drivers of all races, creeds, and colors."

Brady Jackson mopped his brow with a wrinkled white handkerchief. "I'm sure we can work something out here."

"Shut the fuck up," McCoy barked. "If I want any shit out of you, I'll scratch your head."

McCoy looked from Purvis to Owen. "It's a put-up job, ain't it? You bastards knew I had the law on my side, so you set down and figured how to weasle out of your obligations to this here disabled person. Well, fuck you both. And the bus you rode in on." McCoy pulled on driving gloves and wheeled to the head of the table, where a pitcher of water had been placed. "I'll say this, you sorry shits. You ain't heard the last of Hatfield McCoy." He raised his cane and smashed the pitcher to bits.

McCoy swiveled his chair and wheeled out of the courtroom, leaving his lawyer to dab ineffectually at the spreading pool of water.

PURVIS SAT BEHIND the desk in his office, regaling Hollis with his version of Hatfield's tirade while Owen and Mary Beth stood in the doorway. "You ain't heard the last of me," Purvis mimicked. He raised his hands and shook them in mock terror. "Woah there, Mr. Bones. Lock up your crockery. Man's death on glassware. Busted a car mirror and a cut-glass pitcher in the space of an hour."

Hollis laughed, but Mary Beth said, "I wouldn't take him so lightly."

"He's a pathetic old bigot in a wheelchair," Owen said.

"He's a dangerous bigot," Mary Beth said. "And he gets around better in that chair than lots of people on two legs."

"That was brilliant, letting Hatfield know he'd have to ride with Bobby Joe Buford," Purvis said.

"We were lucky," Owen said. "We might not be so lucky again. You better start beefing up your supply of buses."

"Sure, sure," Purvis said. "But first we ought to celebrate. What say we all hit Pokey Joe's?"

"Can I drive you?" Owen asked Mary Beth.

"I'd like that."

Owen's convertible was parked in the alleyway behind the courthouse. A teenage boy leaned over the driver's door, examining the interior, while his companion, a young girl in a black leather jacket, traced a finger along the left front fender. As Owen and Mary Beth approached, the two teenagers backed away quickly and watched.

Two crude arrows were scratched into the fender the girl had just been examining. One arrow pointed downward at the slashed front tire. The other pointed upward at the smashed side-view mirror. The passenger seat sagged under a grimy mound of coal with a tombstone-shaped slab of cardboard protruding from its peak. Smudged charcoal letters on the cardboard spelled out the initials *R.I.P.*

"We didn't do nothing," the teenage boy said.

"Did you see who did?" Owen asked.

The boy continued to back away. "We didn't see nothing, either."

Owen opened the passenger door. Coal spilled out into the alleyway. He grabbed the cardboard tombstone and was about to fling it away when Mary Beth said, "Don't. There may be fingerprints on it."

"You really think the sheriff is going to waste time fingerprinting a vandalized out-of-state car?"

"He will if I ask. I'll call him and Say Ray's garage. While Ray's fixing your tire, I'll drive us both to Pokey Joe's."

Owen put the cardboard in his trunk and slammed the lid shut.

"Looks like Hatfield is a sore loser," Mary Beth said.

"Looks like it," Owen said. But he didn't see how a man in a wheelchair could shovel a seatful of coal over the side of an open convertible without attracting a crowd.

7

THE LAST OF THE INDEPENDENTS

STONY HOBBS WAS LEANING against the bar at Pokey Joe's when Mary Beth came in with Hollis, Purvis, and the bearded stranger Stony had seen outside the Contrary Clinic. When Mary Beth saw him, her eyes focused on the bottle he held in his hand.

"Need to see you," he rasped.

"When? Now?"

"Now's best."

"Stony, look who we got here," Hollis said. "Remember Owen Allison, pitched against us in the state finals?"

Stony tried to imagine the man's face without the beard.

"You remember," Hollis said. "Pitched for Barkley."

"Remembering's not my problem, Hollis," Stony said. He shifted his beer to his left hand, spilling a little on his fatigue pants, and held out his right hand to the man. "Pleased to meet you. I'm Stony Hobbs."

"I figured that out," the man said, shaking his hand.

Stony and Owen stood for a moment facing each other. When it appeared that no one was going to invite Stony to join them, Hollis said, "Come on, I'll whup your ass at shuffleboard."

Before Hollis could lead Stony away, Mary Beth said, "Now. Let's talk now."

"That'd be good." Stony nodded toward the door. "Let's go outside."

Mary Beth smiled at Owen and Purvis. "I'll be right back."

"I still want that shuffleboard game," Hollis said to the back of Stony's fatigue jacket.

Stony took Mary Beth around the side of the road-house, between the wire cage housing a spare generator and a Dempster Dumpster. He hadn't wanted to tell her, and it was hard to begin. "Doc Pritchard says there's a lump growing in my throat," he said finally.

"Oh, Stony."

"He thinks it's not serious. But he says I ought to go to Huntington to have it taken out."

"If it's not serious, why go all the way to Huntington?"

"Doctors there know more about these things."

"Will you go?"

"Don't know. Hardly seems worth it if it's not serious."

A car's headlights swept across the darkened parking lot. Stony flinched at the light. "Thing is, them Huntington doctors won't cut on credit."

"What about your insurance?"

"Don't start in again about insurance. I got enough of that when we were married."

Gravel crunched and a car door slammed. He waited for her to say it.

She picked at the wire cage. "All the company miners get it free. But not you."

"Rosie at Doc Pritchard's said the same thing. You women just can't let it be. You know I ain't no company miner."

"How much do you need?"

He scuffed at the gravel. "Three grand. Maybe four, once you add in the hospital."

"What about the VA?"

"They'll make me take the cure. I won't take the cure."

She put her arms around him, buried her face in the neck of his fatigue jacket. "It's the best thing," she whispered. "Stony, it's the best thing."

He rubbed his cheek against her hair. "Sober, I get the dreams. I won't take the cure."

Headlights swept past them again. He turned his body, shielding her from the light. "Maybe there's other ways."

She sniffled into his collar. "Like what?"

"Doug Fulks said if you thought on it, concentrated real hard, like, you could make it go away. That's what he did. He imagined his blood was full of little crows that ate up all the bad cells."

"Mellie Fulks's husband Doug? He's dead, for Christ's sake."

"His thinking seemed to work for a while. Until Mellie left him."

"He died all alone."

Stony let his hands drop to his side. "Everybody dies alone."

Mary Beth stepped back and clasped his elbows in both her hands. "Not you. You're going to Huntington."

"What'll I use for money?"

"Tell them it's an emergency. They won't turn you away. There's Medicare, all that stuff. You're a veteran. There's got to be something."

He shook his head. "I got to pay my way."

She pulled her checkbook from her purse, paused, and put it back without opening it. "I can't help you now. Maybe tomorrow. I'll need to check a few things at the office. Stop by the house after you finish loading coal. Stuart's got a practice game. You can pick him up."

"Where'll you get that kind of money?"

"I didn't say I could get it. I just said I'd try." She snapped her purse shut. "I'd better get back inside."

He walked beside her. "Who's that new man?"

"He's a fed down from D.C. to check out our buses."

"He the one that spent the night?"

Mary Beth stopped at the roadhouse door. "Seems like Hollis can't keep his mouth shut." She looked him in the eye. "He slept off a drunk. You know all about that. Don't you, Stony?"

BACK INSIDE THE bar Mary Beth rejoined the men in a booth, while Stony ordered a Strohs and stood beside the shuffleboard table, where Hollis joined him.

"Hey, soldier," Hollis said, pulling a punch in the vicinity of Stony's shoulder. "How's the last of the independents?"

"Never better."

Hollis collected the red and black pucks from the gutter of the shuffleboard table, eased a black puck back and forth, and skimmed it toward the end of the table. It came to rest straddling the two-point line. "Ready to get your ass whupped?"

"Take a better shot than that." Barely taking aim, Stony sailed a red puck down the table to knock Hollis's puck off the smooth playing surface.

"Ain't seen you since you took out that biker over to Mullens. That was some show." He aimed at Stony's black puck and missed it completely.

"So they told me. Don't remember much about it."

Across the room, he saw Mary Beth stand up and watched Purvis and the federal guy, Owen Allison, escort her out. She looked back at Stony and mouthed the word *tomorrow*. He raised his beer bottle in a half-hearted salute, turned back to the shuffleboard game, and sailed a red puck viciously down the table, knocking his own puck off the scoring surface.

"Ain't like you to muff a setup like that," Hollis said. Skimming his own black puck down the table, he brought it to rest in the three-point zone. "Gawd dog! Would you look at that." He elbowed Stony in the ribs. "Sweeter than moonshine on a whore's nipple."

"You've been working for Purvis so long you're starting to sound like him. How long's it been since you've seen a whore's nipple?"

" 'Bout as long as it's been since you've seen a nipple that wasn't a whore's."

The two men played in silence, splitting four games and eight beers apiece. Near the end of their rubber match,

Hollis asked, "What were you talking to Mary Beth about? Going to get back together?"

"Doc Pritchard's found something growing in my throat," he said. "He don't think it's serious, though."

"Pritchard don't know his ass from applejack," Hollis said, easing his black puck back and forth for his last shot. "He was any good, he wouldn't stay around Contrary."

"Says I ought to go to Huntington to have it taken out."

"Your throat don't sound that bad to me," Hollis skimmed his puck toward the end of the table. It knocked two of Stony's red pucks into the gutter and came to rest teetering at the edge of the polished surface.

"Gawd dog!" Hollis punched Stony's shoulder. "See that, Stony? See that? Best three out of five! Best lick I ever hit!"

Stony stared at the black puck.

Hollis reared back to punch his shoulder again. Then he unlocked his fist and let it drop to his side.

"Shit, don't worry about it none," Hollis said. "God wouldn't give you that ugly face and cancer, too."

FROM POKEY JOE'S Stony drove by Mary Beth's house. Light from her living room window glinted off the hood of her car in the driveway. He pulled off the road and watched, but he couldn't see anyone moving inside the house. Still, there was something familiar about the scene, as if he'd been watching there before, or dreaming about being there.

He gripped the steering wheel and reminded himself he had no claim on Mary Beth. He'd lost any claim on her somewhere between his first trip to Vietnam and his last barroom brawl. But he still had a claim on Stuart, and if he barged in now or did something stupid, he might lose Stuart as well.

Stony pulled back onto the two-lane road, dodging patches of fog as he headed for his mining shack. The beers he'd had with Hollis tugged at him, causing him to slow down on the hairpin turns. He'd need a few more shots before he'd be able to sleep. His waking life was screwed up, but it was no match for the nightmares he'd have if he went to bed sober.

THE NEXT AFTERNOON, when Stony finished loading coal, thunderclouds capped the ridgetop pines and darkened the hollow. From the look of the sky, Stony doubted that Stuart's team would play nine innings before the rains came. Even so, he stopped at Mary Beth's before going to pick up Stuart at the practice field. He didn't want his son to see him asking his ex-wife for money.

Mary Beth saw him through the screen door and asked, "Where's Stuart?"

"I'm on my way to pick him up. Did you get the money?"

She didn't open the screen door. "Tell me again what Doc Pritchard said?"

"He said he didn't think the thing was serious, but it was big enough so it ought to be cut out of my windpipe."

"But you've got to go to Huntington?"

"Seems best."

"Doc Pritchard would carry our paper. He was good enough for me when I had our baby. How come when it's your neck you've got to go all the way to Huntington?"

"Jesus, Beth. It was Doc Pritchard's idea. He can't

handle it here in Contrary." Bile and doubt rose in his throat.

"Then it must be serious."

"Doc says it's just routine for them Huntington doctors."

Thunder rumbled beyond the ridge. Mary Beth opened the screen door just wide enough to hand him an envelope bulging with money. Fifties, twenties, hundreds.

"It's all there," Mary Beth told him. "Four thousand dollars."

"I didn't expect . . ." He stared at the envelope. "I didn't expect you to have all of it."

"It's Stuart's college fund. I'll need it back."

"Jesus, Beth. I didn't expect all this."

"You hear me, Stony? I'll need it back. As soon as you can manage it."

"Of course. Soon as I get back, I'll finish loading the N & W's hopper cars. I got some money set aside already. I'm good for it."

"I know you are. That much money just makes me nervous, is all."

A blob of rain splattered the flagstone sidewalk. Then another and another, until the stone was polka-dotted.

Stony stuffed the envelope into his overall pocket. "I'd best leave now if I want to see Stuart before his game's rained out."

"Hurry back," Mary Beth said. "I'll have dinner ready."

BY THE TIME Stony arrived at the practice field, rain was pelting down and headlighted trucks and cars were streaming out of the parking lot. Gum wrappers floated on puddles in the empty infield, and Stuart's coach was loading a damp duffel bag filled with bats into his station wagon.

Stony honked twice and Stuart came running from the dugout, holding his chest protector over his head to shield him from the rain.

"How'd it go?" Stony asked as Stuart piled into the pickup.

"They had us by one run when the rains came. I let a pitch get by me with the bases loaded."

"Looks as if it was getting hard to see out there."

Stuart slouched in his seat. "Pitch was in the dirt. I just didn't get in front of it."

"Even the big leaguers have trouble with that play."

Stuart worked his hand in and out of his catcher's mitt. "Coach said it was an easy chance."

"Coach couldn't catch a cold in Alaska."

Stuart laughed. "Sounds like something Uncle Purvis would say."

"Stay around here long enough, everybody sounds like your Uncle Purvis." Stony patted his son's leg. "Don't worry, you'll get 'em next time."

The wipers were fighting a losing battle with the rain, and Stony idled the engine. "I have to go to Huntington for a few days. They want to operate on my throat."

"They're gonna cut on your throat?"

"Seems so."

"What about the mine?"

"Coal's not going anywhere. It'll still be there when I get back."

"I can do some after school."

Stony put his arm around his son. "You've got better

things to do." He nodded toward Stuart's catcher's mitt. "Practice blocking those short hops."

Stuart slid over and hugged his father. "You gonna be all right, Dad?"

Stony clung to his son, inhaling the smell of damp leather. "I been through worse, Jeb Stuart."

8

SUGAR IN THE MORNING

THE MORNING SUN had cleared the ridge, but the parking lot beside the Quonset hut that housed the two Contrary Comet buses was still half in shadows. Purvis left his Dodge at the edge of the lot and walked across the shadowed half of the asphalt toward Hollis, who was talking with a uniformed driver standing next to one of the yellow and white buses. Another driver was siphoning a murky fluid out of the gas tank of the second bus.

"Sugar," Hollis told Purvis. "Some son of a bitch put sugar in the gas tanks."

Squatted at the edge of the spreading murk, Purvis pinched the liquid between his thumb and forefinger and brought it to his nose. It smelled like gasoline, but had the consistency of maple syrup.

"Happened last night sometime," Hollis said. "Wilkins

here couldn't get either bus to move when he showed up for the morning run."

Wilkins shook his head. "Engines both clogged. Deader than Judas's chariot."

Purvis took out his handkerchief and wiped the syrupy gunk off his fingers. "How'd they get in?"

"Bastards busted the window in the office, reached through, and undid the lock," Hollis said. "And that ain't all." He pointed at the bus' side-view mirror, which was a spiderweb of broken glass. "Busted all the mirrors. Driver's side, passenger's side. Both buses."

"Looks like Hatfield McCoy," Purvis said. "Man's death on glassware."

"It was Hatfield all right." Hollis showed Purvis two parallel wheelchair tracks that were plainly visible in the grease and dust on the garage floor. "Bastard didn't even bother to cover his tracks."

"Doubt he'd have tried this alone," Purvis said. "He could have brought some of his kinfolk, though. They stick together like maggots on roadkill."

Purvis turned to the two drivers. "Clean out the fuel lines and have Sully break down the engines. Then get the van from behind the courthouse and cover the routes as best as you can."

When the drivers nodded, Purvis turned to Hollis. "Get on the phone to Mullins and see if we can borrow a couple of their replacement buses. That'll give us some time to get these two back in shape."

"What about Hatfield?" Hollis asked.

"Hatfield's not one to hide his shit under a bushel. Like as not we'll be hearing from him before long."

★   ★   ★

TWO DAYS LATER, Purvis was passing the World War I memorial on the courthouse lawn when he heard a familiar, high-pitched voice calling his name. The voice seemed to come from the sculpted doughboy advancing with fixed bayonet on top of the memorial.

"Pur-vis," the statue shrilled. "Over here, motherfucker."

Purvis saw Hatfield McCoy's face peeking out between the soldier's puttees and found Hatfield and his wheelchair on the concrete bench rimming the monument. A bullet-headed young man with stringy hair dangling from a bald crown had his back wedged against the wheelchair to keep it from tipping off the bench.

Hatfield was chipping away at the name of one of the veterans with the tip of his ebony cane.

"What the hell are you doing?" Purvis asked.

"Just erasing the name of one of Randall McCoy's kin. Sucker probably spent the war shacked up with some French floozy anyhow."

Purvis shook the wheelchair's footrest, upsetting Hatfield's aim. "Cut that out. You're defacing county property."

Hatfield rubbed the cement dust off the tip of his cane as if he were chalking a pool cue. "Never knew you to be so concerned about county property." Then he told the man holding his wheelchair in place, "All right, Snooker, get me down from here."

The balding man encircled Hatfield and his wheelchair in his arms and lifted them off the concrete bench. If the action required any special effort, he didn't show it.

Hatfield pointed at the man with his cane. "You know my cousin Snooker, don't you?"

Purvis nodded and Snooker grunted in reply.

"Notice you're running clunkers on your bus routes," Hatfield said. "What happened to them shiny Contrary Comet buses?"

"They're in the shop."

"Both of them? You'd think they'd be more reliable."

"Somebody mixed a load of sugar in their gas tanks."

"No shit. Who'd do a thing like that?"

Purvis ran his hand over the scratches Hatfield had chipped into the monument. "Some asshole with no respect for public property."

"Sounds like you need somebody to protect your buses from harm. Now you know, that's just the business I'm in."

"I'd think you'd be too busy protecting Irv Carter's still from your own threats," Purvis said.

"Irv Carter don't need me every night. You want references, you talk to him. He had himself plenty of misfortune before he hired me to guard his still."

"We both know the source of that misfortune, Hatfield. If Irv Carter wants to pay you protection money to guard his moonshine, that's his business. It don't hardly seem prudent for a public agency."

Hatfield raised his right hand as if taking an oath. "I'll guaran-god-damn-tee you nothing will happen to your buses any night you pay Snooker and me to watch them."

"Be like paying the town drunk to guard your liquor store."

"You're making a big mistake here, Purvis. There's a world of hurt can befall a bus. Not to mention you and yours."

"I don't have any kids small enough to fit into well

buckets. And I don't see you as much of a threat to anyone bigger. Anyhow, I've already got a watchdog for our buses."

"How's that?"

"I've got Hollis baby-sitting the buses with his ought-six most nights. He's already on the city payroll, and he's got orders to dust anything that moves around the bus barns." Purvis toed the spokes of Hatfield's wheelchair. "Particularly anything that rolls in on four wheels."

"Harm don't have to come at the bus barns. Accidents could happen anywhere along your routes."

"You'd look pretty silly chasing after moving buses with your wheelchair and a sack of sugar," Purvis said.

"No need to chase. I'm a fair shot sitting still. Besides, I got Snooker there to help me." Hatfield nodded at his cousin, who stood a few yards away, chucking stones at the pigeons lighting at the base of the statue.

"Get serious. Snooker there needs crib notes to whack off."

Snooker stopped chucking rocks. "I heard that. What the fuck are crib notes?"

Purvis leaned close to Hatfield. "Working with Snooker's like using a blasting cap with a short fuse. Like as not, it'll blow up in your face."

A stone whizzed past Purvis's head and pinged off the concrete monument. "I never whacked off in nobody's face," Snooker said. He advanced on Purvis, his left hand full of stones, his right hand cocked in a fist.

Hatfield wheeled his chair between Snooker and Purvis. "Back off there, Snooker."

"Make him take it back."

"He's talking about crib notes and blasting caps,"

Hatfield said. "Got nothing to do with you. Now back off and give us room. Purvis and I are negotiating here."

"Nothing short about my fuse," Snooker said. He turned and flung a stone full force at the statue, clanging it off the soldier's bayonet. Every pigeon on the courthouse lawn took flight.

Purvis waited until the fluttering stopped. "You're wrong, Hatfield. We're not negotiating. A negotiation is when you say you'll sell for twenty dollars and I say I'll buy for five dollars and we come to an agreement somewhere in between. I'm telling you here and now I don't intend to do business with you. And I don't give a damn what you threaten or what price you want to stop your threats."

"I'm right sorry you feel that way, Purvis. With my background in law enforcement, I can put myself right into the minds of your perpetrators." He tapped the bill of his grimy Consolidated Coal hat with his cane. "I can think the way they think, anticipate their moves, head off trouble before it starts. Seems like that talent ought to be worth something to you."

"Let me get this straight. You're telling me you can think right along with the pea-brained, corn-holing mammy jammers who dumped sugar in our gas tanks?"

A rock skimmed the surface of the concrete near Purvis. "Watch your mouth, motherfucker," Snooker called.

"Speaking strictly hypo-thetical," Hatfield said, stroking his tobacco-stained beard, "I reckon I could tell you what those sugar dumpers might be thinking right now."

"Wouldn't surprise me a bit."

"For one thing, I reckon they've got a shitload of sugar left over."

"How's that?" Purvis asked, tiring of the game, but wanting to keep Hatfield talking.

"I reckon they must have showed up at the bus barns with enough sugar to fill a whole fleetful of gas tanks. Probably got it wholesale somewhere."

"Somewhere like Irv Carter's still, I imagine."

"He does deal in volume. But the 'where' ain't near so important as the 'what now.' "

"So what now?"

"Well, imagine the perpetrators' surprise when they show up with a shitload of sugar and find only two buses."

"Hardly worth the trip."

"Still, you got to wonder what they might do with all that leftover sugar. For one thing, they might hoard it and do the same two buses over and over."

"And risk getting several loads of buckshot up their sorry butts."

"You got more faith in Hollis as a watchdog than I do. It does make you wonder though, don't it?"

Purvis didn't respond.

"I mean, wouldn't you expect to find more than two buses out there?" Hatfield cocked a threadbare eyebrow under the bill of his cap. "What with all them fancy maps and that big office in the courthouse yonder?"

Purvis hunched his shoulders in a shrug, trying not to put too much into it. "I reckon two buses is all they need to cover the routes on the fancy maps."

"You suppose the feds paying the bills know there's only two buses in the whole Contrary Comet system?" Hatfield asked.

"The feds get a complete report on the system every quarter."

"Last fellow to fill out that report wound up sucking sulphur in the bone pile."

"There's a new auditor to replace the one who died."

Hatfield scratched at his beard. "New fellow don't look to me like he counts too good. Don't you think his bosses might feel a little shortchanged, pouring big bucks into two piddly buses? Ain't that kind of like paying for a whole house and getting a two-hole privy?"

"Hatfield, the bus system carries everybody who needs carrying. The feds audit our books. The money they give us gets spent on city needs. Nobody's lining their pockets. Why would anybody feel shortchanged?"

"Just wondering, is all. It's my duty as a citizen to speak up if I think you're giving the feds a fast shuffle."

"Well now, Hatfield, since you're so good at supposing what lawbreakers might think, how about you let me suppose what a federal bureaucrat might think about our buses."

"Kind of hypo-thetical, still?"

"Still strictly hypo-thetical. Any bureaucrat looking at the Contrary Comet operation is going to say, 'Whooee, you got one efficient bus system there, fellows. Keep up the good work.'" Purvis smoothed his moustache, aping Hatfield's beard-stroking act. "See now, Hatfield, it's a little like your pension. The government doles it out and, long as nothing bounces back on them, they don't much care how you spend it."

"Ain't like my pension at all."

"Still thinking like a bureaucrat here, I'd guess the folks

doling out your pension might be surprised to find a man on full disability is collecting regular pay for guarding a still."

"How they going to find that out? I surely don't report none of that income."

"It's right there in the complaint you filed against the bus system. You claimed Irv Carter was your employer."

"I didn't need to do that. Turns out you have to carry me where I want to go whether I'm employed or not."

"Don't make no never mind," Purvis said. "Point is, you're on the public record as an employee."

"So?"

"So if the feds was to start looking hard at our records, your double-dipping is likely to come out, too. It's like emptying a spittoon, Hatfield. It all comes out in one messy string."

Hatfield hawked a stream of tobacco juice that splattered off Purvis's shoe. "Spit's likely to be messier for you than me. I'd just retire from Irv's official payroll and keep my pension. You'd likely have a tougher time of it, Mr. Mayor. Maybe you ought to think real hard about paying me to watch your buses."

Purvis snatched the Consolidated Coal cap off Hatfield's head and wiped his shoe with it. "You're still mistaking this for a negotiation, Hatfield. In case I haven't made myself clear, I'd rather watch flies fuck than dump a plugged penny of the city's money into your blackmailing lap."

Purvis tossed the crumpled cap into Hatfield's lap and walked toward the courthouse.

"You'll wish you'd hired me, Purvis," Hatfield called. "There's many as wish they had."

Purvis kept walking.

"There's many in Contrary wish they'd never heard the name of Hatfield McCoy."

It's a long damn list, Purvis thought. And I'm at the head of it.

9

CHEATED DEATH ONE MORE TIME

STONY AND HOLLIS HAD the corner booth at Pokey Joe's all to themselves. Empty beer bottles sat in several of the damp rings covering the tabletop in front of Stony. Hollis sipped a jelly glass full of moonshine and listened to Stony worry that he wouldn't be able to fill the N & W cars on time if he went to Huntington for his operation.

"Damned if I do. Damned if I don't," Stony said. "Can't make the money if I take the time off, but I may be fresh out of time if I don't take off now."

"Sounds like an easy choice to me."

"Already made it. Just don't like it. Going to Huntington tomorrow."

"Then drink up and quit worrying it to death," Hollis said.

"Easy for you to say. You don't have to pick the coal to pay the doctor." Stony reached across the booth, took hold of Hollis's necktie, and squinted at the floral design. "How long's it been since you picked an honest day's worth of coal, anyhow? You pencil-pushing, tie-wearing, desk warmer."

Stony dipped the tip of Hollis's tie in the glass of moonshine and squinted at it again. "Moonshine didn't eat it away. Must be a bad batch."

"Long as the rat floats, it's a good batch."

"Long as the rat floats," Stony repeated. "Jesus, Hollis, weren't those the days?"

"Long gone. And you, good buddy, need to put them behind you."

"What's that supposed to mean?"

"For starters, get yourself some insurance. Think about working for Consolidated. They give you days off, too . . ."

"Goddammit, Hollis, did Mary Beth put you up to this? Who'd work my seam if I joined up with Consolidated?"

"Nobody has to work your seam. Coal's coal. Nobody cares where it comes from."

"That's all you know, you ignorant pencil pusher. I been to Norfolk. They got piles and piles of different kinds of coal waiting to be loaded on ships. Four, maybe five hundred different kinds. There's a separate pile for my coal. Labeled Mary Beth, like my mine."

"Well, it's sure as hell all the same after it's been burned."

Stony picked the label off his beer bottle. "It's my coal. It's my mine."

"Yours and the First National Bank of Contrary."

"It'll be mine. Eventually. Free and clear."

"What's the difference if you're dead?"

"Leastways, I don't have to work for anybody. Don't have any assholes telling me what to do."

"Yeah. Well. Everybody has to live with at least one asshole."

"What's that supposed to mean?"

"Nothing. It's just a purely physical fact."

LATER THAT NIGHT Stony paced his miner's shed, trying to recapture some of the assurance he'd felt when Doc Pritchard described the operation in his gravelly voice. Nothing to it, he thought. He'd check in tomorrow afternoon. There'd be some tests. Next day they'd put him to sleep and take out the lump. He'd miss three days of work at the outside. What the hell, he'd faced worse in Vietnam. There, though, he'd been awake and fighting.

He stopped pacing, switched on the naked bulb dangling over his workbench, and rummaged through his father's black oak tool chest. He took out a stubby pencil and pulled the April sheet off the Mullens Hardware calendar over the tool chest. On the back of the calendar sheet, he began writing:

LAST WILL AND TESTAMENT
OF STONEWALL JACKSON HOBBS

This is crazy, he thought. Doc Pritchard says there's no danger. He says it's not serious. Just routine. He wadded the paper and threw it toward the scrap pile. Then he pulled May off the calendar and began again.

Dear Beth,

If you read this, then the operation wasn't as

simple as Doc Pritchard said. They'll call it bad luck, like with Dad. But I had a run of good luck for a while. I come from a wonderful family and had my own for a time.

Give Stuart Dad's miner's hat and all my love. I'm sorry it didn't work out for us and that I won't be around to watch Stuart grow up. You'll do fine with him, I know. Kiss him for me, and have a long happy life.

All my love,
Stony

He folded the calendar sheet once and printed MARY BETH in block letters across the days of the week. Then he put the letter on the top shelf of the tool chest, weighing it down with a spanner wrench. He closed the chest, took his short-handled spade, and headed across the shadowy hollow toward the mine.

Kneeling in front of the receding seam, Stony began chinking the spade slowly against the coal. "It's a shit deal," he said aloud. *(Chink)* ". . . I'm barely forty-five years old. *(chink)* None of the West Virginia . . . *(chink)* . . . line of Hobbses . . . *(chink)* . . . ever died that young. *(chink, thwack)* 'Cept in wars, *(chink, thwack)* car wrecks, *(chink, thwack)* or bar fights." *(Thwack, thwack, thwack)*

He picked up the rhythm and tore into the seam. Sparks ricocheted. Black dust billowed in his miner's light. Chunks of coal and sandstone splintered and fell around his knees. He didn't bother to shovel them back toward the cart. Coal dust made his eyes water as the pile around his knees grew. His breath came in sharp, loud rasps. One final flail with the spade turned him completely around and left him sprawled in the rubble he had created. Panting, he faced the darkening mouth of the mine.

The sound of a car door slamming echoed inside the mine shaft. Stony lay motionless on his bed of coal and sandstone. A speck of light appeared at the mouth of the mine. It bounced in short, tight spirals as it ducked timbers and followed the shaft toward Stony. When the light reached the place where the cart sat and the shaft squeezed down, Stony recognized the face under the miner's hat.

"Hollis," he said. "Whatcha doing here?"

"Thought I'd check up on you. Appears like you could use some help getting this here coal into the cart." Hollis squatted and picked up a few loose chunks. He rose and pitched them into the rusty cart.

"Don't need help." Still lying on his back, Stony kicked more coal out toward Hollis. "Besides, you're not dressed for mining."

"I been thinking on it," Hollis said. "Why don't I drive you to Huntington tomorrow. You can leave your truck here. Then Stuart and I can work this seam while you're away."

"What about Purvis and your buses?"

"I got leave coming. They won't miss me for a couple of days. Come on out of there now. Go home and get some sleep."

Hollis leaned on a timber and reached in toward Stony, who was shoving himself feet first through the rubble. Stony took his hand, pulled himself upright, and started back toward the mouth of the mine.

★ ★ ★

AT THE HOSPITAL, doctors with bright miner's lamps examined Stony's throat, teams of nurses tested the rest of him, and nuns in white ran his ward room. The first day's tests seemed to confirm Doc Pritchard's diagnosis: the growth was a granuloma. His surgeon called it "proud flesh." Not likely to be cancerous, but big enough so it would have to be cut out of the windpipe.

Stony was wheeled to the operating room the morning of his second day. "Sister, honey," he said to the white-robed nun adjusting the respirator, "when they take the lump out of my throat will I be able to sing in the church choir?"

The nun saw the joke coming. "Well now, Mr. Hobbs, did you sing in the church choir before you got your lump?"

It wasn't what she was supposed to say, but Stony plunged ahead anyhow. "No, ma'am, couldn't sing a lick."

"I'll bet you're not much of a churchgoer, either."

"No, ma'am."

The nun smiled and put the respirator over his mouth. "Don't worry, we'll take good care of you, anyhow."

HIS SURGEON SHOWED up at his bedside the afternoon following the operation. "Well, Mr. Hobbs," he said, fingering a large metal clipboard, "we've got some good news and some bad news. The good news is that your growth wasn't malignant."

Stony could sense what was coming. "What's the bad news?"

The doctor pulled an X ray from the clipboard and held it up to the window. It looked to Stony like two sacks of spiderwebs. A blurry spider sat at the bottom of one of the sacks. "It's your chest X ray. Your preop exam shows simple pneumoconiosis. Black lung."

"It's just a flyspeck."

"It's enough to affect your breathing. You must have noticed it. You checked 'shortness of breath' and 'hacking cough' on your medical history form."

"I've cut back on cigarettes."

"Better cut them out all together. Mining doesn't help either."

"Coal mining's all I know."

"The mine where you work. Do they spray to keep the dust down?"

"I've got my own mine. Hobbs Number One. Named Mary Beth. After my ex-wife."

"Didn't know there were any of you independents left."

"Suppose I spray?"

"It'll help, but the only sure thing is to quit."

"Mining's what I do. It's what my dad did, too."

The doctor put the X ray back in the clipboard. He tapped the sheaf of clipped papers. "Says here it killed your father."

"Not till he was fifty-two."

"Well, it might not kill you till then, either. But if I were you, I'd find another line of work."

HOLLIS CAME TO pick him up the next day.

"Cheated death one more time," Stony said, shaking his hand.

"Stuart and I pretty much finished off your last hopper car, so you can take a day off," Hollis said.

"That's fine, real fine. Don't know how to thank you, Hollis."

"Thank your boy Stuart. He did the heavy pick work. It's real tight in there. I mostly helped haul and drove the truck."

"Don't want Stuart doing that anymore. Gotta get him out of mining."

"What'd your doctors say?" Hollis asked.

"Said the lump was God's way of telling me I needed insurance. Gave me some papers." Stony patted the pocket of his Levi's jacket. "Might be I can finance it myself."

Stony didn't say anything to Hollis about his lung. Instead, he told him about the nun and the choir joke. In Stony's version, the nun fell for the straight line and told him he'd be able to sing in the church choir after his operation. "I told her, 'That's wonderful. Never could sing a lick before.'"

Hollis hooted and pounded a fist on the headboard.

By the time Stony reached home and told the story a few more times, it was his version he remembered as real.

10

WHEELCHAIR UNBOUND

OWEN SAT IN THE RECEPTION AREA of Walker Bashford's office, waiting to meet with his supervisor. The reception area was actually Owen's old office. After relocating Owen to Armitrage's cubicle, Bashford had expanded his own office by moving Marge, his secretary, into Owen's old space and converting it into a waiting room.

"What's he want to see me about?" Owen asked Marge, who was half hidden behind her computer monitor.

"No idea. You know how he is."

On the first visit to Contrary, Owen had given Purvis Jenkins a week to clean up his act. By signing his invoice, though, he'd effectively given him three months. That time was almost up and nothing had changed. Soon Owen would have to process another invoice. Or blow the whistle. The longer the scam went on, the more likely it was to be uncovered. And the longer it went on without Owen blowing the whistle, the more likely he was to be considered a coconspirator.

At least his name wasn't on the invoice. So far as he knew, Bashford still hadn't bothered to get the approvals needed to take Armitage's name off the signature list and replace it with Owen's. That was just like Bashford. He let details slip through the cracks, then ignored his mistakes and hoped everyone else would, too.

Marge peeked around her monitor. "His highness will see you now."

Walker Bashford sat on one edge of his desk, riffling the pages of Owen's report on Hatfield McCoy as if he wanted to shake the words free and sweep them under his new Oriental carpet. "Owen, I must say I'm surprised at you. This Contrary business is becoming an embarrassment to the department."

So the meeting was about Contrary. Had someone uncovered the scam? Owen felt clammy with apprehension. If someone had uncovered the scam, he knew that Bashford would deny ever authorizing him to sign Armitrage's name.

Bashford rolled up Owen's report and held it like a club. "And this report on the McCoy incident doesn't help matters much."

"How's that?" What did his report on Hatfield McCoy have to do with anything?

Bashford nodded toward a stack of letters on his desk. "This man McCoy is still complaining. The secretary gets one or two letters a week."

"McCoy's a chronic malcontent. I thought I made that clear in my report."

Bashford slapped the rolled report into his palm. "I

can't possibly show this to the secretary. Your language is inappropriate and insensitive."

"Insensitive? How?"

"How do you think?"

"McCoy said he wouldn't ride with a dinge. Those were his exact words. It's all there in the transcript."

"Couldn't you have simply written that the man used a 'racial epithet'? In view of the fact that our secretary is a person of color, it seems particularly insensitive to quote McCoy verbatim."

"I thought it best to be precise. It's a simple trip report. I'm surprised the secretary would be interested."

"The secretary is sensitive to the high level of complaints. Actually, I'm much more concerned about your own choice of words than about Mr. McCoy's racial epithets."

"How's that?"

"On the very first page, you refer to Mr. McCoy as 'wheelchair-bound.' "

"He is wheelchair-bound, Walker. That's his disability. That's why he thinks he's entitled to special bus trips and door-to-door service."

Bashford rubbed his eyes with his thumb and forefinger. "You just don't get it, do you Owen? 'Wheelchair-bound' is a pejorative, a put-down. Such people prefer to be called 'wheelchair users.' "

"So it's okay for McCoy to use the word *dinge*, but it's not okay for me to call him wheelchair-bound?"

"Neither is okay, as you put it. And neither is appropriate in a department report. Particularly a report that I will have to show the secretary." Bashford handed the report to Owen. "Fix it, please. Remove the offending references.

And get it back to me before my three o'clock meeting with the secretary."

"Walker, even if I change every word in my report so it wouldn't offend a physically challenged, politically correct Puritan, it's not going to stop McCoy's complaints."

"I'm sure you're right about that." Bashford lifted the stack of letters from his desk and handed them to Owen. "After you've edited your report, start in on McCoy's complaints. The secretary expects us to put a stop to these letters."

"What am I supposed to do? Steal McCoy's stamps?"

"Go back to Contrary. Address the issues. Hold a hearing. Confront the problems."

"What problems?"

"Apparently there's a long list. Read the letters. Everything from faulty equipment to rude drivers. Mr. McCoy has no end of complaints."

BACK IN HIS office Owen put through a call to Purvis Jenkins. "What the hell's going on with Hatfield McCoy? He's filling the secretary's office with complaints about your system."

"No shit. What's he saying?"

"Your buses are late, your passengers smell, your drivers are rude, your equipment's dirty, and you're not meeting your ADA obligations. And that's just the top three letters in the stack."

"Well, Hatfield should know about our problems. He's caused most of them. He's sugared our gas tanks, broke our mirrors, slashed our tires, shot out our windows, and painted graffiti on the sides of our vans. And that's just the top of my list."

Owen remembered the broken mirror and slashed tire on his own convertible. "You're sure it's Hatfield?"

"Him and one of his kinfolk. My cousin detailed a deputy to watch the buses. He found out it was easier just to watch Hatfield. We got photos of him doing some of that stuff."

"Then why not prosecute?"

Purvis exhaled a long stream of air. "Ain't that simple. Our boy Hatfield suspects we're overcharging the government for our services."

"Oh, Christ."

"I don't think he's got anything concrete. Just a grifter's nose for the grift. He's been sniffing around, trying to get at our books, talking trash about how our britches are too big for two buses."

"He knows, Purvis. He must know."

"Don't think so. If he knew, we'd know it. Hatfield ain't one to keep a secret long. Point is, if we jail his ass for petty vandalism, his mouth's still free to shout 'fraud' to the feds. Hatfield don't know it, but what we got is a Mexican standoff."

"You mean a Hispanic confrontation."

"Say what?"

"I just got a sensitivity lecture. Along with orders to visit Contrary and sort out your problems with Hatfield McCoy."

"You're coming down? That might be just what we need to settle Hatfield's hash."

"How's that?"

"All you got to do is let on like the two buses we got is what you're paying us for and what you expect us to have. That should stop Hatfield's grift-sniffing."

"Purvis, we'll have a court stenographer there. I'm not going to lie for you in front of a stenographer."

"Nobody's asking you to lie. You may not have to say anything at all. Just let on like everything's hunky dory between the Contrary Comet and the Federal Department of Transportation. I'll coach you when you get here. There'll be no surprises from Hatfield. He's snake mean, but he's predictable as a rattler on a hot rock."

"There's still the stenographer."

"Shit, Owen. We pay the steno. She ain't going to transcribe anything that threatens her paycheck."

"Purvis, you amaze me. Have you ever done anything honest in your life?"

"Once or twice by accident. Honesty's not exactly in my nature. But sometimes it slips through by pure chance."

PURVIS ARRANGED TO meet with Owen and Hatfield McCoy in the same courtroom where Hatfield's lawyer had pleaded his earlier case. The two of them arrived early to go over Hatfield's complaints and work out strategies to defuse his threats and deflect his distrust. The more Owen listened to Purvis, the more he felt drawn into the plan.

"We got more than enough to nail Hatfield's balls to the wall," Purvis said after going through his arguments. "What we got to do, though, is leave him feeling lucky we left him with a pecker to point. We can't have him sniffing out any difference between the money we're getting from you feds and the money we're paying to run buses."

By the time Hatfield arrived, Purvis and Owen were sitting at opposite ends of the oblong defense table with the court stenographer between them. Hatfield pointed his cane at Owen, and a hulking young man pushed his wheelchair to the vacant spot next to Owen at the defense table. Hatfield shook Owen's hand and introduced the young man as his cousin Snooker. Snooker acknowledged the introduction with a short grunt and took a seat in the rear of the courtroom, across the aisle from Mary Beth.

Owen opened the meeting by explaining for the benefit of the stenographer and those present that he'd been sent by the Department of Transportation to hold an informal hearing regarding complaints lodged against the Contrary Comet Transportation System by Hatfield McCoy. Turning to McCoy, Owen said, "The last time we met you were represented by counsel. Am I correct in understanding that you are no longer so represented?"

"Nosiree," Hatfield said. "Once you gave me to understand my rights, I realized that an honest man didn't need no lawyer in this here hearing."

Owen asked Hatfield to set forth his complaints against the Contrary Comet. Hatfield shifted in his wheelchair, reached under his seat, and pulled out a manila folder dented with the imprint of his left buttock. The sheaf of papers he took from the folder retained their concave shape as Hatfield began reading.

Pausing at intervals to scratch his beard and clear his throat, Hatfield twanged out a litany of late buses, rude drivers, and filthy equipment, noting on several occasions that there were only two buses serving all of Contrary and wondering aloud whether the citizens were getting their money's worth.

Purvis slouched through most of Hatfield's testimony, head tilted back, eyes following the slow circling of the ceiling fan. From time to time he would scratch his forehead, rub his eyelids, or wipe his nose with a handkerchief he kept wadded in his vest pocket.

"Just to cap this off," Hatfield said finally, "seems to me there's at least four things Purvis and the other bus bosses ought to do to service this county better." Hatfield paused and glared until Purvis roused from his slouch. "First thing, they ought to lay on more buses than the two they're using now."

Purvis stroked the bridge of his nose, winked behind his hand at the stenographer, and slouched back into his chair.

"Second thing is, they ought to be more mindful of security. A citizen just don't feel safe on their buses, what with random shootings and all. What's more, I understand there's been a lot of vandalism at the bus barns that's cost them some downtime. Now, I've suggested what they need is a night watchman, but I might as well be talking to a tombstone for all the good it does."

Purvis bolted upright, slapped the table with both hands, and shouted, "I'll see you under a tombstone before we hire you as a watchman, you two-faced, turd-wheeling peckerhead. We wouldn't need a watchman if it weren't for your shenanigans."

Owen rapped hard on the table. "That's enough, Mr. Jenkins. You'll have a chance for rebuttal when Mr. Mc-Coy has finished."

"I apologize for my outburst," Purvis told Owen. Then, to the stenographer, "And I'd like to ask that it be stricken from the record."

"Don't make no nevermind to me," Hatfield said. "Third thing is, I still believe under this here new Disability

Act I'm entitled to daily door-to-door service between my house and Gobbler's Knob."

"We done mined that seam," Purvis said. "It's played out and sealed off."

Owen held up a cautioning hand.

"Oops." Purvis winked openly at the stenographer. "Apologize again."

"Finally," Hatfield said, ignoring Purvis. "These here bus bosses ought to give an accounting of their spending. There's nothing on record since the last auditor bit the bone pile, and we taxpayers got a right to know where our money's going."

Purvis closed his eyes and exhaled a long sibilant hiss that ended with a barely audible "shit." Then he opened his eyes, lifted a worn leather briefcase to the table, unstrapped it, looked from Hatfield to Owen, and announced, "My turn."

"First off," Purvis said, pulling a manila folder from the briefcase, "let's just take up the sheer volume of Hatfield's complaints. Over the past three months, I counted twenty-five letters from Hatfield bitching about one damn thing or another." Purvis tapped the folder. "Know how many complaints we get over that same period from all the rest of our riders?"

Without waiting for an answer, Purvis held up four fingers. "Four, that's how many. Just four. Twenty-five from Hatfield, four from everybody else."

"Don't mean the rest didn't have no complaints," Hatfield said. "They just needed somebody to take the lead in speaking out."

"Mr. McCoy, please," Owen said. "You had your say."

"Anyhow," Purvis went on, "Guess what three of the

four letters that didn't come from Hatfield were complaining about?"

Purvis paused, then pointed at Hatfield. "Hatfield," he said. "Three of the four letters complained about riding with Hatfield. Or at least about riding with that mangy hound Hatfield takes with him from time to time." Purvis pulled a sheet of paper from the folder. "Says here Hatfield's hound stinks, drools, and pees on the wheelchair restraints."

"Jiggsie's got gum disease," Hatfield said. "He can't help drooling."

"The one person who wasn't complaining about Hatfield was complaining about something Hatfield already brought up," Purvis said, taking another letter from the folder. "Buses were late on May eighth. Real late. That's true enough. Problem was, when the early shift got to the garage to take the buses out, they found all the tires slashed."

"Told you, you need a watchman out there," Hatfield said.

"We had a watchman out there." Purvis reached in his briefcase for a set of 8 x 10 photographs. "And this is what he saw." He spread the photos on the table. "These pictures were taken by Deputy Sheriff Dave Bauer early on the morning of May eighth. They show Snooker Hatfield and Hatfield McCoy slashing the tires on both our buses."

There was a commotion in the spectator seats. Owen looked up in time to see the courtroom door slam shut. "Let the record show," he told the stenographer, "that Snooker Hatfield has just vacated the premises."

"Easiest thing in the world to doctor photographs," Hatfield said. "Don't see that these pictures prove anything." He shoved the glossy photos to the far corner of the table, out of everyone's reach but his own. "What about all the money the feds are paying to run these here buses?"

Owen stood, walked to the end of the table, and scooped up the photographs. "Mr. McCoy, in following up on your complaints, I've checked out the Contrary Comet's subsidy. Every time you pay a dollar to take a trip, federal and state taxpayers chip in four dollars. That's a fairly high rate of subsidy, but it's not uncommon for systems this size." He returned the photos to Purvis. "I do think, though, if you were really concerned about the cost of the bus service, there are some fairly simple steps you could take."

Owen went back to the head of the table and sat down. "First," he said, raising one finger, "stop slashing their tires. Second, stop demanding special service. And third," he concluded, spreading Hatfield's letters on the table in front of him, "stop bogging the system down with these absurd complaints."

"I just want what's due me," Hatfield said.

"It's our aim to see you get just that," Owen replied.

"On that note, I'm not quite through here," Purvis said. He fished in his righthand trousers pocket and pulled out a plastic Baggie holding two lead slugs. "On May fourteenth, somebody put two thirty-seven-caliber slugs through the windows of our double-ought-two bus. The slugs lodged in the rear seat and scared the crap out of the driver and Donnie Huss, the only passenger left on the late run.

"Donnie ain't rode with us since." Purvis raised his left hand like a magician showing he had nothing up his sleeve. Then he dipped it ceremoniously into his other trousers pocket and pulled out another plastic Baggie. The lead slugs in the new Baggie clunked as he shook it.

"Now the bullets in this here bag were retrieved by Deputy Bauer after Hatfield McCoy had spent some of his watchman time using the dump behind Gobbler's Knob for target practice."

"You got no right to invade my privacy that way," Hatfield objected.

"Dump's public property, Hatfield. Deputy Bauer was just tidying it up, doing his job. On a hunch, though, he ran ballistics tests on your slugs, and guess what?"

Hatfield was silent.

Purvis held both bags of slugs aloft. "Tests showed the bullets we dug out of our bus seats came from the same gun you was using for target practice."

Hatfield backed his wheelchair away from the table. "Half the county uses the dump for target practice. You got no way of knowing which slugs were mine."

"Deputy Bauer has pictures of you taking potshots at a crib mattress, and he's more than willing to testify he got the right slugs." Purvis turned to the rear of the courtroom. "That so, Dave?"

Two burly deputy sheriffs, one male and one female, had entered the courtroom and stood near the main door. The straps on their mountie's hats were cinched tightly in the creases of their double chins, and the polished butts of their holstered guns gleamed across the room. The male deputy grinned and nodded in response to Purvis's question.

"I want me a lawyer," Hatfield said.

★   ★   ★

PURVIS TOSSED A crumpled paper towel in the receptacle by the men's room door while Owen ran cold water over his hands and splashed some on his face. It all seemed too easy, Owen thought. It hardly seemed worth all the worrying, rehearsing, and dissembling he'd put into meeting with Hatfield McCoy.

"Whooee," Purvis said. "I knew we had his pecker in our pocket when Hatfield started whining that he needed a lawyer."

"He needs professional help, all right," Owen reached for a paper towel. "He could also use a shrink, a barber, and a vet for his hound."

"And when he asked you where the subsidy money went, it was a stroke of genius to break it all down in dollars per trip."

"I figured he'd never be able to add it all up that way."

"But giving him the numbers made it seem like we had nothing to hide."

That was the trouble, Owen thought. They did have something to hide. And he was helping them hide it.

"Don't look so glum," Purvis said. "We nailed the bastard's balls to the wall."

"Guess I'm just a sore winner."

They pushed through the men's room door to find a glowing Mary Beth waiting in the hallway. She gave Owen a quick hug and a look that cheerleaders give quarterbacks who have just won the big game.

"See, winning's not so bad," Purvis said.

"Cahoots, by God. You're all in cahoots." Hatfield careened his wheelchair down the hallway toward them, leaving the two burly deputies in his wake.

Hatfield skidded to a stop just short of the end of the corridor, pinning the three of them in the corner between the men's room door and the rear stairwell. "I saw that hug. Been taking it out in trade, ain't you?" he asked Owen. "Cozying up to Contrary cooze and filching my tax money."

He leered at Mary Beth and stroked his tobacco-stained beard. "Can't say's I blame you, though. Lips like those, I bet she could lick the label off a Louisville slugger."

"Watch your mouth, Hatfield," Purvis said.

Hatfield hooked the hem of Mary Beth's skirt with his ebony cane and started to raise it. "Let's just see what you're getting in return for all those federal bucks."

Owen planted his foot between Hatfield's knees and propelled the wheelchair backward. Hatfield waved help-lessly as the chair rocketed in reverse and crashed against an upright water cooler. The cooler toppled to the floor, flooding the hallway.

Hatfield lurched unsteadily from his wheelchair and flailed at Owen with his cane.

Owen was so surprised to see Hatfield on his feet that he was late protecting himself. As the cane smashed down against his cheekbone, a flash of light pierced his retina.

When Owen's vision cleared, the two deputies were maneuvering a kicking Hatfield back into his wheelchair.

"Jesus Christ," Owen said. "You can walk."

Hatfield bit the wrist of the female deputy, who jerked free of him and slipped in the spreading pool of water.

"Of course I can walk," Hatfield shouted. "Thank God I don't have to."

The deputy recovered her balance and looped her billy

club around Hatfield's neck from behind, pinning him against his wheelchair. Hatfield's legs jerked twice, then fell limp against the wheelchair's footrest.

A flashbulb popped, and Owen realized it had been a flash camera, not Hatfield's glancing blow, that had caused him to see stars. A chubby cigar-chomping photographer moved in on Hatfield and the deputies, crouching and focusing.

Purvis retrieved Hatfield's cane from the spreading pool of water and tapped the cameraman's arm with its silver tip. "That's enough, Rupert," he said. "We don't want people thinking the deputies here used undue force in subduing Mr. McCoy."

Purvis wiped the cane dry with a wadded handkerchief. "You've made quite a mess here, Hatfield. Appears to me you owe an apology to my sister and Mr. Allison."

Hatfield planted his feet in the footrests and strained against the billy club pressing down on his Adam's apple. "Arrgh," he said, eyeballs popping.

"We'll accept that apology for the time being," Purvis said. He slapped the handle of the cane hard against his own palm. "Now Hatfield, consider what we got here. We got pictures of you slashing bus tires, a misdemeanor. We got ballistic tests that show you shot up our buses, a felony. We just got a picture of you assaulting Mr. Allison, another felony, and, finally, these pictures show you standing on both your legs to swing this here cane, a supremely stupid act for somebody collecting full disability payments from the county."

"You fuckers are cheating me out of my rightful due."

"I'm powerful sorry you feel that way, Hatfield, because if I hear one more word about your rightful due, or if you send one more complaining letter to DOT, or if you so much as fart within fifty feet of our buses, or if you come within a cane's length of my sister again . . ." Purvis flexed the ebony cane. "I'll break your pecker off at its flabby roots and see you do hard time in the county jail."

Purvis snapped the cane in two over the arm of the wheelchair. "Do I make myself clear?"

Hatfield made a hawking noise deep in his throat, tried to spit, and came up dry.

Purvis handed the two halves of the cane to the male deputy. "Keep these around in case we need to press charges and get this sorry shit out of my sight."

The two deputies wheeled Hatfield off down the corridor, leaving a trail of footprints straddling each wet tire track.

Purvis shook his head at the shattered water cooler. "That Hatfield's death on glassware." He linked arms with Owen and Mary Beth and started back down the corridor, allowing as how the day couldn't have worked out better if he'd staged it himself.

11

THINGS THAT GO BUMP
IN THE NIGHT

OWEN TOLD HIMSELF that he didn't have to lean on Mary Beth, that he could make it to her couch all by himself, in spite of the glasses of moonshine he'd consumed at Pokey Joe's. He was sure he could walk. Thank God he didn't have to. Wasn't that what Hatfield had said? He stumbled over a standing lamp and sank heavily to the couch, pulling Mary Beth down beside him.

Mary Beth half rose and caught the teetering lamp before it fell. "Shh," she whispered. "You'll wake Stuart."

"Can't believe it. Can't believe I kicked a cripple."

"You were defending my honor."

"Did I say cripple? 'Scuse me. I meant a physically challenged person with a disability."

"Cripple's the right word for Hatfield. He's a mental, moral, and physical cripple."

"I kicked a cripple and lied in a court of law."

Mary Beth ran her tongue along the edge of her handkerchief and dabbed at the red incision Hatfield's cane had cut into Owen's left cheek. "It wasn't exactly a court of law, and you didn't exactly lie."

"Kicked a cripple, lied in a court of law, forged federal documents, drank too much moonshine." Owen held up four fingers, one for each transgression. "Know what?"

"What?"

"I feel great."

"A life of crime must agree with you."

"No, I think it's the company I'm keeping." Owen stared at his four upraised fingers. "Know what else?" Owen raised his right hand. "I've got a whole 'nother hand left to count more sins."

"What did you have in mind?"

Owen looked from his left hand to his right. "Man starts with drinking, lying, forging, and cripple-kicking, no telling what he might end up doing."

Mary Beth traced the outline of his wound lightly with her finger. "No telling."

Owen captured her finger and kissed its tip. "Pretty soon he's liable to find himself taking the Lord's name in vain and procrastinating."

"Not procrastinating. Anything but procrastinating."

"Know what else?" Owen whispered, nuzzling her neck.

"No, what?"

"I'm not as drunk as you think." He undid the top buttons of her blouse. She shifted on the couch, clearing his way to the lower buttons. "Just needed a drink or two to get past being nervous."

"Nervous about what?"

The blouse fell away. "About what we're about to do."

Mary Beth reached down and unbuckled his belt. "There's nothing to be nervous about," she whispered, unzipping his trousers.

OWEN FELT A cover being pulled from his body and opened his eyes. Mary Beth stood at the living room window, clutching the quilt from the sofa against her breasts. The quilt shielded her from anyone in the darkness outside, but left Owen with a clear view of her slim hips and bare buttocks.

"What's the matter?" he whispered.

"I thought I heard something moving outside."

Owen fished his underpants from the floor and pulled them on.

Mary Beth turned from the window and shrugged. "I must have dreamed it." She returned to the couch and ran her index finger along the elastic of Owen's briefs. "It's past two. You'd better be going."

"Can't I spend the night here?"

"I don't want Stuart to see you in the morning."

"He saw me here once before."

"You were sleeping off a drunk then."

Owen nuzzled the hair at the nape of her neck. "We can say I'm sleeping off a drunk again."

Mary Beth combed his hair lightly with her fingers. "I don't want to lie to him."

"Saying I was drunk isn't much of a lie."

"He'd guess what happened if he finds you here. I'm no good at lying."

The quilt dropped in her arms, exposing one bare breast. Owen bent and kissed it. "In a way, we're lying by not telling him."

She pulled away from him and stood up. "If he doesn't ask the question, it's not lying. And if he doesn't find you here, he won't ask questions."

She retrieved his trousers from the floor and handed them to him. "I'll drive you back to your car."

"No need. The walk will clear my head."

"You sure?"

"It can't be more than half a mile back to Pokey Joe's. There's no need for you to bother getting dressed."

She pulled the quilt around her with one hand and kissed him. "Thank you."

He reached under the quilt and drew her to him. "I'm the one who should be thanking you."

THE ROAD BACK to Pokey Joe's had been slashed into the side of a hill above a winding creek bed. Owen could hear the creek gurgling below, but it was hidden from view by scrub brush and dark clumps of spindly cedar. On the up-hill side, denser stands of cedar stretched from the rocky gash at the road's edge to the crest of the ridge, shredding the moonlight into pale slivers. A small animal skittered onto the road ahead of Owen, paused in a patch of moon-light, and disappeared into the scrub brush. Startled, Owen shivered.

Beyond the bend where the animal disappeared, the bone pile began. Instead of scrub brush and cedar, the slope down to the creek bed was covered with smoldering slate. Thin wisps of smoke rose from the slate and blended with ground fog from the creek to blanket the bone pile with a murky haze.

Owen heard the whine of a truck grinding its gears to make it up the hill behind him. The truck's headlights threw his shadow into the fog as it swept around the bend toward the bone pile. Owen stepped off the road to give the truck room when he felt it bearing down on him. A horn blared, and he dove headfirst onto the matted grass at the edge of the bone pile.

Skidding to a stop against a pile of slate, Owen crawled to his knees and watched the truck careen down the road. Headlights flashed off something metallic as it disappeared around a bend. Brakes squealed and he heard tires biting asphalt, followed by a sudden silence. Then the truck door slammed, and the night was quiet again.

Owen rose shakily to his feet and peered into the murk where the truck had vanished. The path rustled behind him, and a nasal voice said, "Over here, motherfucker." He had half turned when he felt a sharp blow behind his right ear and blackness closed over him.

SULPHUR BURNED IN his nostrils and someone was tugging him backward by his armpits over a bed of loose slate. Owen could hear the man's labored breathing, somewhere between a grunt and a gasp. When the gasps outnumbered the grunts, the man laid Owen back on the smoldering slate and rested before he started in again. It was like being dragged over the dying coals of an endless barbecue pit by an asthmatic giant.

Owen let his hands dangle loosely by his sides and ran his fingers over the shards of loose slate. He closed his right hand over a chunk the size of a hockey puck and waited. When the man stopped to rest again, Owen sat up, pivoted, and swung the chunk at the place where he expected to find the man's head. The blow caught the man on the shoulder and knocked him sideways. Owen scrambled toward him, raising the slate for another blow.

The man scuttled backward, raising his left arm to ward off the attack. "For Christ's sake, Owen! I'm trying to help get you out of here."

Owen recognized the voice. "Hollis?"

"It's me, yeah. Can you walk?"

Owen got to his knees. His vision swam and his legs buckled when he tried to stand. "Don't know if I can walk. I'm having trouble just standing up." He took a deep breath, and his nostrils filled with the stench of rotting eggs.

Hollis helped Owen to his feet and supported him while he moved one foot forward on the slippery slate and started up the slope. They were about a hundred feet from the stationary headlight beams swimming in the murk at the top of the slope when a second pair of headlights pulled in and a car door slammed. A flashlight played over the bone pile, coming to rest on Hollis and Owen. "Hello, down there," a young male voice shouted. "Can we help?"

Hollis swore under his breath and shouted back. "We're making it okay."

The flashlight holder scrambled down the bone pile toward them, kicking up a small avalanche of loose slate. When he reached Hollis and Owen, he played the light over their faces. "Your friend here looks stewed to the gills."

"I got it under control," Hollis said.

The man shoved the flashlight in Owen's face. "Is that blood?"

"He had a small accident."

"I'll help." The man shouldered Owen's weight so that he and Hollis could carry him up the hill. Just before they reached the top, the flashlight picked out something shiny below the roadway.

"What's that?" the man asked.

"Don't see nothing," Hollis said.

"Goddamn, it's a wheelchair." The man focused the flashlight beam and Owen could see that the wheelchair was overturned, tilted forward on its armatures and head-rest with its wheels in the air.

"Goddamn," Hollis echoed.

The two men set Owen down on the grass and picked their way back to the wheelchair. A crumpled body lay about twenty feet below the chair.

In the beam of light Owen recognized the straggly beard of Hatfield McCoy.

THE COUNTY SHERIFF'S office was spare and neat. The only items on the wall were a calendar from the Colt Firearms Company, a pair of dueling pistols encased in glass, and a framed citation from the United States Marine Corps bearing the name of the sheriff, Travis Jenkins, in hand-lettered script. The sheriff's crewcut was graying at the temples, but his uniform at five in the morning was as buttoned down as his office, and he looked to Owen as if he could still pass the corps physical.

The sheriff sat at attention behind his metal desk, his large manicured hands forming a steeple over a tiny tape recorder. "Let me get this straight, Mr. Allison," he said. "You say you were walking past the bone pile around two this morning when somebody coldcocked you, and the next thing you remember is Hollis Atkins trying to haul you out of the slate dump."

Owen winced at the sheriff's recitation, which sounded questionable even to him. "I'm afraid that's all I remember."

"And you've no idea how Hatfield McCoy came to be there with a broken neck?"

"No idea."

"You didn't see Hatfield when you got to the bone pile?"

"I told you, somebody hit me from behind just as I got there."

"So Hatfield could have been there already?"

"I guess so."

"But you didn't see Hatfield out there?"

"I told you, no. What's this all about? You think I had something to do with Hatfield's death?"

"Let's put it this way," the sheriff said. "Hatfield didn't strike me as being suicidal. And even if he had been, I doubt he would have wheeled himself all the way out Route 12 and rolled full tilt downhill into the bone pile on the off chance he'd break his neck or suffocate. Somebody sure as shit killed him."

"Why me?" Owen asked. "I gather he had lots of enemies."

"I'll grant you half the county had reason to wish Hatfield dead. But you're the most recent." Jenkins nodded toward the cut on Owen's left cheek. "That gash from his cane hasn't even started to scab over. And you were out there at the bone pile."

"I was out cold at the bone pile."

"So you say."

"Ask Hollis if you don't believe me."

"Hollis says that's the way he found you. Says he was driving by the bone pile, saw Hatfield's wheelchair, and stopped to help. Didn't say much about what happened before that."

"I'm afraid I can't help you there either."

The sheriff poured himself a cup of coffee and set it on a coaster bearing the Marine Corps insignia. "Where were you earlier last night?" he asked.

"Pokey Joe's. That's where I left my car."

"Just decided to walk from Pokey Joe's to the bone pile for exercise?"

Something in the sheriff's tone told Owen he knew exactly where he had spent the evening. "No, I went from Pokey Joe's to Mary Beth Hobb's house. I was walking back to my car when a truck forced me off the road and somebody hit me from behind."

"And you didn't get a good look at the truck or whoever hit you?"

Owen shook his head.

"What time did you leave Mary Beth's?"

"A little after two in the morning."

The sheriff stared into his coffee cup, then fixed his eyes on Owen. "Let me tell you something. Stony Hobbs is a genuine war hero. That means something in these parts. Most folks hereabouts are hoping he'll get back together with Mary Beth. So even if your story checks out, it doesn't sit well."

"I can't help that."

"There's something else you should know. My cousin Purvis is outside right now with Hollis Atkins. He's taken great pains to let me know you're a friend of his."

"The two of you don't seem like cousins."

"Because I'm not folksy like some TV bumpkin, you mean? Hell, Purvis is folksy enough for six generations of Jenkinses." The sheriff warmed his hands over his cup of coffee. "Actually, we're only second cousins. And I can get just as folksy as Purvis around election time."

The sheriff sipped his coffee and returned the cup to the exact center of the coaster. "The point I want to make is this: I know Purvis likes to trade on our relationship. But you better not expect any favors from me because he and I are related. Hell, I'm probably related to half the people in this county. That's how I got elected in the first place. But it's not how I stay elected. And it's not how I do my job."

"I take your point."

"You better. This county's not exactly a high-crime area. Typical month, we get a few serious bar fights and more than our share of DUIs. Nothing we can't handle. Since you feds started nosing around, though, we've had two unexplained deaths at the bone pile."

"Two unexplained deaths? You think Armitrage didn't die accidentally?"

The sheriff rubbed his hand across his mouth, as if he felt he'd said too much. "Besides that, there's been a disappearance. Nobody seems to be able to find Snooker Hatfield."

"Could be he had a falling out with Hatfield McCoy."

"More likely, he got spooked by those pictures Purvis turned up showing him slashing tires out at the bus barns."

"But he's a suspect?"

"In Hatfield's death? Hell, I told you, I've got a county full of suspects. But that hardly lets you off the hook." The sheriff pointed toward the door. "I'd like you to stop and see my deputy on the way out. First door on the left. She'll take a cast of those shoes you're wearing. Maybe help us sort out what went on at the bone pile. She'll want some blood and fiber samples, too."

"Maybe I should take a cup for a urine sample?"

The sheriff's steel gray eyes didn't waver. "Buddy, if I find out you had anything to do with Hatfield's death, we won't need a sample to recognize your urine. You'll be pissing pink." He unlocked his office door and let Owen out. "First door on the left. Keep in touch."

12

BEST LICK I EVER HIT

As THE MORNING FOG LIFTED from the hollow, Stony loaded rail ties, timber, and fence posts into the back of his trunk. Then he picked up Stuart and drove to the bone pile.

"I thought we were headed for the mine," Stuart said.

"Not this Saturday."

"This here's where that man died, isn't it?"

"Two men, recent," Stony said. "People been dying here ever since Hollis and I were kids."

"What are we stopping here for?"

Stony took a spade from the back of the truck. "Gonna fence off this here path. Save me a drunk or two. Maybe even a careless schoolkid."

Their shoes slid on the dew covering the matted grass path. Two crows nibbled at the carcass of a jack rabbit between the path and the smoldering shale. Stuart shied a rock at the crows, who took flight, cawed furiously, circled, and returned to their meal. Stony began spading a hole alongside the path.

"Isn't that the county's job?" Stuart asked.

"County hasn't done anything here in the last forty years. Not likely to in the next forty."

Stony brought a fence post and sledge down from the truck. His son held the post upright while Stony rested the sledge against his crotch and spat on his hands. Then he arched the sledge and drove the post cleanly into the center of the hole. The sharp crack of the sledge echoed off the hillside and sent the crows flying.

"Wow, that was some lick, Dad," Stuart said.

Stony spat on his hands again. "Best lick I ever hit."

AFTER FOUR HOURS, a row of upright fence posts skirted half the bone-pile path. Sweat dribbled down Stony's bare chest and soaked the waistband of his jeans. "Too hot to keep at this. I'll finish the day off in the mine." When he and Stuart had loaded their tools in the back of the truck, Stony said, "I'll drop you at your mother's house."

"I can help you at the mine."

"Don't need you there."

"I helped Hollis when you were in the hospital."

Stony ground the gears to brake a downhill skid. "Don't want you there. You get in, you never get out."

"What's that supposed to mean?"

"Means I don't want you down in the mine."

"But Dad . . ."

"Don't 'but' me, Jeb Stuart. You're not so old I can't still take a strap to you."

They drove in silence to Mary Beth's house. Stony

pulled into the driveway and said, "Tomorrow's Sunday. How about I stop by and give you some practice blocking short hops behind the plate?"

"Can't."

"What do you mean, 'can't'?"

Stuart shifted in his seat. "Going to Barkley with Mom."

"What's in Barkley?"

"Going to meet Mr. Allison's mother. I promised I'd go along."

"Thought this Allison guy was back in D.C."

"His mother still lives in Barkley."

"Your mom seeing a lot of this guy?"

Stuart shrugged. "I guess."

"You guess? Don't you know?"

"Why don't you ask Mom?"

Stony saw the curtains part in the front window. He waited for Mary Beth to come out, but the door didn't open. "I'm asking you, Goddammit."

"I don't know, Dad. She sees him some. Not a lot."

"Well, get yourself out, then. I got to get on to the mine."

"Maybe we can go back to the bone pile next Saturday. One more day, we ought to be able to finish off that fence."

Stony reached across and pulled the truck door shut. "Yeah. We'll finish it off."

STONY AND HOLLIS were into their fifth round of beers at Pokey Joe's when Stony brought up the subject of his son.

"Boy wants to help out in the mine. He don't understand how it sucks you in and chews you up."

"Show him the letter," Hollis said.

"My Uncle Vic's letter? It didn't stop me."

"Stopped me," Hollis said. "I got out as quick as I could. Still got the letter?"

"Still in the same drawer where my daddy kept it."

"Show it to Stuart. That drawer and the bone-pile path scared the piss out of me when we were his age."

Stony remembered the first time he and Hollis snuck into his father's bedroom to find the .45 automatic he kept tucked under his wool socks in his dresser. Stuck in one corner of the top drawer was a horseshoe-shaped box that held a starched white collar, a gold-plated watch, and the letter. The letter was written by his great-uncle on the back of a store receipt while he waited for rescuers to tunnel to him and two other miners caught in the cave-in of 1919. The awkward printed capitals were pinched and squeezed to fit on the small scrap of paper, and the lines sloped downward as if they'd slide off the sheet.

"I am in God's hands now," the letter read. "Please take the clothes and the collar box from my room to my parents, Wayne and Mildred Hobbs of Contrary. There is $136.52 and a gold watch in the collar box. I want them to have it, with all my love." The signature, Victor Hobbs, overran the last line, as if he'd signed the note as an afterthought and couldn't see what he'd written before.

"I used to think about that letter a lot when I was in 'Nam," Stony said. "Reckon he knew he wasn't going to make it out when he wrote it."

"He must have had some hope. There's always hope."

"When he wrote that note, he knew. There's a peace comes with knowing." He finished off a Strohs and ran his shirttail across his mouth. "In the tunnels in 'Nam, the not knowing was what got to you. That's when I'd think about Uncle Vic, sitting there in the dark, knowing."

"A hundred and thirty-six dollars."

"Seemed like all the money in the world when we were kids, didn't it?"

"Don't seem like so much anymore," Hollis said.

"It was a lot back then. Specially to a miner. It helped my granddaddy buy our mine."

"Same mine you want to keep Stuart out of," Hollis said.

"Mining's killed every Hobbs that ever took a pick into a hole. Killed Uncle Vic. Killed my granddaddy. Killed my daddy. I don't want it killing Stuart."

"You're making a go of it."

"The hell I am. Best I can hope is to break even. And I'll only do that so long as my health holds and the regulators look the other way."

Stony turned toward the bar to signal Reba for another round. Between him and the bar he saw a hulking biker wearing a handlebar moustache, a black leather jacket crisscrossed with silver chains, and a German helmet with a protruding spike.

The biker used his teeth to pull a black leather glove off his left hand. "Which one of you's Hobbs?"

Stony placed his hands carefully on the tabletop. "That's me."

The biker pulled off his other glove. "You the motherfucker sucker-punched my brother over to Mullens?"

"Can't say I remember that."

"Why don't you come outside with me, see if I can't refresh your memory?"

"We don't want no trouble here," Hollis said.

The biker ground his right fist into the palm of his left hand. "Ain't talking to you, pussy mouth."

Stony held up both hands, palms outward, and said, "It's all right, Hollis. Man wants to go outside, we'll go outside."

Stony edged out of the booth with his palms still raised and facing outward. As soon as he cleared the booth, he pivoted and hit the biker in the face with a short right cross. He wasn't able to get much on the punch, but it took the biker by surprise and he felt the man's nose pop.

The biker brought his hands to his face, saying "Son-bitch." Blood dribbled out between his fingertips.

Stony followed with a short left to the stomach. Pain shot through his arm as his fist collided with the chains crossing the biker's midsection. The biker doubled over, expelling a stream of blood and spittle.

The pain in his fist enraged Stony. He twisted the biker's wrist behind his back, grabbed the helmet spike, wedged the biker's stomach against the bar, and swung the spike downward.

The bar's patrons grabbed their drinks and backed away. Stony lifted the man's head by the helmet spike and smashed it against the bar again. The third time he jerked the head upright, the chinstrap broke and the helmet came free in his hand. He shifted his grip on the spike and was about to use the helmet as a club when Hollis caught him from behind.

"Cut it out, Stony," he said, pulling him backward. "You'll kill the guy!"

The bar was dead silent. Reba reached under the cash register and held up the stock of a twelve-gauge shotgun. "That's enough, boys. Take it outside."

The biker groaned, slid off the bar, and thudded to the floor. Stony grabbed him under the armpits and motioned for Hollis to take his feet. They dragged him toward the door, clearing a broad path through the dried sawdust and peanut shucks.

Reba ran a damp cloth over the blood on the bar. "Show's over," she announced. "Let's see if we can't put the bar to its proper use."

Stony and Hollis dropped the biker's limp body at the edge of the gravel parking lot. Ground fog had settled in, and it was difficult to make out the cars in the lot. "Must be a bike around here somewhere," Stony said.

"Harley, most likely," Hollis said.

A lone headlight pierced the fog, followed by the whine of an engine. More engines kicked to life as single headlights blinked on all around them. They were in the center of a half-circle of motorcycles, and the circle shrank as the bikes moved forward.

"Oh, shit," Hollis said.

"Get back inside," Stony shouted to Hollis. "Call Travis Jenkins."

Hollis ran for the door but a motorcycle cut Stony off and herded him back to the center of the circle.

"Let the other guy go," a voice behind Stony said. "We got the one I want."

The biker standing in the center of the throbbing machines was the spitting image of the man Stony had just laid out. His right forearm was in a cast, and his left was covered by a studded leather wristband. "What'd you do, sucker-punch my baby brother, too?"

Stony stood frozen in the circle of headlights.

"It ain't gonna be so easy this time, motherfuck," the man said. He drew his cast back and whipped it across Stony's jaw.

Stony fell to his knees, and two bikers grabbed him by the arms. While they held him, the man with the cast measured the distance to Stony's belt buckle and kicked him squarely in the stomach.

Then all three bikers were stomping and kicking him. Stony curled up into a ball. So long as he kept both eyes open, he thought, he could wriggle away from the worst blows. A boot caught him in the cheekbone, closing his right eye. He concentrated on keeping his left eye open. So long as he could see, he knew he was still alive.

A shot thundered, and a motorcycle on the perimeter spun and toppled. With his one good eye, Stony could see Hollis framed in the lit doorway of Pokey Joe's, holding Reba's twelve-gauge.

"Back off, there," Hollis shouted. "Next man to touch him gets the other barrel."

Stony lowered his face to the gravel and closed his eyes. In the distance, he could hear a siren winding uphill from the hollow.

STUART AND MARY Beth were sitting in the front pew of the chapel. In the row behind them were Hollis, Purvis, and Purvis's cousin, Sheriff Travis Jenkins. Then came Doc Pritchard, his nurse Rose, and the nun from the Huntington hospital.

The preacher was ranting on about hellfire and damnation. The Dundee twins sat on the other side of the aisle, still in their combat fatigues. Behind them were a moustached biker balancing a German helmet on his lap, the bearded guy from the federal government, a miner holding a crumpled sheet of paper, and two small Vietnamese children. An empty wheelchair sat in the center aisle beside the back pew.

The preacher was likening the fires of hell to the fires of the bone pile; or maybe he was likening the fires of the bone pile to the fires of hell. Stony couldn't quite follow the sermon. Something was wrong. It wasn't what the preacher was saying, it was where he was saying it. Or, rather, where Stony was listening to it. The preacher was standing behind the pulpit, where he usually stood. But Stony was beside him, on the altar, staring out at the congregation through a picket fence of lit candles.

It was a goddamn memorial service. Stony struggled to move, but he'd been strapped into some kind of box. He mouthed the word *goddamn*, then said it out loud. Nobody paid attention to him. "Goddamn," Stony said again, but the preacher went on ranting. "Goddamn," he shouted. "Goddamn, goddamn, goddamn!"

He awoke shouting the words, strapped into a hospital bed, his chest wrapped in elastic bandages, and gauze covering half his face.

Hollis moved to Stony's side. "Easy there, hoss. You've got two cracked ribs and were thrashing around so much they had to strap you down."

"Something's wrong with my face."

"Busted cheekbone," Hollis said. "Lucky they missed the eyesocket. Doc Pritchard filled you with painkiller."

Mary Beth stood at the foot of the bed. She had pulled a baggy sweater over the sweats she used to sleep in. "Bloody damn fool. Won't it ever stop?"

"Not my fault," Stony said. "They came after me."

"Because you'd gone after them."

"Can't remember."

"You sure coldcocked the one in the bar," Hollis said. "He's three rooms down. Sheriff's got a guard on both your doors."

"Oh, grow up," Mary Beth said. "Who cares who cold-cocked who? Grown men, still seeing who's the fastest gun. One day Travis won't be around to save you."

"Hollis saved me," Stony said. "Shot the lights out of one of them Harleys. Kapow."

"Kapow," Hollis laughed.

"Jesus, you're as bad as he is," Mary Beth said.

"I'll go see if I can find Doc Pritchard," Hollis said.

As Hollis left the room, Mary Beth moved to the side of the bed and took Stony's immobilized hand. "I thought I was through with this."

"Thanks for coming down."

"Travis stopped by. Stuart wanted to come. Only way I could get him to stay home was to come myself."

"He's a good boy."

"He shouldn't have to see his father drunk and beat up."

"I was just drinking with Hollis, minding my own business."

"Why do I think I've heard that before?"

"This means it'll take a while longer for me to pay you back. For the operation, I mean."

Mary Beth sighed and squeezed his hand. "We'll get along."

Hollis returned with the doctor, who asked to be left alone with Stony.

"What's so bad you can't talk about it in front of Hollis

and Mary Beth?" Stony asked when the door closed behind them.

"I think you know," the doctor said.

"Shit, Doc, I've had my ribs busted before. They'll heal fine."

"It's not your ribs I'm worried about. Didn't those doctors in Huntington give you a chest X ray before your operation?"

"Yeah, sure."

"What'd they tell you about it?"

"Showed me a picture of a spider in my lung. Told me I had miner's asthma."

"It's black lung, Stony. You know what that is."

"It killed my daddy. You didn't find out about it in time."

"We found out about it in plenty of time. He wouldn't stay out of that mine of yours."

"It was all he knew."

"It killed him, Stony. Don't let it kill you, too. That spider in your lung thrives on coal dust; you keep feeding it, it'll eat you alive."

"I've stopped smoking. I can't stop mining. I got debts to pay."

"You try to pay them by mining, your debts will outlive you."

"Okay, I get the picture." Stony twisted under his restraints. "When can I get out of here?"

"I want to keep you a couple of days for observation."

"A couple of days? Jesus Christ. I can't stay here that long."

"You couldn't go back to the mine with those ribs, anyhow. Take it easy for a while."

"It's just . . . I get restless is all."

"You won't have to stay strapped down. Let's just see where we are after a day."

"Thanks, Doc. Could you maybe give me something to help me sleep? I've been having trouble lately."

"I can do that."

"Maybe now? Before Mary Beth and Hollis get back."

The doctor left the room and came back with a hypodermic needle. He unstrapped Stony's arm, swabbed it, and inserted the needle.

Stony took a deep breath and closed his eyes. In his dream, the preacher was still ranting about hellfire and bone piles. But at least now Stony was back in the congregation where he belonged.

13

IF THE BONE IS YOURS

OWEN LIKED THE WAY his convertible leaned into the curving backwoods roads and the way Mary Beth's blonde hair rippled in the wind. He was glad she hadn't imprisoned it in a scarf. He had hoped, though, for more interaction with Stuart than he was getting. Shoehorned into the narrow backseat, the boy hadn't said a word since Owen had picked them up to drive to his mother's home in Barkley.

As they passed the bone pile, Stuart pointed to the freshly planted row of fence posts and said, more to his mother than to Owen, "Dad and I put up those posts. Gonna fence off the path. Keep drunks from wandering down there."

"Good idea," Owen said.

"Mr. Allison was at the bone pile the night Hatfield McCoy died," Mary Beth said, raising her voice in the wind.

"Oh, yeah?" Stuart said. "What happened?"

"Don't know," Owen answered. "Somebody clobbered me."

"Somebody clobbered my dad last night, too."

"Lot of that going around," Owen said. He turned onto the main road, a four-lane highway slashed through the country-side. Deep gashes in the mountain left scarred limestone walls on the uphill side of the straightaway. After a while, the road narrowed and followed the natural terrain. Here hillside cuts were more shallow and covered with small white patches of chalky gravel. Stands of stiff beech trees covered the slope beyond the chalky patches. Isolated homes sat in half-hidden hollows and on cleared knolls. Well-to-do home owners had satellite dishes and separate garages, while the not-so-well-off had makeshift antennas and hoodless cars.

Owen took the convertible over a rise and downshifted as the road dropped to follow the contours of a winding creek bed. "My father called this God's country," he said as the beech shadows enveloped the car.

"Is your father still alive?" Mary Beth asked.

"No, he worked for the Highway Department. He drowned trying to control the flooding when a makeshift dam let go."

"Like Buffalo Creek?" Stuart asked.

"Like Buffalo Creek, except not so many died. It was one of those jerryrigged dams formed by mine dumpings."

"How awful," Mary Beth said.

"He was working with the Corps of Engineers to put a string of real dams up and down the state," Owen said. "Now that they're built out, flooding's not the problem it used to be."

After an hour on the road, Owen pulled up in front of a two-storey frame house at the end of a cul-de-sac cut into the side of a steep hill. The screen door opened, and a small black bundle darted through, cleared the porch steps in two bounds, and sped to Owen's side. Standing on its hind legs, tail wagging, the black dog barely cleared his kneecaps.

Owen knelt to pet the dog. "Buster, I'd like you to meet Mary Beth and Stuart Hobbs."

Buster stayed on his hind legs, panting and wagging his tail, his coal black eyes focused on Owen.

"My goodness," Mary Beth said. "What kind of dog is that?"

"Poodle."

"Doesn't look like the poodles you see on TV," Stuart said.

"Mom doesn't believe in those fancy fluffy cuts," Owen said, "She trims him to look like a regular mutt."

"What do I have to do to get introduced?" Owen's mother stood on the porch, wiping flour-covered hands on the front of a checkered apron.

"Stand on your hind legs, wag your tail, and pant a lot," Owen said. "Works every time."

"I can do the hind legs part," his mother said. She waved a white hand and said, "Hi there, I'm Ruth Allison."

Owen led Mary Beth and Stuart up the steps of the brick porch and introduced them. As they shook hands, Buster bounced in circles around the newcomers, yapping and pawing at Owen's pantleg.

"You'd best take that dog out back and let him work off some of his energy," Ruth said.

Owen took Stuart to the garage behind the house,

where he found a baseball bat and a plastic bucket full of used tennis balls. Buster leapt and yapped at the sight of the bucket and followed Owen and Stuart to the field behind the garage. It was overgrown with broom grass, but bare patches of dirt could still be seen marking the bases and pitcher's mound of an abandoned baseball diamond. The field ended a short distance beyond second base, where a two-foot retaining wall made of railroad ties formed the outfield fence. On the slope above the retaining wall, Owen's mother had planted a terraced garden. Delicate white roses bloomed beyond the right-field fence, where balls rarely landed, with heartier rose-purple rhododendron bushes in centerfield giving way to white and yellow daisies on the left-field terrace. The flowers were backed by a steep limestone wall topped by a grassy slope.

Owen stood at home plate and lobbed a tennis ball beyond the bare patch that had once been second base. Buster sped through the grass, leapt, caught the ball on the first bounce, and shook his head once to kill it. Then he trotted back over the pitcher's mound, stopped at the edge of the bare patch marking the batter's box, dropped the ball, and nudged it with his nose so it rolled right to Owen's feet.

"Wow," said Stuart. "Where'd he learn to do that?"

"I trained him when we were in California. There's no room for a dog where I live now."

Stuart picked up the ball and threw it in a low arc over second base. Buster took off when Stuart cocked his arm and caught the ball as it caromed off the wooden retaining wall.

"Gets a good jump on the ball," Stuart said.

"Yeah. Too bad he can't hit a lick."

Stuart laughed. It was the first time Owen had been able to coax so much as a smile out of him.

"Looks like you had a ballfield here once."

"Enough for pitching and infield practice. The field is too short for much else." Owen threw the tennis ball into the outfield and waited as Buster retrieved it. "If we wanted to hit, we had to use tennis balls. Buster's grandfather fielded for us."

"How'd that work?"

Owen explained the rules while they took turns throwing balls for Buster to track down. A batted ball hitting the railroad-tie retaining wall on the fly or first bounce was a single. A ball over the ties into the garden was a double, unless it hit the limestone wall behind the garden on the fly, in which case it was a triple. Anything onto the grass slope above the limestone facing was a home run.

Stuart pointed to the stand of cedar beyond the grassy slope. "What about the trees? Anybody ever reach the trees?"

"We called that a Wes Whitfield wallop. Wes was the only one of us could hit a tennis ball that far. Signed a contract with the Reds right out of high school."

"The Cincinnati Reds? Whatever happened to him?"

"Killed in Vietnam."

"My dad knew lots of guys killed over there," Stuart said.

"Your dad was over there himself, wasn't he?"

"Two years," Stuart said. "Weren't you?"

"I was in graduate school. It kept me out of the draft."

"What's that?"

"Graduate school?"

"Yeah, that."

"I stayed in college after I got my bachelor's degree. Took more courses and got a master's in engineering."

"Was it hard?"

"In lots of ways it was easier than being an undergraduate. The instructors were better."

"No, I mean was it hard not going to Vietnam?"

Owen didn't know how to take the question. "Not at the time, no. It wasn't something I was real eager to do."

"Oh."

Owen handed Stuart the bat. "Want me to pitch you a few?"

"Sure." Stuart dug into the batter's box while Owen carried the bucket of tennis balls to the bare patch of ground that marked the pitcher's mound. Buster scampered back and forth between the mound and second base, tail wagging.

Owen stood on the mound and looked in at Stuart standing at home plate, looping the bat in a relaxed arc. A nasal voice in the back of his mind announced, "Now pitching for the Cincinnati Reds—Owen Allison." Owen smiled. He was surprised to find that there was still a press box announcer somewhere in his subconscious, and that the announcer still sounded like Waite Hoyt, who broadcast the Reds' games when he was in high school.

Owen lobbed an easy pitch toward the plate, getting the feel of the motion, and Stuart slammed the ball off the limestone facing into a rhododendron bush. Buster leaped over the short retaining wall into the terraced garden, bounded into the bush, retrieved the ball, and brought it back to the mound.

"Triple," Owen announced. "Man on third, nobody out."

Stuart lined Owen's next pitch off the short retaining wall.

"Single," Owen announced in Waite Hoyt's nasal twang. "One run in, man on first."

Owen swiped the ball across his pantleg to get rid of some of Buster's saliva, gripped the ball at the end of his fingertips, and threw a knuckleball toward home plate. Unstabilized by its lack of rotation, the ball fluttered toward Stuart, dripping sharply as he swung over it.

"Wow," said Stuart. "What was that?"

"Knuckler. A scuffed and slimy tennis ball will do all sorts of tricks if you know how to throw it."

"Will you show me?"

"Wait till it's your turn to pitch."

Owen tried to throw another knuckleball, but his fingers slipped and the ball flew over the garage backstop.

"That's the trouble with my knuckler. Never could control it."

The game settled into a clear pattern, with Stuart crushing any ball Owen threw near the plate. When the score reached twenty to nothing, the announcer's voice in the back of Owen's head clicked off, too proud to broadcast the play-by-play for a game so lopsided. Owen thought even Buster looked tired, although the dog's tail hadn't stopped wagging.

Owen went into an elaborate windup and threw his best fastball toward the plate. Stuart met the ball cleanly and drove it in an ascending arc over the limestone wall, across the grassy slope, and into the cedars well beyond the property.

Stuart stood at home plate watching the ball disappear. "There you go! A Wes Whoosis wallop."

"Whitfield," Owen said. "A Wes Whitfield wallop."

Buster, who had run to the retaining wall to watch the ball disappear, trotted back to the infield and pawed at the yellow ball bucket just as Owen's mother called them in to dinner.

The aroma of freshly baked bread blended with the heavy smell of roast beef as they joined hands to say grace. With Mary Beth holding his right hand lightly and his mother clasping his left hand in a firm, remembered grip, Owen felt something he hadn't felt in years. He felt safe, safe at home.

Lying in the corner, Buster gnawed on a shoulder bone that had been worked clean.

"That's some smart dog," Stuart said.

"Poodles are a smart breed," Ruth Allison said. "I read somewhere they're the second-smartest breed in the world."

"What's the smartest?"

"I believe it was border collies."

"But you've got to think herding sheep was a big part of the final exam," Owen said. "Right, Buster?"

Buster looked up at the sound of his name. When it appeared Owen wasn't offering him any food, he turned his attention back to the bone between his paws.

"We had a dog once," Stuart said. "A coonhound named Trixie. She got old and died."

"Sounds like you miss her."

"Yes, ma'am," Stuart said.

"Of course you do," Ruth said. She reached out and ran her finger lightly over the scar on Owen's left cheek. "Owen, whatever happened to your cheek?"

"A man hit me with his cane."

"Whatever for?"

"He disagreed with some things I said in a court hearing."

"A court hearing?" Ruth Allison said. "Well, I hope the man's in jail."

"He's not a worry anymore."

"That's so, ma'am," Stuart added. "He's dead."

"Stuart!" Mary Beth interrupted.

"Is this true, Owen?" his mother said. "The man who struck you is dead?"

Owen swallowed and wiped his mouth. "It's true."

"There's got to be more to it. How did the man die?"

"He died out to the devil's bone pile," Stuart said.

"You still have bone piles?" Ruth said. "I thought the federal government was going to clean them up."

"My dad says, best they can do is keep the miners from starting any new ones."

"So this man's death was an accident?" Ruth asked.

"Nobody knows," Owen said.

"My dad and I are fencing off the bone pile so's it won't happen again," Stuart said.

"Your father works for the county, then?" Ruth asked.

"He works his own mine. I'm going to help him when I graduate high school."

"Stuart, that's not at all certain," Mary Beth said.

"I'm afraid I'm not following all this," Ruth said. "Just how did this man die?"

"Nobody knows," Owen repeated.

"They found him dead at the bone pile," Stuart said. "Same night Snooker Hatfield disappeared and somebody clobbered Mr. Allison."

"My God, Owen," his mother said. "What have you gotten yourself involved in?"

"I'm not involved in anything, Mother. Hatfield McCoy was a mean old SOB with dozens of enemies. One of them evidently did him in."

Ruth Allison reached for her son's hand. "But Stuart here says somebody attacked you as well."

"Somebody clobbered my dad, too," Stuart said.

"Stuart, hush. That was something else entirely," Mary Beth said.

Owen took his mother's hand and returned it to her lap. "Let's just drop it, okay? It's over and done with."

"What kind of a name is Hatfield McCoy?" Ruth Allison asked.

"It's a dead man's name," Owen said. "Let him rest in peace while we finish our meal."

AFTER DINNER, OWEN sat on the concrete steps of the front porch throwing a tennis ball to Buster while Mary Beth and Stuart helped with the dishes. Fireflies were just beginning to glimmer in the dusk when his mother came out the screen door.

"Everything all right, son?" she asked. "Seems like a lot's been happening to you lately."

"Stop worrying about me, Mom. Half the things you worry about never happen."

"Trouble is, I never know which half." Ruth smoothed her apron and sat on the porch steps beside her son. "What do you hear from Judith?"

"Not much."

"She dropped in to see me last week. On her way to try

some big lawsuit in D.C. I thought she'd get in touch with you."

"Divorce doesn't make for good pen pals."

"Never held much with your breakup. I don't think Judith's as hot for it as she once was, either."

"Give it up, Mom. I'm finally getting on with my life."

"I can see that. Stuart seems like a nice young man."

"He is. It's his mother I'm really interested in, though. What do you think of her?"

Ruth cocked an ear to listen to the clinking sound of dishes in the kitchen. "I once asked your Great-Aunt Lizzie that same question about your father when we were courting. Remember what she told me?"

Owen nodded. "If the bone is yours, no other dog will drag it away."

"Words to live by."

"Doesn't exactly answer my question."

"I guess Aunt Lizzie didn't want to answer mine, either."

OWEN PUT THE convertible top up for the drive back to Contrary, imposing a low ceiling on Stuart's backseat prison. The boy scrunched sideways behind the two bucket seats, drawing his knees up to eye level and dozing fitfully.

"Your mother's an awfully nice woman," Mary Beth said. "What was that mysterious medical problem she mentioned over dessert?"

"She had colon cancer a couple of years ago. They operated in time, but she still has regular checkups and needs more rest than she's used to getting."

"Oh. She never said cancer."

"She's funny that way. She's buried one child and fed hot meals to divers dragging the river for her husband, but there are some words she can't bring herself to say. Cancer's one of them."

"There are others?"

Owen recalled his mother's front-porch questions about his ex-wife and let loose a short laugh. "Divorce, for one."

"She doesn't believe in divorce?"

"Marriages lasted in her family. They took their troubles to Catholic priests instead of marriage counselors."

"What about you? Are you still Catholic?"

"Me? Hell, I'm divorced. But I stopped going to church long before we split up."

"Do you still believe in God?"

"I guess so. We just haven't had much to say to each other lately."

"What about heaven and hell?"

"Back when I worried more about such things, I came across an argument by Pascal that appealed to the statistician in me." The shadows of the surrounding trees covered the road and Owen switched on his headlights. "Pascal argued that the odds against an afterlife made heaven a real long-shot, but the rewards were so great, you might as well bet on it. Even if you're wrong, it helps you lead a better life."

"If you believe in heaven and hell, how do you feel about signing off on our invoices?"

"How do you feel about sending the invoices?"

Mary Beth glanced backward to make sure Stuart was still asleep. "It bothered me at first. Now it's just part of the job. And the town really needs the money."

"That's funny. It bothers me more now than it did at first. At first, I was just getting back at some dumb bureaucrats. I didn't even have to sign my own name. Now it seems like I've been sucked into something bigger."

Mary Beth laid her hand lightly on his thigh. "But you'll sign our next invoice? You're not having second thoughts?"

Owen covered her hand with his own. "I'm having second and third thoughts. I just don't see an easy way out. It would help if Purvis bought a few more buses."

"He can't do that without cutting back on something we really need."

"But it can't go on like this. Somebody's sure to find out. If we don't do something, we're just waiting for the ax to fall."

"What ax?" Stuart asked from the backseat.

They passed the rest of the trip in silence. When they pulled into Mary Beths' driveway, she squeezed Owen's hand and ducked out of the car. "It was a wonderful day. Thank you for inviting us."

Stuart unwound himself and edged sideways out of the backseat. "Yeah. I had a good time."

"You should have," Owen said. "You sure cleaned my clock on the backyard diamond."

"You just never got to bat. Wait till next time."

IT WAS ONE o'clock in the morning before Owen made it back to his Washington, D.C., apartment. As he put the key in the lock, he thought he heard the strains of Willie Nelson singing "On the Road Again." Had he left his CD player running? Sometimes he left it on to entertain potential burglars, but he didn't remember doing so this weekend. He turned the key and swung the door open.

The music blared out at him. His reading lamp was lit on one side of the couch that faced the CD player. A pair of familiar hazel eyes topped by brunette bangs peered out over the back of the couch.

"Judith," he said. "What are you doing here?"

"Your super let me in. I told him I was your wife. I've still got some papers that prove we were married once."

"Some papers and a house in California. That's *how* you got in. I asked *why*."

"Well, Scout," she said, holding up a folded copy of *The Washington Post*, "I'm a damn good lawyer. And it looks to me like you're going to need one."

14

THEY COULD MAKE A HERO OUT OF DILLINGER

THE WASHINGTON POST SECTION was folded to a short column headlined "Disabled Activist Meets Mysterious End." The picture below the headline showed Hatfield McCoy brandishing his cane in Owen's face. The photo was cropped at McCoy's shoulder, and because Owen was much the taller of the two men, it wasn't clear whether McCoy was wielding the cane offensively or defensively.

"Read it," Judith said.

Wheelchair-bound activist Hatfield McCoy, a long-time advocate of the rights of the disabled, was found dead last week in a public dumping ground in McDowell County, West Virginia. McCoy was recently involved in a fight to make the county transportation system fully accessible to persons with disabilities. Above, he defends himself with his cane against an unidentified Department of Transportation Official following a hearing regarding his demands. The cause of Mr. McCoy's death is currently being investigated.

Owen twisted the newspaper as if trying to wring some sense out of the words. "Where do they get this 'disabled activist' shit? The man was blackmailing, vandalizing scumbag. And he wasn't defending himself. He was attacking me with his goddamn cane."

"You can't tell that from the picture."

"There are lots of witnesses." Owen pointed to his cheek. "And I've got the scar to prove it."

"Still, you're on record in a violent argument with a man just before he turned up dead."

"Whose side are you on?"

"I'm just trying to make you see how it looks to somebody who doesn't know you."

"Half the voting population of the county had it in for Hatfield McCoy. Nobody's charged me with anything. What makes you think I need a lawyer?"

Judith took the newspaper and untwisted it. "Grow up, Scout. *The Washington Post* doesn't have stringers in McDowell County. Somebody down there planted this story."

"But why?"

"Damned if I know. But it probably wasn't to fill out Hatfield McCoy's scrapbook."

"Even supposing I needed a lawyer, what makes you think I'd choose you?"

"Don't make me sorry I came, Scout. I'm the logical

choice. I'm good, I'll work cheap, and I'm the only lawyer you'll find who knows you're so honest you don't even fudge your tax returns."

"If there is a case here, I'd think it would have too low a profile for your high-powered firm."

Judith yanked on her black pumps and started for the door. "Up yours. My firm has nothing to do with this. And you better hope the profile of this case stays low. If it gets any higher, you'll be in over your head."

Owen moved to head her off. "Wait. Stop." He captured the doorknob before she reached it. "I'm sorry. Stay. Please. It's just . . . I'm having trouble processing all this."

Owen took Judith's arm to lead her back to the couch. Just before they reached it, he dropped her arm and said, "Mom. It's Mom, isn't it? She must have called you. That's why you're here."

Judith folded her arms. "She knew you were in trouble and she hadn't even seen this article."

"But the article doesn't even mention my name."

"Don't worry. It'll be spelled right on the warrant."

"What makes you think there'll be a warrant?"

"Humor me. For the sake of your mother. Tell me what this is all about. If there's no warrant, you won't have lost anything."

Owen went to the CD player and turned off Willie Nelson.

"How come you wound up with all the good country CDs?" Judith asked.

"You want to listen to me or not?"

Judith raised her hand, palm outward. "I'm sorry. I was just trying to lighten things up."

"Funny you'd expect reminders of our divorce settlement to lighten me up."

"I said I was sorry."

Owen started a pot of tea and joined Judith on the couch. He told her what had happened to him in Contrary, starting with his first trip there and ending with Hatfield McCoy's death, omitting only his affair with Mary Beth Hobbs. She interrupted him only twice, once to express disbelief that he'd been reduced to counting buses, and once to ask why he felt it necessary to forge another person's name on an invoice he had the right to approve himself.

"Jesus, Scout, I wouldn't have believed it," Judith said when he'd finished. "You'd have been better off signing your own name. At least then you could claim you'd been duped. Like this guy Armitrage before you. Signing his name makes it seem like you knew you were involved in something fishy."

"Duped or not, what's the big deal? I'm not pocketing any money."

"It's fraud, Owen. Pure and simple. Somebody's pocketing a hell of a lot of money."

"I told you, they're using it to run the town."

"That's what they're telling you. Did they tell you about Santa Claus and the Easter Bunny, too?"

"I trust them. They're good, hardworking people."

Judith set her empty teacup on the coffee table. "Let's say they are. Let's say all the money is going to widows and orphans. It's still fraud. Your signature is misdirecting two million a year in taxpayer money."

"Would it be better if they used the money for buses they don't need?"

"Listen to me, Owen. Even if I give them the benefit of the doubt, you're still up to your neck in fraud. And that's putting the best possible face on it. Look at the other side. Suppose all that money's not going to widows and orphans and the good of the town. Two men are dead. One of them held the same job you're holding. Somebody knocked you out and left you sucking sulphur fumes. I'd say you're already in way over your head." She took his hands in hers. "What in the world got into you?"

"They're good people. And my DOT bosses are assholes of the first order."

"Owen, if working for assholes were a legal defense, Howard Hunt and Charles Colson would have walked and the Nuremberg trials never would have gotten off the ground."

"What's that supposed to mean?"

"It means you don't have a legal leg to stand on. You're the point man in a two-million-dollar swindle."

Owen pulled his hands free.

"I don't get it," Judith said. "When we were married you were stiff-necked about right and wrong. Santa Clarita wanted you to change a couple of sentences in their light-rail report, but you wouldn't do it. You could have saved your consulting business, but you wouldn't change that damn report."

"It was more than a couple of sentences."

"I pleaded with you, but you wouldn't change the report."

"My name was on that report. I couldn't sign off on what they wanted."

"But you're signing off on a two-million-a-year fraud."

"It was only one invoice. And my name's not on it."

"Grow up, Scout. You're the one who signed it. Maybe the system is so screwed up you could sign Mickey Mouse's name and keep the money flowing. But you're the one with the pen and the authority."

"I'm not pocketing any money."

"You keep saying that. I told you it doesn't matter." Judith stood up and began pacing in front of the coffee table. "You're sleeping with her, aren't you? You're sleeping with that Hobbs woman."

"That's none of your business."

"Jesus Christ, that's what's going on here." Judith laughed once and shook her head. "If I'd known you could be bought for a blow job, we'd still be married and you'd be rolling in consulting jobs on the West Coast."

"Speaking of blow jobs, how's what's-his-name?"

"His name, as you well know, is Phillip McKenzie Davis. And he left me flat in the fast track six months ago." Judith stopped pacing. "You haven't cornered the market on dumb mistakes."

"Can't say I'm sorry for your loss."

"I wouldn't expect you to be. I'll even sit still for a little gloating." Judith returned to the couch. "But I came here to see if you needed help. And from what you've told me, you need a bucketful."

Owen ran both hands hard down the sides of his beard as if he were trying to adjust it. "What do you suggest I do?"

"First thing tomorrow, call your buddies in Contrary." Judith tapped the *Post* article. "Find out what's behind this little press notice. And tell them it might be a good idea to start shopping for more buses."

"Anything else?"

"If the press tracks you down, don't talk to them. Even if you don't say anything wrong, they'll misreport it. You're the bad guy here, the unfeeling bureaucrat who hounded a disabled rights advocate to his untimely death."

"But that's bullshit."

"That's the tack they'll take. They're not going to let the facts bother them." Judith checked her watch. "Christ, it's three in the morning. I've got a busy day ahead. I'll call you tomorrow night. In the meantime, get me copies of all the paperwork you've got on Contrary. And Scout, if you have to sign more invoices, at least use your own name from now on."

"What good will that do?"

"It's one less count against you if this blows up." Judith fished in her purse. "Here's my card. I'm staying at the Jefferson. Call me if there are any new developments."

Owen read the card. "Partner! You made partner. Congratulations."

"It's no big whoop. After Phillip dumped me, I found our grand passion seemed a lot like sexual harassment. When I said so, they made me partner."

"You blackmailed McKenzie, Davis and Stapleton?"

"It wasn't the proudest moment of my life. But it got me tenure. And it means I can handle your case without anybody squawking."

"My case? You think it will come to that?"

"Believe me, Scout, unless you're awfully lucky, it will come to that. Somebody's going to bring charges."

"As long as we've got a lawyer/client relationship going here, would you do me a favor and stop calling me Scout? You know I've always hated it."

Judith paused, pointed her index finger at his beard, and made a popping noise with her lips. "Glad to. After what you've been up to, the uniform and merit badge sash probably won't fit anymore, anyway."

THE NEXT MORNING Owen left his cubicle and found a phone booth so he could call Purvis Jenkins in Contrary without being overheard. "Purvis, this is going to sound strange, but is somebody down there putting out press releases making a martyr out of Hatfield McCoy?"

A giggle that gave way to a full-fledged guffaw came from the other end of the line. "That would be Brady Jackson. He wrote an obit for the *Contrary Crier* that made Hatfield out to be the Second Coming in a wheelchair. Gave those of us that knew the man quite a little laugh."

"Who's Brady Jackson?"

"You recall Brady. He was Hatfield's lawyer at the first hearing down here. White suit and more Latin than the pope's prayerbook. He's brought a wrongful death suit against the county of behalf of Hatfield's momma. Guess he figures the settlement might go up if somebody believes Hatfield was a real loss to the world."

"What grounds can he possibly have for suing the county?"

"The county's been under federal orders to clean up its bone piles for some time. The feds thought it'd be nicer for the environment. 'Course, they didn't give us any money for the clean up or anyplace else to dump our mine shaving."

"So he might win?"

"Depends on lots of things. Whether the judge remembers Hatfield, for one. And what my cousin Travis turns up in his investigation, for another."

"Travis didn't turn up much on the death of Dwight Armitrage."

Purvis didn't respond right away. "That was another matter entirely," he said finally.

"So is Travis doing better with Hatfield McCoy's death?"

"Travis doesn't exactly confide in me. I do know there's still no sign of Snooker Hatfield. You shouldn't worry, though. Travis is keeping a tight lid on it so's nothing splashes your way."

"It's already splashed my way." Owen described the squib in *The Washington Post*.

"The Washington Post?" Purvis said. "Sounds like old Brady's been doing some tall farting. Didn't think he had it in him."

"Well, somebody planted the story. And if it goes national, Travis won't be able to keep a lid on anything. Contrary is likely to be swarming with a lot of wannabe Woodwards and Bernsteins. Some of them may even start counting buses."

"That's a whole 'nother kettle of shit."

"My lawyer thinks you ought to buy enough buses to bring your operations in line with your invoices."

"Your lawyer? What're you doing with a lawyer?"

"It's just my ex-wife," Owen said. "She saw the *Post* story and wanted to help."

"So you told her all about us?" Purvis asked.

"It's all covered by attorney/client privilege."

"My ex-wife pees on my leg every chance she gets. You're telling me you trust yours to give you legal advice?"

"If it makes sense," Owen said. "From where she sits,

she sees two unexplained deaths at either end of a two-million-a-year swindle. If one of those deaths gets to be national news, it's going to be hard to keep the rest of it covered up."

"We're not swindling anybody. We're just spending federal money where it's most needed."

"Purvis, any reporter that thinks Hatfield McCoy was a martyred disabled activist isn't likely to appreciate the finer points of that argument."

"Maybe we should start educating the press as to Hatfield's true nature."

"Maybe you should stop spending federal money on stuff it's not earmarked for."

"You telling me you're going to stop approving our invoices? It's a mite late for that, isn't it?"

Owen felt as if the phone booth were closing in on him. "I'm telling you I'm approving money for running buses, not your own pet projects."

Owen hadn't expected to issue an ultimatum. Evidently Purvis hadn't expected to hear one, because there was a long silence at the other end of the line. Finally Purvis said, "Well, don't that take the sheen off of the weenie."

THE REST OF the morning dragged by without incident, bolstering Owen's hope that no one in the department had recognized his photograph in *The Washington Post*. Just before lunch, though, Walker Bashford thrust his head over the edge of Owen's cubicle and demanded that Owen come to his office immediately.

As soon as Owen entered Bashford's office, his supervisor closed the door and shoved the *Post* photograph under his nose. "In heaven's name, Owen," Bashford asked, "how could you assault this man?"

"I didn't assault him, Walker. He assaulted me."

"The man's a cripple."

"I know. He hit me with his cane."

"The article says he was defending himself against you. It says he's wheelchair-bound."

"Maybe you should tell the *Post* that 'wheelchair-bound' is a pejorative, Walker. In any case, it's inaccurate. Look at the picture. The man's up on his feet swinging a cane."

"You can't tell that."

"There are witnesses, Walker. Look at the scar on my cheek."

"I've just spend an hour with the secretary," Bashford said. "The incident wasn't written up anywhere in your report."

"He attacked me after the hearing was over. I didn't see any point in reporting it."

"Not worth reporting? A man files twenty-two complaints against the department, turns up dead, and you don't think it's worth reporting?"

"I gave you a complete report on the complaint hearing. That was my job as I saw it."

"Your job is what I say it is." Bashford slammed the folded newspaper down on his desk. "Give me your report now, Owen. Tell me what happened after the hearing."

Owen told the story of Hatfield's hearing, his lurching assault, and the deputies' efforts to restrain him. Then he told what he remembered of the night at the bone pile, leaving out his liaison with Mary Beth Hobbs.

"So this McCoy vandalized our equipment and shot at a moving bus?"

"That's all in my report, yes."

"And his friend, this Snooker Hatfield, is still missing?"

"So far as I know, yes."

Bashford rose and stalked his desk like a predator. "All right, here's what we're going to do. I've got a friend at the *Times*. I'm going to feed him the dirt on McCoy." He pounced on *The Washington Post* article and karate-chopped the folded newspaper. "Better than that, I'll suggest that this fellow Snooker Hatfield killed Mccoy in a flare-up of the old Hatfield–McCoy feud."

Owen folded his arms across his chest. "That's all very nice, except Hatfield McCoy wasn't a real McCoy. Snooker Hatfield was his first cousin. They were on the same side of the feud."

Bashford shoved the crumpled newspaper aside. "What difference does that make? It's a good story. It'll fly with the press. It'll get them sniffing somewhere else." Bashford paced behind his desk, more animated than Owen had ever seen him. "Smear and steer. Worked like a charm when I was running the president's campaign in south Georgia."

"This isn't politics, Walker."

"I've told you before, Owen. Everything is politics."

THAT EVENING, OWEN found four phone messages waiting on his answering machine. One was from a *Washington Post* reporter, two were from names he didn't recognize, and one was from Judith. He returned Judith's call.

"Seen this week's *Time* magazine?" she asked as soon as he'd made contact.

The phone felt heavy in his hand. "Oh God, it's gone national."

"Full-page article under the heading *Investigations*. It starts, 'Dead under mysterious circumstances in a West Virginia slag heap was disabled rights activist Hatfield McCoy.' "

"Do they have the same picture as the *Post*?"

"No. Their picture shows McCoy being held down in his wheelchair by two burly deputies. One of them has him in a chokehold. Looks pretty brutal."

"That was after he attacked me."

"They don't mention any attack. The caption says he's being restrained by local law enforcement following a protest against ADA violations."

"Good Christ. Where do they get this 'disabled activist' shit? How can they make a hero out of that scumbag?"

"It's easy for the media. They made heros out of John Dillinger, Clyde Barrow, and O.J. Simpson. And those guys didn't even need wheelchairs."

"Neither did Hatfield McCoy."

"So you say he could walk. You sure can't tell it from the *Time* article. There's a quote from somebody named Brady Jackson that makes McCoy out to be a rolling Robin Hood."

"Jackson. That's the guy that started all this publicity. He's got a wrongful death suit going against the county on behalf of McCoy's mother. Thinks the suit will be worth more if he can make it seem McCoy's death was a loss to society."

"Well, he's doing a good job of it. This whole article makes McCoy sound like a crippled crusader persecuted by local bureaucrats."

"Do they mention me or the department?"

"Nothing about you. Listen to this, though: 'Four months ago, Dwight Armitrage, a Department of Transportation worker sent to investigate McCoy's allegations, was found dead at the same site, suffocated by sulphur fumes.' "

"But nothing about me?"

"Better they should mention you than Armitrage."

"Why's that?"

"Think, Owen. There are people at DOT who might wonder how Dwight Armitrage has been signing Contrary's invoices if he's been dead for four months."

Owen twisted the phone cord into a tight knot. "Oh, God."

"Maybe they don't read *Time* at DOT. In any case, you can't worry about it. Get me your paperwork to review. And don't talk to strangers."

"Reporters are already calling."

"Take my advice. Don't answer."

"I can tell them the truth about Hatfield McCoy."

"Believe me, they won't want to hear it. They want to know who killed their crusader. And you can't help them with that. You're the bad guy to them, Owen. Anything you say will be used against you."

"That sounds like an official warning."

"It's not a warning. It's a statement of fact. Pure and simple."

AFTER JUDITH HAD hung up, Owen let the phone dangle from its cord and watched it untwist slowly. Then he listened to the rest of his messages. One from a *Washington Post* reporter and two other callers who didn't identify themselves, probably reporters as well. He wondered if Judith wasn't overreacting by warning him against talking to the press. Somebody had to set the record straight on Hatfield McCoy. He was writing a list of the points he wanted to make about Hatfield when the phone rang. It was the *Post* reporter, asking for an interview.

Owen scanned the list he'd been writing and agreed. It was his chance to set the record straight.

"Now then," the reporter began. "I understand Mr. McCoy lodged a number of complaints with the Department of Transportation. Can you tell me the nature of those complaints?"

"He was at war with the Contrary bus service. He complained about rude drivers, dirty equipment, late buses, ADA infractions . . . there was a long list."

A keyboard clacked at the other end of the line. "And it was your job to adjudicate those complaints?"

"Yes. I found them groundless."

"So the drivers were polite, the equipment was clean, the buses ran on time, and everything was fully accessible?"

"I didn't say that."

"You said claims were groundless. Wasn't he just trying to make the system work for people with disabilities?"

"He was trying to make the system work for Hatfield McCoy."

"But Mr. McCoy was disabled, wasn't he?"

"Not as much as he pretended for his pension. He was a chronic malcontent. A troublemaker." Owen checked the list he'd prepared. "He vandalized the system. Slashed tires. Shot up buses. His complaints were a form of extortion. Your story made him sound like a saint." Owen sensed that he was saying too much and stopped. There was no keyboard noise on the other end of the line.

"So you didn't like the man. Did you kill him?"

"Certainly not." Owen could see the headlines he was generating: "DOT Man Denies Killing Disabled Activist."

"The police report says you were there the night he died."

"I was unconscious."

The keyboard clacked. "And how did that happen?"

"I don't know." The headline "DOT Man Doesn't Know Shit" flashed through his mind.

"Didn't you threaten Mr. McCoy with bodily harm?"

"Never. He threatened me. The county deputies had to restrain him."

"How much harm could he do from a wheelchair?"

"Plenty. Look, you're missing the point here. Hatfield McCoy was a . . ." Owen checked his list, found that he'd already exhausted it, and finished lamely, ". . . a scumbag."

"So you think he deserved to die?"

"Of course not. I didn't say that."

"Just what are you saying?"

"I guess I'm saying, 'no comment.' "

The keyboard clacked. "Well, if you change your mind, you've got my number."

Owen hung up, crumpled the notepaper where he'd written the numbers of the two other reporters, and threw it in the wastebasket. Judith was right. The press was off and running and the best thing he could do was stay out of its way.

OWEN READ THE *Washington Post* cover to cover for the next three days, but his phone interview wasn't deemed newsworthy by the paper. After a week had gone by with no coverage, Owen began to hope they were home free. Then he received a call from Mary Beth Hobbs.

"They're sending somebody to audit our bus system."

Owen felt trapped in his cubicle. "Who is?"

"Your accounting office. Why can't they send you?"

"It's a different department. They'll be sending a CPA to go over your accounts. That's not what I do. I look at how the system operates on the road."

"But they sent you last time."

"It's a different kind of audit. They'll be looking at your books. It may not be anything to worry about," Owen said, trying to put more confidence than he felt in his voice. "Your books were good enough to fool Armitrage. Just hope they don't count your buses."

"But what if they do? What if they find out?"

"Tell them the truth. Tell them Hollis made a mistake on your first invoice and we paid it. After that, it just snow-balled. Show them the money is supporting the town. Show them nobody's lining their own pockets." When Owen heard nothing but silence at the other end of the line, he added, "That's true, isn't it?"

"As far as it goes."

"Is there something you're not telling me?"

"Oh, Owen. I took some money. Four thousand dollars. To pay for Stony's operation. I thought he'd pay it back before anybody missed it. He's paid back some, but he's hurt now, and I'm still short."

"How short?"

Owen heard a chair scrape. "Fifteen hundred dollars."

"Does Purvis know?"

"Oh my word, no. He'd go ballistic."

"When's the audit?"

"Next week sometime. They haven't set a date."

"I'll wire you the money."

"I can't let you do that."

"You can pay me back when Stony starts working again."

"Oh I will, I will." Owen heard a massive intake of breath. "Oh, thank you."

"Don't worry about it. What's the name of the auditor who contacted you?"

Owen could hear a drawer opening. "His name's Young. Craig Young. Do you know him?"

"We've met." Young was the man from Accounting who sent invoices on for Armitrage's signature. He must have read the news accounts of Armitrage's death. He must be wondering who signed a dead man's name to Contrary's last invoice. Judith had warned him that was likely to happen when she'd called him the point man in a fraud. Owen rested his head in his left hand and massaged his eyelids with his thumb and middle finger. It was about to blow up, and he had no place to hide. For the first time since he'd signed off on Contrary's invoice, he felt like a fraud.

15

BETWEEN THE BALANCE SHEETS

PURVIS LOOKED THROUGH the glass window of the conference room door at the auditor poring over printouts and Mary Beth's balance sheets. "Man looks about as happy as a pallbearer with a bad back. He been here long?"

"Since a little after nine o'clock," Mary Beth said. "Drove all the way from D.C. this morning. Said he would have been here earlier, but Cletus Longacre stopped him for doing thirty miles an hour in a school zone."

"Cletus gave him a ticket?"

"Well, you know Cletus. And he did have out-of-state plates."

"Christ, what a welcome committee. Guess that took the glaze off his day."

"He didn't seem any too happy to be here."

"You keeping him supplied with sharp pencils, hot coffee, and sexy smiles?"

"He brought his own supplies. Including that box of doughnuts." While Mary Beth and Purvis watched through the window, the auditor took a powdered doughnut from a pink pastry box, centered it on a broad white napkin, cut it into four equal sections with a pocket knife, and plopped one section into his mouth. "He's more interested in his doughnuts than in anything I say or do."

"Well, don't take it personal, darlin'," Purvis said as the auditor sucked thoughtfully on the doughnut. "Looks like he's got at least one vice we can work on if we have to."

"Maybe we won't have to. He's not the brightest bulb they've sent."

"He ask for anything special?"

"Just my balance sheets."

"Man wants to slip between your balance sheets? Maybe he's got more than one vice after all."

"Purvis, this isn't a joking matter."

"What makes you think I'm joking?" Purvis knocked on the conference room door and, without waiting for an answer, opened it and introduced himself.

Startled, the auditor pulled the napkin holding the doughnut sections behind the screen of his laptop computer.

"Finding everything you need?" Purvis asked.

"Yes, your staff has been most helpful."

"I understand one of our local police officers made you feel a little less than welcome this morning?"

"The man gave me a ticket. I'd just slowed to cross the railroad tracks when I heard his siren. I couldn't have been going more than twenty-five miles an hour."

Purvis held out his hand. "I'll take care of it if you'd like."

"Take care of it?"

"In addition to running the Comet, I'm also Contrary's mayor. Cletus Longacre, the officer who ticketed you, works for me."

"So you can fix it?"

"It's a mayor's privilege."

The auditor licked powdered sugar from his thumb and forefinger, retrieved the ticket from his vest pocket, and handed it over to Purvis. "And it won't show up on my driver's record?"

"It'll be just like it never happened." Purvis pocketed the ticket and held up both hands, palms outward, like a magician completing a trick.

"I don't know how to thank you."

"Don't mention it." Purvis hesitated with his hand on the doorknob. "Mr. Young . . ."

"Call me Craig, please."

"Craig, my staff and I were wondering, well, why this sudden audit? It seemed to come out of the blue."

The auditor straightened the edges of Mary Beth's printouts and aligned them with the edge of the conference table. "We became aware of certain irregularities."

"Irregularities?"

"Oh, not here. In Washington. Questions arose regarding approval procedures."

"I see. But in Washington, not here. Not among my staff?"

"Oh, no. Your books appear to be quite in order. So far at least."

"That's good for me to hear. How much longer will you be with us?"

"The way things are going, I should be through by midafternoon."

"Then perhaps you'll join my staff and me for lunch. There's a place in town that serves good home cooking and the best corn bread this side of the Mason-Dixon line."

"Sounds delightful."

THE WAITRESS AT Longacre's Diner greeted Purvis by name and led Purvis, Mary Beth, Hollis, and the auditor to a corner booth away from the press of the lunchtime crowd.

"Looks like a popular place," the auditor said.

"Deserves to be," Purvis said. "Ma Longacre's the best cook in three counties."

The auditor ran a pudgy finger over the name on the plasticized menu. "Longacre must be a common name in these parts."

"Not really. Just Ma and her two kids. You had the misfortune of meeting Cletus this morning. Her daughter Rose is a nurse over at our clinic. Dad Longacre's been dead for years."

"Their family tree don't branch much," Hollis said.

"Not like us Jenkinses, huh Mary Beth?" Purvis put a hand on his sister's arm. "Our ancestors left their name on half the county."

"Other half's related in ways they won't admit," Hollis said.

"You two shush now," Mary Beth said. "Mr. Young's not interested in county genealogy."

"Just seemed I'd run into a lot of Longacres in my half day here," the auditor said.

"At least one too many," Purvis said. "But Ma'll make up for Cletus. Here comes her corn bread now."

The waitress brought an oval basket heaped with steaming squares of corn bread under a gingham coverlet. Purvis took the basket, lifted a corner of the gingham, smiled as if he'd discovered gold, and offered the corn bread to Craig Young.

The auditor took a square of corn bread, slit it lengthwise, and slathered butter on the bottom half. He lifted the yellow morsel, briefly inhaled its aroma, bit off a corner, tilted his head back, and closed his eyes. His Adam's apple barely bobbed as he swallowed and a beatific smile played across his face. After a short pause he exhaled slowly, opened his eyes, and nodded approvingly at the piece of corn bread left in his hand.

"Didn't I tell you?" Purvis said. "If that corn bread were any moister, the humidity in this town would be unbearable."

The auditor finished off the bottom half of his slice of corn bread, slathered butter on the top half, and paused to inspect his handiwork.

"Go on, eat up," Purvis said. "There's plenty more where that came from."

The four diners worked their way through a platter of fried chicken, gobs of garlic-laced mashed potatoes, and three more baskets of corn bread. Craig Young was buttering the last square of corn bread when Purvis asked the waitress for the check. "Sherlyn, honey, bring Mr. Young here a fresh slab of corn bread to take home and put the whole thing on my tab."

The auditor raised his butter knife. "I can't let you do that, Purvis. We're not allowed to accept any sort of gratuities from clients."

"It's only corn bread, for Christ's sake. Guaranteed noncorrupting."

"It's the meal, too. I can't let you pay for my meal."

Purvis held up his right hand, palm outward, as if to stop oncoming traffic. "Now look here, Craig. I know the government's not going to reimburse you for your lunch on a day trip. And you've already told me our books are clean as a hound's tooth, so there's no way I'm trying to influence your audit." He leaned forward and made a steeple of his fingers. "Down here we pride ourselves on our hospitality as well as our corn bread. Now I've just bought lunch for you and my coworkers." He shook his head slowly over the steepled fingers. "There's absolutely no obligation and no paperwork involved. Just my thanks for everybody's efforts on behalf of the town of Contrary. I'd take it mighty poorly if you refused to accept our hospitality."

Craig went back to buttering his corn bread. "Well, since you put it that way."

"I do. I do indeed."

"Then I thank you." Craig swallowed a corner of the corn bread. "I've just got to run a few more balances. I should be out of your hair within an hour."

"No hurry. No hurry at all."

"I'd like to make it back to D.C. at a reasonable hour."

Purvis rose and handed the auditor a cakebox full of corn bread. "We'd best be getting back to the office, then. So you can have daylight for most of your drive home."

As PURVIS AND his party walked back to the courthouse after lunch, Travis Jenkins pulled his blue and white sheriff's car up alongside them and kept it abreast of the walkers for a full block.

"Better look out, Craig," Purvis warned the accountant, "the sheriff may be fixing to ticket you for walking too fast through a business zone."

Hollis laughed and Mary Beth smiled, but the accountant didn't change his expression.

"Don't worry," Purvis added, "it's my cousin Travis. He doesn't have a quota on out-of-towners."

At the corner stoplight, the sheriff rolled down his window and asked Hollis to get into the patrol car. Alerted by the sheriff's drill-sergeant tone, Purvis followed Hollis to the car and asked, "What's happening, Cuz?"

"Those two peckerwood motorcyclists that had a run-in with Hollis and Stony Hobbs have filed charges. I want to take Hollis out to Pokey Joe's and clear up a few things."

"Mind if I ride along?"

"Don't see that it concerns you," Travis said.

"My town, my employee."

"Get in, then."

Hollis ducked into the front seat next to the bracketed shotgun. Purvis asked Mary Beth to see that the auditor got everything he needed before he left and slid into the rear seat. Travis smiled at Mary Beth, touched the tip of his mountie's hat, and pulled away from the stoplight.

"Who's that with Mary Beth?" Travis asked as they crossed the railroad tracks on their way out of town.

"Auditor down from D.C.," Purvis said. "Cletus Longacre welcomed him with a ticket this morning."

"Cletus cherry picking at the school zone again?"

"Don't suppose you'd like to take care of the ticket for me?"

"You'll have to take that up with Cletus yourself," Travis said. "Local ticket, local traffic cop. I'm strictly a county mountie."

"I just thought it might go down easier coming from a fellow officer. You know how Cletus gets sometimes. His bonus depends on those tickets."

"You pay him the bonus. Your town, your employee."

The early afternoon sun beat down on the asphalt as Travis sped over the few straight stretches. Passing the bone pile, he downshifted and looked back over his shoulder. "Did you see that?"

"Where?" Hollis said.

"There. In the bone pile."

"Don't see nothing," Hollis said.

Travis spun the wheel and slewed the car into a U-turn. Then he headed back past the bone pile. "There it is," he said, slowing to a near stop. "See it now?"

"Still don't see nothing," Hollis said.

"Just that wood fence Stony built," Purvis said. "The bone pile slopes away pretty fast."

Travis pulled onto the loading platform trucks used to dump slag into the bone pile. "Let's go look." He led Purvis and Hollis to the edge of Stony's wood fence and pointed down into the bone pile. "There. See it now?"

Hatfield McCoy's wheelchair lay upended about ten feet down the slope.

"Why's that still there?" Hollis asked.

"I put it back there," Travis said. He cinched his mountie's hat tight around his chin and looked directly at Hollis. "Something's been bothering me, Hollis. The other night you said you were driving by the bone pile at two in the morning, saw Hatfield's wheelchair, and stopped to help."

"Yeah, right," Hollis said.

Travis shook his head slowly. "Hollis, we just drove by the bone pile twice in broad daylight and you couldn't see the wheelchair from the roadway. None of us could. And we were looking for it."

"I don't know," Hollis said. "I sure saw something that night."

"Maybe the wheelchair was closer to the road when Hollis drove by," Purvis said. "Maybe Hatfield was still in it. Maybe it tumbled downhill after Hollis stopped to help."

"I don't know," Hollis repeated. "I sure saw something."

"Maybe he caught sight of Hatfield's killer leaving," Purvis said. "By the time Hollis parked and got back, the wheelchair was all that was left."

"That and Hatfield," Hollis said.

"And Owen Allison," Purvis added.

"That's enough speculating from you, Purvis," the sheriff said. "I want to know what Hollis really saw."

"I don't remember."

The sheriff took Hollis by the arm. "All right, Hollis. You're loyal to Purvis here. I admire that. Loyalty's always been your strong suit. But I know you're lying about the wheelchair. I know you know more than you're telling. That makes you an accessory to murder. That's serious business."

"Wheelchair don't mean nothing, Travis," Purvis said. "There's lots of ways it could have happened."

"Don't make me sorry I brought you, Purvis." The sheriff tightened his grip on Hollis's arm. "And don't be thinking I'll cut you slack because you're my second cousin. If you're involved in this, it'll go hard with you."

Purvis said nothing.

"All right, Hollis," the sheriff said. "You can't tell me what made you stop that night. What happened after you stopped?"

"I seen Hatfield was a goner and went to help Mr. Allison."

"And where was he?"

"Further down."

The sheriff pointed out a gnarled outcropping about halfway down to the muddy creek bed. "And to that stump?"

"Guess so."

"There's signs a body was dragged there."

"Then that's where it must of been."

"Hollis, I marvel at your eyesight. First you see a wheel-chair nobody could have seen. Next you spot a body nearly two hundred yards away in the dark of night."

"Maybe Allison moaned," Purvis suggested.

"That so, Hollis?" the sheriff asked.

"Maybe so," Hollis said. "I don't rightly remember. It all happened pretty fast."

"Well, you better remember, and pretty damn quick." The sheriff released Hollis's arm and pointed at his cousin. "And Purvis, you better help him remember."

"I wasn't even here."

"The two of you are never that far apart," Travis said. He pointed down the slope. "Hollis, bring that wheelchair back up here for me."

As Hollis climbed down the slope to the wheelchair, Travis turned to his cousin. "All right, Purvis, I'm through looking the other way. This time I've got piles of reporters up my ass who think Hatfield was some kind of saint just because he sat in that wheelchair. Do we understand each other?"

"I've told you all I know."

Travis nodded at Hollis, who was struggling to shove the wheelchair up the slippery shale. "Well, that buddy of yours sure knows more than he's telling."

"I'll talk to him," Purvis said.

"You do that. Soon."

Hollis pushed the wheelchair over the crest onto the truck platform. "What now?"

"Pack it up and put it in the truck," Travis said.

Hollis looked at the wheelchair as if it were a crossword puzzle in a foreign language. Then he bent to examine the wheelchair's fittings.

Purvis watched Hollis fumble with the wheelchair footrests. Finally he stepped forward, snapped open two spring fasteners, and folded the wheelchair into a compact unit. "Travis wanted to know whether you'd ever folded up Hatfield's wheelchair before this," he told Hollis. "Congratulations. It's the first test you've passed today."

"Well, one of you passed, anyhow," Travis said. "Put the chair in my trunk and let's get back to town."

"I thought we were going to Pokey Joe's," Hollis said.

Purvis shoved the wheelchair into the squad car's trunk and slammed the lid shut. "We never were going to Pokey Joe's, numbnuts. Travis found out everything he wanted to know right here."

MARY BETH MET Purvis and Hollis as soon as they got back to the Contrary Comet office. Her balance sheets trembled in her hands. "Purvis, it's the auditor."

"Shouldn't he be on his way home by now?"

"He's counting buses. He knows."

"What the hell happened?"

"Right after lunch he came into my office. Wanted to know how Cletus Longacre could be working as a cop when he was on our payroll as a full-time bus driver. The same with his sister Rose at the clinic."

"We're carrying Rose Longacre as a driver, too?"

"We had to pay her somehow."

"Is it too late to bribe him?" Hollis asked.

Purvis sank into his office chair. "Probably not enough pastry left in the county."

Mary Beth shook her head. "I tried to stop him, Purvis. Truly I did."

Purvis took the morning's traffic ticket from his jacket pocket and smoothed it on his desk. "That damn Cletus." Then he leaned back in his chair and propped his feet up on his desk. "Well, I may not be able to get the corn bread back, but at least that son of a bitching auditor will have to pay his own speeding ticket."

16

TALE OF THE COMET

THE WASHINGTON POST broke the story Sunday morning under the headline "Tale of the Comet." Their coverage opened with the question "How many West Virginians does it take to run a bus line?" And went on to provide the answer "Thirty, counting six policemen, three librarians, four nurses, one family doctor, four mechanics, two administrators, one accountant, a secretary, two street cleaners, and six drivers." The photo accompanying the article was captioned "Slipped Decimal Saves Town," and showed a beaming Purvis Jenkins holding up a spreadsheet and pointing at the bottom line. There was no mention of either Hatfield McCoy or Dwight Armitrage, no hint that the local windfall was anything more than a lucky fluke overlooked by a bumbling federal bureaucracy.

Judith showed up at Owen's apartment a little before noon carrying a loaf of freshly baked cinnamon bread and copies of *The New York Times* and *Washington Times*. While she fixed tea and broke out marmalade for cinnamon toast, Owen sat on the couch and leafed through the coverage in the two newspapers.

"They're all pitching the 'Hillbillys Outfox Feds' story line." Judith leaned over Owen and pointed a corner of toast at the *Times*' second lead, "Slick Hick Tricks Fix Clinic."

Owen felt her familiar weight against his back as he brushed a few toast crumbs off the newspaper. " 'Hillbillys Outfox Feds,' that's good for us isn't it?"

Judith moved to sit beside him. "It's good if you're from Contrary and don't mind being called a hillbilly. It's not so goof if you're a fed. Your bosses are likely to be mad as hell."

Owen had a fleeting image of Walker Bashford reading the *Times* and *Post* articles. "Oh, God." He spread all the articles out on the coffee table. "At least they didn't try to tie the bone pile deaths to the Comet story. The *Times* is the only newspaper that mentions Hatfield McCoy."

"My guess is your buddies in Contrary leaked their version of the story to a few reporters with short memories and tight deadlines. They just didn't make the McCoy connection."

"Why would the people in Contrary leak the story?"

"Preemptive strike. Pretty smart, really. The government's not likely to prosecute what seems like their own oversight. They already look pretty silly, and they might even find a way to keep the money flowing to the nurses and librarians."

"If they did that they'd get invoices for bloated bus fleets from every city in the state."

Judith tugged the telephone to the couch and handed

Owen the receiver. "Let's call your mom to see how the hometown papers are handling the story."

While Owen dialed, Judith removed an earring and held the telephone earpiece between them so they could both listen. The slow tilt of his ex-wife's head as she took off her earring had once been a prelude to lovemaking, and Owen found it hard to concentrate on his mother's conversation. She was reading a story from the *Charleston Gazette* that viewed Contrary's bus scam as an admiral ploy to recover some of the excess taxes West Virginia sent to Washington. Owen recognized much of Purvis's leaky bucket theory, and guessed that he must have been the source of the story. The state capitol's newspaper mentioned Hatfield McCoy's death and ran a statement from the governor, who vowed to appoint a task force to determine whether Contrary was entitled to continuing payments from the federal government.

After reading the governor's statement, Owen's mother paused and cleared her throat. Owen and Judith sat with their cheeks separated only by the telephone receiver.

"That's all there is," Ruth Allison said. "Owen, what's your connection to all this?"

Owen stood up, taking the telephone with him. "I approved their invoice, Mom."

"Oh, dear. Did you do it for the Hobbs woman?"

"It's nothing like that, Mom. I saw they needed the money and approved it."

"But you knew the money wasn't going for buses?"

Owen looked at Judith, wishing she could coach him in a guilt-deflecting answer. "I knew."

"Well, I'm sure you had your reasons," his mother said. "Is Judith still on the phone?"

"Not right now."

"May I talk with her?"

Judith held the receiver so that Owen could hear snatches of his mother's voice. He couldn't make out her first question, which Judith answered by saying, "I don't know. It depends on what action the feds take. He could lose his job, yes. But I don't think that's very likely."

He could barely hear his mother's response, but he recognized the word *jail* in her next question.

"I certainly don't think it'll come to that," Judith answered.

She turned her head away from Owen, but he heard his mother say something about "that Hobbs woman."

"Ruth, Owen's a big boy now. He's responsible for his own actions." Judith handed Owen the phone and slid to the other end of the couch.

The first thing his mother said was, "Owen, Judith's a good woman and a good lawyer. Promise me you'll let her help you."

"She's already helping, Mom."

"Good. I feel better knowing that. You'll ride this out. Don't worry. I'll remember you in my prayers."

When he hung up, Owen said, "She's going to pray for me."

Judith licked a small dab of marmalade off her thumb. "Can't hurt."

"What was all that about responsibility?"

"Your mother can't believe her good little boy could do anything wrong. First she blamed those bureaucrats you work for. Then she blamed the Hobbs woman."

"If we're going to work together, you can knock off

that 'good little boy' shit. I heard enough of that when we were married. And the Hobbs woman has a name."

"I know she does. I was just quoting your mother."

"What does Mom have against Mary Beth?"

"How would I know? Divorce, probably."

"We're divorced, and she doesn't hold that against you."

"That was your mistake." Judith gave him the open "gotcha" smile that he'd loved once. "Even your mother admits that."

OWEN DELAYED HIS trip to the office Monday morning as long as he reasonably could. He stopped for coffee at the delicatessen outside his Metro stop and read through both *The Washington Post* and *The New York Times*. Neither newspaper had followed up their Sunday coverage on Contrary. While riding the Metro to work, however, he found the following comment at the bottom of *The Wall Street Journal*'s editorial page.

ASIDES

A small West Virginia town was upbraided last week by the Department of Transportation for using its bus money to keep its library, clinic, and police department solvent. This so-called misuse of funds had been going on for at least four years, raising two important questions. First, what sort of an audit system does DOT have that allows their funds to be derailed so easily? And second, why shouldn't the local city fathers spend their tax money wherever they want? Pumping tax dollars through the Beltway siphon introduces a lot of waste and misguided priorities into the pipeline. We think the locals have their priorities straight. In this as in so many other spending decisions, the federal government is on the wrong trolley track.

Owen usually walked up the steep escalator leading from the Metro to L'Enfant Plaza. Today he stood holding the rubber railing while the escalator clanked slowly upward and other late-arriving employees puffed past him. He blinked away the piercing sunlight that confronted him at the Metro exit, folded *The Wall Street Journal* to hide its editorial comment, and crossed the street to the Department of Transportation quadrangle.

As he was leaving the elevator at the ninth floor, he met Walker Bashford's secretary. She'd been poised to push the "down" button, and jerked her hand back at the sight of him. He said "Good morning" and stepped aside, holding the elevator door open to let her enter. She just stood still, staring at him. Finally she said, "That's all right, Owen. I'll go later. I just remembered something I left in my office."

Owen let the elevator door shut and headed down the corridor toward his office. About halfway there he became aware that Bashford's secretary was following him. "Is everything all right?" he asked.

"Oh, yes. I just remembered something I forgot."

Owen continued down the corridor, sensing that she was still following him. When he turned the corner to his office, he understood why. The entrance to his cubicle had been criss-crossed with bright yellow tape reading DO NOT ENTER, making the enclosed office space look like a giant Easter present hurriedly wrapped by a harried parent.

He turned to face Bashford's secretary. "How could you possibly forget this?"

Without waiting for an answer, he stormed into Walker Bashford's office. Bashford was seated behind his polished oak desk, talking with a middle-aged man wearing wire-frame eyeglasses and a clipped back moustache.

"Good of you to join us, Owen," Bashford said, checking his watch. "Actually, we were expecting you a little earlier." He nodded toward the prim man seated at the side of the oak table. "This is M. Estes Brown, with our legal department."

"What the hell's going on, Walker? My office is trussed up like a portable crime scene."

"Crime scene. Well now, I'd say that's an appropriate description. Wouldn't you agree, Estes?"

"I need to get into my office, Walker," Owen said. "I've got work to do."

"I'm afraid that's impossible, Owen. Your office has been quarantined. And as for work, you're suspended until further notice. Estes here has drawn up the official papers."

Estes reached into his briefcase and handed Bashford a sheaf of papers which he passed on to Owen.

Owen glanced at the top sheet. "This says there's an investigation pending. What are you investigating?"

Bashford slammed his hand down on a stack of newspapers on one corner of his desk so hard that a pen popped out of its holder at the other end. "What do you think we're investigating?" He picked up a section of Sunday's *Washington Post* and brandished it under Owen's nose.

"Forgery. Gross malfeasance. Misappropriation of funds."
His hand was still shaking when he returned the newspaper to the stack. "By God, you've made this office a
public laughingstock."

"I'm sorry you feel that way, Walker. I'd still like to get
some personal items from my office."

"Everything in there is federal property! And don't expect to find anything there about Contrary. I went through
your files last night. Your files, my files, Marge's files.
Shredded everything that mentioned that damned town."

"Shredded?" Owen asked.

Estes Brown clutched his briefcase to his chest.
"Walker, that's not proper procedure."

"Procedure be damned," Bashford said. "Nixon never
would have resigned if Rosemary Woods had used her
shredder. Ollie North had Fawn Hall, who shredded all
night and kept the wolves off Reagan. Clinton should
have shredded more than he did. I know my duty to this
administration."

"How can you have an investigation if you've shredded
all the evidence?" Owen asked.

"It'll be my word against yours," Bashford said. "I've
been on to you all along, with your Ph.D. twaddle and
your goody-goody reports. They didn't fool me. Not one
bit. You've been forging Armitrage's signature from the
start. And my initials, too." Bashford's eyes bulged.
"Dwight caught on, didn't he? Is that why he had to die?
Well, by God, I'm on to you."

Estes Brown said, "Walker, that's enough. This is a
simple suspension proceeding. Section 2406B of the Federal Employee's Handbook applies. You've served Dr. Allison his papers. Let it rest."

"*Dr.* Allison," Bashford sneered, spitting out the title. "You career types think you're so superior, with your titles and degrees. Well, you weren't appointed by the president. I was. I can show you his signed letter. And I'm not letting him down. You're finished here, Owen. Through. You can't make me a laughingstock and get away with it."

The attorney moved between Bashford and Owen. "Walker, please. Dr. Allison is only suspended pending an investigation. He's not being fired."

"He's not coming back if I have anything to say about it," Bashford said.

"I'm sorry, Dr. Allison. We'll notify you well in advance of any hearings," the attorney said.

"Tell him not to talk to reporters. Tell him," Bashford said.

"We do prefer to keep these matters internal," the attorney said. He turned his back on Owen and pressed Bashford backward.

"I'm sure you'd prefer that," Owen said. He realized he was still carrying *The Wall Street Journal* and held it out to Bashford. "Here's one newspaper that's not in your collection. Check out page fourteen. More laughs for a laughingstock." When Bashford made no move to accept the newspaper, Owen added it to the stack on the corner of the desk.

"You son of a bitch! Get out of here," Bashford yelled.

"It really is best if you go," the attorney said.

"I'll go," Owen said. "But I'm coming back with my own lawyer."

OWEN CALLED JUDITH'S office as soon as he got back home. She said she was tied up with depositions for the rest of the day and had an early dinner with a client, but promised to come over right after the dinner. In the meantime, she suggested he go back to DOT, talk to a representative of the employee's union, and pick up a copy of the handbook Estes Brown had cited.

It was nine-thirty at night before she rang his doorbell, wearing a black sheath and smelling of wine and plum blossoms. She gave him an unlawyerlike hug and apologized for being late.

He pointed out the Federal Employee's Handbook on the coffee table in front of the couch. "I tried to read it. But it's too obscure and I'm too pissed off."

Judith gathered her sheath and slid onto the couch. "That's why you have a lawyer," she said, leafing through the two-inch handbook. "To read stuff like this."

Owen went to the refrigerator. "Can I get you anything?"

"Maybe later." She slipped off her pumps and dipped her head to remove her pearl earrings. The movement tugged again at Owen's memory.

He poured himself a glass of Chardonnay and joined her on the couch.

She raised her eyebrows at the full wineglass.

"Thought I'd try to catch up."

"I'm not that far ahead."

He nodded toward the Employee Handbook. "Anything there?"

"I'll need to spend more time with it. Seems like pretty standard stuff, though. Look Owen, I know you're concerned. But a federal job is a safe haven. They can't fire you for being incompetent, chronically late, or a drunken jerk. I can't imagine that they can fire you for approving payments you had every right to approve."

"But I forged Armitrage's signature."

"Your boss told you to do that. It was just a stop-gap measure to keep the funds flowing until the paperwork on his death caught up with the paperwork on your desk."

"Bashford denies telling me to sign the invoice. As far as I know, he never officially put me in charge of the Contrary file. He even accused me of forging his initials."

"But he told you to do that, too."

"Hell, it was standard operating procedure. Bashford would nitpick us to death on anything likely to cross the secretary's desk, but he wasn't interested in mundane office details. He left us peons to deal with invoices from accounting. He's just waiting to trade in his time for a bigger entry in *Who's Who* and a stake in next year's state Senate race."

"So it was standard operating procedure. Do you know if anybody else copied Bashford's initials on invoices?"

"I'd guess Armitrage did."

"He won't make much of a witness. Anybody else?"

Owen shook his head. "I just don't know."

Judith squeezed his hand. "It sounds to me as if your boss just overreacted. Did he really shred everything?"

"That's what he said."

"Good thing you'd already made copies for me. You didn't tell him, did you?"

"He wasn't in a listening mood. And I hated to spoil his fun. He saw himself right up there with Ollie North and all the other famous shredders."

"Like W. K. Kellogg and John Deere?"

"Yeah, those guys. Shredder's Hall of Fame."

The doorbell rang. Owen checked his watch; it was nearly ten-thirty.

The doorbell rang again.

"Who is it?"

"Federal marshals. Open up please." Two burly men wearing identical blue suits stood in the hallway. When Judith asked for ID, the man nearest the door showed them a badge with a photo that could have been either of the two men.

"Mr. Owen Allison?" the ID holder asked.

"Yes."

"I'm Federal Marshall Nelson James, and this is Marshal Brownie Stephens. We're here to arrest you for the murders of Snooker Hatfield and Hatfield McCoy."

17

BILLINGSGATE

OWEN AWOKE TO the strong smell of Lysol, unable to make out where he was. He was head-high to a toilet, as if he were still in college, passed out in the dorm john. But he wasn't on the floor. He was on some sort of narrow pallet, covered with a thin institutional blanket of brown wool. The morning sun played parallel shadow patterns on the brick wall at the foot of his pallet. Bars. Oh, God. Bars. Then he remembered his late-night ride through the hills, handcuffed to a door handle while one federal marshall drove and the other slept. They'd delivered him to Contrary just before dawn, where the drill-master sheriff had marched him down a short hallway to the cramped cell he now shared with a chipped toilet and a dented metal chair.

The sheriff stood at parade rest outside Owen's cell

door, watching him through the bars. "Most inmates sleep with their feet to the toilet. You'll get the hang of it."

Owen gathered the threadbare blanket around him and sat upright. The stone floor was cold under his bare feet. "What's going on?"

"Couple of leaf peepers found Snooker Hatfield's body in a sinkhole off the road to Barkley. That's where you're from isn't it? Barkley?"

"There are twenty-five thousand people in Barkley. Why pick on me?"

"That's right," the sheriff said, "your file says you're a statistician. Well, Mr. Statistician, they found fibers from your tweed jacket under Snooker's fingernails. That sort of sets you apart from the crowd."

"Impossible. I'd barely met the man."

The sheriff flexed his back slightly without taking his eyes off Owen. "You had an argument with him the afternoon before he died. With him and his cousin Hatfield McCoy."

"Hatfield McCoy attacked me."

"And you got back at him later that night. Him and his cousin both."

Owen pulled the blanket tighter around his bare shoulders. "That's ridiculous. Hatfield McCoy must have had a hundred enemies here in Contrary. Are you rounding all of them up?"

"I'll grant you Hatfield was a piece of shit. But he was our piece of shit. And we aren't about to let you get away with his murder."

"I want to see my lawyer."

"The feds said you were with a lawyer at ten-thirty last

night. In my experience, innocent men don't need lawyers at that hour."

"The lawyer happens to be my ex-wife."

"Ahh. So you're porking your ex-wife in Washington at the same time you're romancing Mary Beth Hobbs down here."

"I don't see that's any of your business." Owen pointed to his clothes, which were strewn across the dented metal chair. "Mind if I get dressed?"

The sheriff said, "Go right ahead," but he didn't budge from his position.

"How about a little privacy?"

"What's the matter? Afraid I'll see that stud muscle you've been exercising from here to D.C.?"

When the sheriff still didn't move, Owen gathered the blanket around him and hobbled across the cold floor to his clothes. He tried to pull his pants on under the blanket, but it fell away as he balanced on one bare foot.

"Don't see how what little's under those Jockey shorts could satisfy one woman, let alone two," the sheriff said.

"It doesn't surprise me you wouldn't understand how to satisfy a woman."

The sheriff moved his hand to the shiny black riot club at his belt. "Don't get smart with me, boy. I'm in a position to do you a world of hurt."

Somewhere a door opened, letting in street sounds and Purvis Jenkins's voice asking, "Have I come at a bad time?"

The sheriff's hand dropped from his leather holster. "You came at a good time for your buddy here. His smart mouth was about to get to me."

"Maybe you could let us have a little privacy. I could

make him aware of some of our local customs regarding jail etiquette."

"Prisoner wants privacy. You want privacy. If privacy is so damned important to you, stay the hell out of my jail."

"Believe me, Travis, we'd love to do just that," Purvis said.

Owen thought he saw a hint of a smile on the sheriff's face as he edged past Purvis.

"Don't let Travis get to you," Purvis said. "The marine in him still swaggers some, but he's about as straight as sheriffs get in this state."

"He acts as if he'd be happy to see me hanged."

"Probably doesn't like it that you're seeing my sister."

"What's that to him?"

Purvis checked the outer office to make sure Travis wasn't listening. "Travis was sweet on Mary Beth all through high school. He'd have dragged his balls through three miles of broken glass just to finger-fuck her shadow, but she only had eyes for Stony. When Stony and Mary Beth got engaged after graduation, Travis joined the marines. Did two hitches in Vietnam, then was a trainer down at Camp Lejeune. Left the marines all of a sudden, I never knew why. Just showed up back here one day, went to work for the sheriff."

"Did he get an honorable discharge?"

"Must have. Old Sheriff Crain never would have taken him on if Travis had bad paper. Probably wishes he hadn't taken him on anyhow. Travis ran against Crain first chance he got and won."

"How'd that happen?"

"Crain was crooked as they come, even for West Virginia. Everybody knew it."

"But your cousin is straight?"

"Never heard of him being bought outright." Purvis smiled. "Well, hell. He might rent himself out for a while, take a little here and there, but only to do something he's already decided it's right to do."

"Somehow that doesn't seem like much comfort right now."

"Hell's bells, boy. I never thought it would come to this." Purvis glanced toward the outer office, then grasped the cell bars with both hands. "They ought to give you a medal for whacking Hatfield," he whispered.

"Jesus Christ, Purvis. What makes you think I killed Hatfield?"

"Stand back from that cell there Purvis," the sheriff shouted from the other room.

Purvis raised both his hands to show the sheriff they were empty. "Travis says the feds have lots of evidence. He's usually pretty savvy about these things."

"If they've got evidence, somebody must have planted it. I was out cold in the bone pile until Hollis woke me up trying to drag me out."

"That's what I come to tell you. I wouldn't count too much on Hollis's testimony."

"You mean he's likely to lie?"

"Not exactly. Hollis likes you just fine. And he don't have the imagination for a big lie. But Travis has already caught him in a little lie. And he can use that to explode anything else Hollis has to say."

Owen exhaled slowly. "What passes for a little lie in this part of the state?"

Purvis told Owen about their trip to the bone pile with Hollis, when none of them could spot Hatfield's wheelchair from the roadway.

"What's that mean, really? The wheelchair might have been closer to the road when Hollis drove by. Maybe he saw something else and figured later it must have been the wheelchair."

"I told Travis that. Point is, it looks like he's caught Hollis in a lie. And that puts his whole testimony up for grabs. If it's favorable to you, they can blow holes in it because of that one lie."

"And if it's not favorable?"

"Then they probably won't work very hard to discredit him. It's just a damn shame this had to happen. We were just about home free. It looks like the governor's gonna pressure the feds to keep the money coming, so it's not likely they'll be pressing any fraud charges. And, hell, ridership's up twenty percent. Mostly tourists, but it just goes to show what a little publicity'll do."

"Time's up, Purvis," the sheriff yelled.

"Since when is there a time limit on visits, Travis? Where'd that rule come from?"

"My jail, my rules," Travis said.

"I'd best be going, Owen. Mary Beth wanted to come, but I thought it best that she stay home. Be like waving a red flag in front of Travis there. You understand."

Owen leaned back against the cell wall. "Purvis, I don't understand a damn thing."

Around midafternoon Travis escorted a shambling prisoner past Owen's cell to the cell next door. The prisoner was a shoeless man of indeterminate age, with straggly blond hair and bare soles so black they might have been vulcanized rubber. The sleeves of his grimy buckskin jacket had been joined by knotting the fringe to form makeshift handcuffs. The sheriff handled the man like an exasperated parent, holding a nightstick under his armpit as he passed Owen's cell.

Owen watched through the bars separating the two cells as Travis settled the new prisoner on his pallet.

"Try and get some sleep, Samuel," the sheriff said. "I'll bring you dinner in a few hours."

Metal keys clanked, and Travis stopped in front of Owen's cell. "That boy was worth ten of you once," he told Owen. "They took him fresh out of high school, sent him to 'Nam with a lieutenant who didn't know shit, had him crawling in tunnels and burning villages no worse than some we got up Eight-Pole Creek. Then they brought him out, checked him for drugs and VD, and sent him home.

"When they get him back here, do they thank him?" Travis fished in his hip pocket for a handkerchief and rubbed his face. "Hell no. Do they give him a job? Hell no. Instead they tell him he was a sucker. Or worse, a whacked-out baby killer.

"Fucking VA's no help, either. First they ignore him, then they dope him up. Like that's what he needed."

The sheriff poked his nightstick through the bars at Owen. "Here's a statistic for you, Mr. Statistician. West Virginia lost more boys per capita in Vietnam than any other state. Dumb ridgerunners, didn't know no better. Went over with pictures of John Wayne and Gary Cooper dancing in their heads. Didn't take long to learn it wasn't like the movies. Didn't take long to die."

The sheriff pulled his nightstick back and slapped it against the palm of his hand. "Hell, they're still dying. Lost more since the war ended than while it was going on. Suicides, OD's . . ." He nodded toward the next cell, ". . . zombies like Samuel there.

"And where were you while this was going on? Huh, Mr. Statistician?" The nightstick slapped against the palm once more. "Back here in the States, sitting on your fat little college deferment, so's you could take our jobs and screw our women."

The sheriff paused, distracted by something outside Owen's view.

"I hope you're not threatening my client with that nightstick," Judith said. A slim black briefcase hung from her left shoulder and a gray garment bag was slung over her right arm. "I'm Owen Allison's lawyer." She pulled a card out of the briefcase and handed it to the sheriff. "I'd like to see my client alone."

Travis waved his nightstick toward the garment bag. "What's in the bag?"

"A change of clothes for our bail hearing tomorrow."

"Take them off their hangers one at a time."

For a moment, Judith looked at the sheriff as if he'd asked her to perform some obscene act. Then she set her briefcase on the floor, unzipped the garment bag, and handed the sheriff a black suit with a wavering pinstripe. Owen recognized it as one of the last suits they'd bought together while he and Judith were still married. He knew that Judith had always like the suit, and it didn't seem the right time to tell her that the pants no longer fit.

The sheriff patted down the suit, put a hand in each of the pockets, and passed it through the bars to Owen.

A tie Judith had bought in Los Angeles to go with the pinstriped suit followed. Owen hadn't worn the tie since their divorce.

Travis held the tie up to the light and examined the pattern, a tangle of white and yellow loops. "Pretty fancy. Like a mess of shiny spaghetti."

Instead of passing the tie through the bars, the sheriff draped it on his nightstick. "Had me a prisoner once down in Camp Lejeune, hanged himself with a noose made of two shoelaces and two neckties. I see you're wearing loafers, though. Probably be a hard thing to hang yourself just with one fancy necktie and no shoelaces.

"Nobody knew how my Lejeune prisoner got ahold of two neckties. It being against regulations for a prisoner to have even one." The sheriff poked his nightstick through the bars and let the tie dangle. "I guess I can trust you with this one necktie, though. Not that I want to give you any ideas about hanging yourself." When Owen didn't reach for the necktie, the sheriff tilted the nightstick and let the tie slide to the cell floor.

The sheriff went through the other items in the garment bag, examined the contents of Judith's briefcase, made a show of letting her keep her tape recorder, and finally called a deputy to open the cell door. As the deputy locked the cell behind Judith, the sheriff said, "I understand you were once married to the prisoner. I just want to make it plain that this is in the nature of an attorney/client visit, not a conjugal visit. Do I make myself clear?"

Judith reddened. "Perfectly."

When the sheriff and his deputy left the corridor, Judith sat down in the dented metal chair. "That man seems to have something against you."

"It's that I'm a draft-dodging, murdering, defiler of West Virginia womanhood," Owen told her.

"Womanhood in general, or does he have someone particular in mind?"

"It seems the sheriff has had a crush on Mary Beth Hobbs ever since high school."

Judith opened her briefcase. "Then we'd better figure out how to get you out on bail."

OWEN'S BAIL HEARING was held in the same courtroom where he'd listened to Hatfield McCoy complain about the Contrary Comet. Then he'd sat on the other side of this same defense table, looking out at the courtroom. And there had been no judge overseeing the proceedings from a raised platform behind the ornate wood railing. Now there was a judge with the gaunt, hollow-eyed face Owen associated with coal miners; he wouldn't have been surprised to find that he was wearing bib overalls under his black robe.

The prosecutor's table had also been empty when Owen had last used the courtroom. Now it seated the district attorney—a squat, balding man Purvis claimed had been "bought and paid for by big coal,"—a black-suited federal attorney who reminded Owen of a young George C. Scott, one of the federal marshalls who had brought Owen back to Contrary, and two legal assistants, one male and one female.

Owen sat alone with Judith at the defense table, feeling outnumbered and uncomfortable in his too-tight suit. He stood as she entered a not-guilty plea to the murder charges and asked that he be released on bail, citing his lack of a criminal record, his ongoing history of employment, and his ties to the communities where he worked and was raised.

The local district attorney conferred with the black-suited George C. Scott look-alike; then he rose and addressed the bench. "Your Honor," he said, overdoing the nasal twang that marked local speech, "the prosecution asks that the defendant be held without bail. The charge of dual murder is a serious one, and we have evidence that the defendant poses a significant risk of flight if he is released."

Judith jumped to her feet. "Your Honor, I object. We know of no such evidence."

The judge addressed the district attorney. "Can the prosecution be more specific regarding the risk of flight?"

The balding DA stooped while the black-suited federal attorney whispered in his ear. The DA nodded three times before he turned to face the judge. "Your Honor, we have evidence that the defendant has diverted over two hundred and fifty thousand dollars of taxpayer money to his own private account. Were he to . . ."

"Your Honor, this is preposterous," Judith interrupted, on her feet again.

Owen gripped the table edge. His too-tight pants squeezed stomach bile up into his throat.

"These allegations," Judith said, "we deny wholeheartedly. They are not a part of the State's charges. We have no prior knowledge of them and have seen no evidence to support them."

"Is this true, Mr. Alexander?" the judge asked the DA. "Did you or did you not inform the defense of these allegations?"

"This is just a bail hearing, Your Honor," the DA answered. "Evidence regarding the embezzlement would have been shared in due course as part of the pretrial discovery process."

Judith leaped to her feet again, but the judge silenced her with an upraised hand.

"Mr. Alexander," the judge said, "you couldn't wait for the trial to bring the subject up. You brought it up today. If you're going to play a card in my courtroom, I expect you to let the defense examine the deck first."

He flipped the file in front of him closed. "I'm going to adjourn for two days. In the meantime, I expect you to acquaint this good lady with any and all evidence you have pertinent to your arguments at this bail hearing. Do I make myself clear?"

The DA glared at Judith as if she were the one lecturing him. "Yes, Your Honor. Perfectly clear."

"Good. Then we'll adjourn until the same time Thursday."

THE SUN HAD gone down and the harsh light from the recessed overhead bulb turned the jail wall into a pitted lunar landscape. Sounds of retching came from the cell next door. Owen's microwaved dinner sat untouched on the metal chair. Judith had said she would come to see him as soon as she had reviewed the prosecution's evidence; but that had been nearly five hours ago. They couldn't have that much evidence. They couldn't have any evidence. He hadn't killed Hatfield and he'd only seen Hatfield's cousin once.

They'd have to let him go if there was no evidence. Right? Wrong. Look at all those high-profile trials in the news the last few years. Juries made mistakes. They could as easily convict an innocent man as let a killer go free. Maybe there's a thermodynamic law governing the conservation of justice. For every killer a jury sets free, another jury has to convict an innocent person. Conservation of justice. That kind of thinking could drive him crazy. Where the hell was Judith?

A door opened, and he heard Judith's voice in the outer office. She seemed to be arguing with the deputy in charge. The two of them finally appeared, and the deputy ordered Owen to stand away from the cell door as he unlocked it to let Judith in. Then he removed Owen's untouched dinner without asking whether he intended to eat it.

"Crappy service," Judith said after the deputy had left. "I wouldn't leave a tip if I were you."

When Owen didn't respond, she said, "Sorry. Bad joke. I brought you a tuna sandwich and a shake, but the gatekeeper out there wouldn't let me bring it back."

"That's okay. I don't think I could keep anything down. What've you got?"

Judith took two bulky manila folders from her briefcase. "I made copies for both of us."

The size of the files surprised him. "You mean they actually have some real evidence?"

"What looks like evidence to them. We'd better go over it and see what it looks like to us."

Owen reached for the top folder.

"Just wait a minute," Judith said. "There's not much here about the murders; just what we already know. Your jacket fibers were under Snooker's fingernails, you'd argued with Hatfield, and you were at the scene of his murder."

"I was out cold. I barely knew the victims. What was my motive?"

"They think you've been draining money from the Contrary Comet subsidy for the last four years. They think you killed Hatfield because he caught on to what you were doing."

"That's preposterous! I haven't been working on that job for more than four months, let alone four years."

"Well, it seems clear that all that extra bus money isn't going to doctors, nurses, and street cleaners. Somebody's been pocketing sixty-five grand a year, regular as clockwork. They think it's you."

"Why me?"

"The whole thing started about the time you moved to Washington."

"So did the Redskins' string of losing seasons. Have they blamed that on me, too?"

"That's the kind of response I need to make as your lawyer," Judith said. She handed him one of the folders. "You need to look at what they consider to be evidence and help me to discredit it."

The top sheet in the folder was a photocopy of the fifteen-hundred-dollar personal check Owen had written to Mary Beth Hobbs. "First of all," Judith asked, "did you write this check?"

"I wrote it, yes."

"Did you know that your friend Ms. Hobbs turned around and put it into the Contrary Comet's cash fund?"

"She told me what she needed it for. But that's putting money in. That's not taking it out."

"Come on, Owen, she was covering her tracks before the auditor hit town."

"She'd borrowed the money for her husband's operation. I helped her pay it back."

"Let's not call it borrowing. It's embezzling, pure and simple. And your check implicates you."

"I can't help that. I was just loaning money to a friend."

"To cover up a crime."

"Have it your way." Owen pulled out a sheaf of papers. "These are my credit card invoices. What the hell are they doing with my credit card records?"

"They're using them to show you made frequent visits to Contrary. There's a regular pattern of receipts from the gas stations on Route 64 that goes back four years."

"I was visiting Mom."

"You and I know that. They don't. We can make them look foolish if they use it in court."

"That's not so bad, then."

"No, it could be a good thing." Judith pulled out more invoices. "Your home and office phone bills show an abnormal number of calls to your Ms. Hobbs."

"We can explain that, too."

"I imagine you can. But that's not all. They know about Billings, Gates." She watched for Owen's response.

"They know what about billingsgate?"

"That's what I thought you'd say." She handed Owen a business letterhead. "It's not billingsgate, it's Billings, Gates and Associates. It's a bogus consulting firm using a D.C. post office box."

"So?"

"So every July, at the start of the fiscal year, the Contrary Comet has been sending Billings, Gates and Associates a check for sixty-five thousand dollars."

"In return for what?"

"Nobody's quite sure. Purvis thought it was for an annual system report that was actually prepared internally. Mary Beth thought it was part of a maintenance contract. She just paid their invoices.

"So Contrary got nothing in return for their sixty-five grand?"

"Nothing anybody can put their finger on."

"Sounds like a hell of a consulting deal. A few like that and I'd still be in business."

"I wouldn't joke about it, Owen."

Something in her tone stopped him cold. "Why not?"

"Because the FBI found a dozen copies of that letterhead hidden in your office."

18

MINER'S ASTHMA

A STREAKED STEM OF BLOOD led from the rail tie to the flower of phlegm in the dust at Stony's feet. Bent double, clinging to the half-ton coal cart for support, he stared at the blood, remembering his father in this same position. He straightened, closed his eyes, and took two great gulps of air, imagining he was drowning the spider-web the doctors had shown him in his left lung.

The doctors had told Stony it wouldn't get better, but they hadn't told him how quickly it would get worse. He'd stopped smoking, but he couldn't stop working his mine. The mine was his livelihood, and he still owed Mary Beth the money.

Even after he'd emptied the cart into the dump truck, the truck was still only half full. Just half full, and he'd been working since dawn. Time was, he'd have taken a full load to the tipple and been back for more by now.

Stony kicked the empty cart. Reddish-brown flakes of rust floated around the shiny rails. He wedged his back against the cart and began moving it slowly uphill toward the mine. His ribs ached under their tape, and he looked forward to the short downhill stretch just after he entered the cool blackness.

There was barely enough room at the mine face to work the seam from a kneeling position. In the light of his miner's cap, black dust swirled as he picked the coal free and loaded it into the cart. The seam had narrowed, giving him less coal for each swing of his pick. Soon he'd have to blast deeper into the earth, and you never knew what might happen then. He had to do something though. Between the narrow seam, his taped ribs, and whatever his ribs were protecting in his lungs, he wasn't pulling out enough coal to pay his tab at Pokey Joe's, let alone to pay back Mary Beth.

He stopped loading and hacked away at the seam, letting the chunks of coal and shale fall around his knees. Coal dust clogged his throat; he dropped his pick and gasped for air. Waving futilely at the clouds of black dust, he managed to inhale a lungful of soot and air. Then nothing. He couldn't exhale. He tore at his throat, crawling through chunks of coal and shale toward remembered daylight. As he squeezed between the cart and the mine wall, the air in his throat wheezed like a slow leak or a faint scream. Then a racking cough sprayed sticky sputum over his grasping hands and let him inhale again.

He clawed his way gasping and wheezing toward the light at the end of the mine shaft, scrambling on his hands and knees even when the shaft opened out to allow him to stand. Each time he inhaled, he felt as if he were going to suffocate until a strangled cough cleared his lungs for another breath.

Using the rail ties as a horizontal ladder, he climbed out of the mine and sprawled facedown between the rails, coughing up a mixture of blood and bile. He lay still and practiced breathing. In and out. In and out. He didn't move until he heard running footsteps and Stuart's voice asking if he was all right.

Stony pulled himself to one knee and waved off his son. "I'm fine. Just resting."

Stuart stopped beside the blue dump truck and saw that it was only half full. "Been to the tipple and back already?"

"Got a late start," Stony lied. "Not much seam left."

"Let me help load."

Stony stood up shakily to keep Stuart from the mouth of the mine. "Don't want you in there."

"I worked the seam when you were in the hospital."

"I don't want you mining."

"Where's the cart?"

"Still in the mine."

"You didn't bring it out?"

"I had to piss. I left in a hurry."

"Let me go get the cart."

Stony grabbed his son, as much for support as for restraint. "I said I don't want you going in there."

"I'll just get the cart and come right out."

"All right. Just wait there a minute before you go in."

Stony retreated to the side of the dump truck away from Stuart, ducked down, and hawked red liquid into his handkerchief. He remembered his father doing that, too.

Then he opened the glove compartment and pulled a surgical mask from a packet Doc Pritchard had given him.

"If you're going in, wear this," he told Stuart.

His son groaned. "Oh, come on, Dad."

"Wear it, or you're not going in."

"You never wear one."

"I will from now on." Stony tied the mask so it covered Stuart's nose and mouth and fitted his own miner's lamp onto his son's forehead. "In and out. Just get the cart. No picking or loading."

After Stuart disappeared into the mine, Stony listened for the sound of the cart moving on the rails. Nothing. He remembered letting his son ride in the cart and sort shale when he was still in grade school. He never should have got him started. "Stuart, get that cart and your ass out here. Right now."

Stony heard the screech of metal wheels on metal rails deep within the shaft and waited for Stuart to appear. "What the hell kept you?"

Stuart's cotton mask bore sooty circles around his nostrils. "There were chunks of coal all over. Did you leave them there?"

"I had to leave in a hurry."

They rolled the cart downhill and loaded its coal into the dump truck. Then Stony threw their shovels behind the truck's seat. "Come on. I'll give you a ride home."

"But the truck's not full yet."

"Let me worry about that. I want to give you some practice catching short hops while it's still light out."

"That'd be great."

Stony eased the truck into gear and jounced it down the

narrow winding road, trailing puffs of coal dust at each pothole.

"If you want to stop at the tipple, I'll help you unload," Stuart said.

"I'll dump the load later," Stony told him. "That's my job. Your job is to finish high school and find a college that needs a good catcher."

As the truck gained speed, Stony said, "I hear your mom's still seeing that guy from D.C."

"Mr. Allison."

"Heard he was all hole and no coal."

"No, that was the other one. Mr. Allison's okay. Except they've got him in the county jail."

"What for?"

"They say he killed Hatfield McCoy."

Stony swerved to avoid a chuckhole. "They ought to give a man a medal for killing Hatfield. What makes them think he did it?"

"Don't know. He sure doesn't seem like a killer. He's never even been in a war."

Stony was still considering his son's answer when he pulled into Mary Beth's driveway. "Go and get your catcher's gear," he said to Stuart. "I want to talk to your mother."

"You're trailing coal dust all over town," Mary Beth said. "Why didn't you dump that load at the tipple?"

Stony waited to be sure Stuart was out of earshot. "That money I owe you. It's going to be a while longer before I can give it back."

"That's all right."

"Last few weeks you were near frantic about it."

"I got a loan."

"You got a loan? Where from?"

"That's my business."

"It's that D.C. guy, isn't it? That Allison guy?" Stony took a step toward Mary Beth, then moved away and pounded his fist against the side of the dump truck. The coal shifted and slid toward the rear gate. "Bad enough he's spending the night and shining up to Jeb Stuart. Now I owe the bastard money on top of it."

"He's not spending the night. Who told you he's been spending the night?"

Stony felt a cough coming and tried to hold it in. It exploded from his lungs, leaving a sticky red streak along his rear fender.

"My God, Stony. Have you seen the doctor?"

"Can't afford to. Still paying off my last visit."

"You told me you'd finally got insurance."

Stony took Stuart's cotton mask from his pocket and wiped off the rear fender. "Accidental death was all they'd sell me."

"What about health insurance?"

"Wouldn't sell me any. Said I had some kind of precondition."

"A preexisting condition? What kind of preexisting condition?"

He turned to face her. "Miner's asthma."

"Oh, Stony, black lung killed your father."

"Guess it runs in the family."

Stuart appeared at the screen door, wearing blue jeans, white athletic socks, and an old Cincinnati Red's uniform top. He was carrying spikes, shin guards, a chest protector, and a catcher's mask with three baseballs wedged inside. "Is something wrong?"

Stony took the catcher's mask and shin guards. "Nothing's wrong. Let's get to the ballfield while we've still got some daylight."

THE BASEBALL DIAMOND was sandwiched between two softball fields alongside a dry creek bed. A pickup game was in progress on one of the two softball fields, and the clear evening air carried the game chatter across the shared outfield. Cries of "Hey, batter, batter" reached Stony as he stood on the pitcher's mound and waited for Stuart to pull on his chest protector. He remembered hearing the same sounds on the same diamond when he was in high school, fresh and full of promise.

Stuart squatted behind home plate and gave Stony a low target with his catcher's mitt. "Okay, let's see your fast one."

Stony took a short windup and aimed the ball at the dirt to the left of home plate, releasing it easily.

The ball bounced beside the plate and Stuart caught it with a backhand swipe of his mitt.

"You've got to slide your whole body over," Stony said. "Don't just swipe at those short ones."

"I caught it, didn't I?"

"You're better off blocking it. If I'd put more on the pitch, it might have gotten through."

Stony continued to bounce half-speed pitches in the dirt to the left of home plate, making each pitch wider than the last, trying to force Stuart to move his body in front of the ball. More often than not, Stuart would catch the ball the same way he'd caught the first pitch, with an arcing backhand swoop of his mitt. "Goddamm it, block it with your whole body," Stony shouted.

Stony decided to throw harder and make it more difficult

for Stuart to field his pitches backhanded. He took a full windup, swung his right arm behind him, and felt something tear under the tape on his rib cage. He followed through feebly, clutched at his ribs with his gloved hand, and watched the pitch plop in the dirt halfway to home plate.

As Stony flexed his right arm, pain shot through his chest. "I don't think I can throw anymore. Let's rest a bit."

While Stuart went to the cooler in the dump truck for a Coke and a couple of Strohs, Stony sat in the bleachers behind home plate and poked gingerly at his taped ribs.

"You all right, Dad?"

"I must've pulled a few ribs loose."

"Where those bikers stomped you?"

Stony nodded.

"Hollis says you coldcocked one before they got you outside."

"Hollis saved my ass," Stony said. "Not the first time. Won't be the last."

A great whoop came from the softball diamond. A boy and girl in yellow T-shirts were running full tilt around the bases, while a shirtless teenager chased the softball. By the time the teenager got the ball back to the infield, the boy had scored and the girl stood on third with a triple, clapping her hands.

"Have things changed much since you played here?" Stuart asked.

"Some," Stony answered. "Girls hit better." He took the catcher's mitt from his son's lap. "Catcher's mitts are bigger."

"I would have tried catching your way."

"That's all right. You were doing fine."

"Hollis says you and he hit against Mr. Allison in the state championships."

"He was a last-minute sub. Some fireballer was supposed to pitch for Barkley, but he racked up his motorcycle the night before the game."

"Wes Whitfield."

"How'd you know the name?"

"Mr. Allison told me. How'd you do against him?"

"Double and a homer. Struck me out once on dinky stuff, though. He wound up winning the game."

"I got lots of hits off Mr. Allison." Stuart told Stony about the backyard diamond at Owen's mother's house in Barkley, with the flower garden in the outfield and the ball-retrieving dog.

"Sounds like you get along fine with this guy Allison."

"He's okay. Think you and I could train a dog to do that?"

"We had Trixie. She used to fetch sticks."

"Not all the time. And she got old and died."

"I had to put her down. Hardest thing I ever did."

"You shot her? That wasn't what Mom said."

"You're old enough to know now. She had cancer. Snapped at most everybody that last year. Your mother was after me to do her in for a long time, but I couldn't."

Stony stretched and winced at the pain shooting through his chest. He never should have tried pitching to Stuart. All he'd wanted to do was get the kid away from the mine. He fingered his taped ribs again and felt his right leg jerk at the pain. "Where was I?"

"Talking about Trixie. You said Mom wanted you to put her down."

"Oh yeah. You could see she was in pain. Growled at everybody but you. But you know, every morning, when I'd be frying bacon, she'd hear the sizzle and come and wag her tail under the stove, waiting for a piece."

"Mom didn't like you to feed her bacon."

"Well, hell. It was her last pleasure. One morning, though, I was frying bacon and she didn't come. Just laid there on the porch, all stifflike, trembling. That's when I knew it was time."

Stony finished the Strohs and cradled the empty bottle between his feet. "Point is, no matter how much pain she was in, I never would have put her down so long as she still took some pleasure in things."

They watched the softball game together. The girl in the yellow T-shirt was pitching now, lofting high arcs that caught the dying sunlight and dipped into shadows as batters swung too soon or too lustily. Usually there was nothing Stony liked better than watching a ball game, any ball game, but he was finding it hard to concentrate.

Across the diamond, a batter swung mightily under a looping pitch and popped it high in the air.

"That's it, third out," Stuart said.

"The shortstop's still got to catch it."

"It's a sure thing."

"Nothing's sure."

The shortstop closed his glove around the pop-up and the others ran off the field. "See, what did I tell you?"

Stony slid down one tier of bleacher seats and retrieved the beer bottle. "Time to go home."

★   ★   ★

BACK IN THE mining shed where he slept, Stony swallowed two quick shots of Jack Daniel's. He poured himself a third drink, turned off the naked bulb that dangled over his cot, and propped himself against pillows in a position that didn't pull at his rib cage. Sipping the third Jack Daniel's left-handed, he stared at the far corner of the darkened shed, waiting for the pink edge that helped him separate dreams from reality.

His mind drifted, and he found himself in an underground cavern dimly lit by four candles that flickered from a lack of oxygen. He could make out the shapes of three other men besides himself. One was his father, blood and spit caked in his beard, tied to a shiny intravenous feeder. One was his Uncle Vic, writing a note to rescuers that he knew would never get through in time. The third figure was indistinct, slumped in a far corner of the cavern. He could tell it was a much younger man, but as he approached, the four candles snuffed themselves with a thin hiss. He knew who the third figure was, but he had to be sure. He fumbled with a book of matches, finally lighting one on the third try. As the match consumed the last of the available oxygen, he recognized the face of his son Stuart.

He awoke sweating and gasping for breath. It was still dark, but he sensed that dawn was not far off, and he didn't want to risk another dream. Stony swung his feet off the cot and tested his rib cage. The pain was still there, but it seemed to have subsided in the night. He switched on the overhead bulb and moved about gingerly in its harsh light. When he was dressed, he pulled a wooden packing crate out of the sawdust and grime under his workbench and counted out a dozen sticks of dynamite. He wasn't quite ready yet. He'd need to get blasting caps and attend to a few other chores, but he knew what he had to do.

19

NO GOOD DEED GOES UNPUNISHED

Owen HANDED THE COPY of the Billings, Gates and Associates letterhead back to Judith. "What can I say? Someone must have planted it in my office."

"Who could have done it? Isn't your building secure?"

"You have to pass a guard at the entrance, but it's easy enough to get in if you know somebody on the inside. And once you're in you can wander anywhere."

"I thought you said your boss had roped off your cubicle."

"Hell, he trussed it up with yellow tape." The memory renewed Owen's outrage. "But anybody could have gotten through. Besides, the letterhead might have been planted before Bashford taped the office shut."

Judith returned the letterhead to her briefcase.

"Where was it found, anyhow?" Owen asked.

"In an envelope taped to the bottom of a desk drawer."

"I'm surprised they didn't sprinkle it with Hatfield's blood. Why didn't you give me the letterhead with the rest of this stuff?"

"I wanted to see how you'd react if I sprung it on you." Judith shrugged. "I'm sorry."

"Trust is a wonderful thing."

Judith raised her voice. "Don't you dare talk to me about trust." She saw that the prisoner in the next cell was staring at her and she lowered her voice. "I said I was sorry. Billingsgate. It just sounded like a name you'd make up."

"If the press gets hold of it, will it be Billingsgate Gate? Or is that redundant?"

"See what I mean? It sounded like you."

"If bad jokes were grounds for imprisonment in this state, these cells would be full to bursting and Purvis Jenkins would be doing life. Is there anything else you're holding back?"

"No, I showed you everything." She pulled a copy of a ruled sheet from an accountant's ledger out of her briefcase. "Except his, but it's not really evidence against you."

"What is it?"

"It's a record of deposits and withdrawals from the account Billings and Gates maintained at First Federal in Washington."

"Looks like they took in sixty-five grand every July, regular as clockwork."

"That came from your friends in Contrary."

"Then they took out about two grand a month, except for two or three splurges."

"That was all cash issued to Billings."

"You mean somebody walked out of the bank with

twenty and thirty grand at a time here in July and here in August?"

"The feds were looking for evidence of a change in your lifestyle during those months. They seemed disappointed not to find any."

"They're disappointed? Hell, I'm disappointed. I sure could have used a thirty-grand change in my lifestyle."

"There's only about eighty grand left. And there's been no activity at all in the account for the past four months."

"That's about how long I've been responsible for Contrary's payments," Owen pointed to the ledger. "But look here. Every time sixty-five grand came into the account from Contrary, they paid out sixty-five hundred dollars right away."

"That went to another First Federal account. It hasn't been touched."

"Withholding tax?"

"None of this ever got reported to the IRS. They've got no record of Billings or Gates."

"It's exactly ten percent. Maybe these guys had an agent."

"Or an accomplice."

Travis Jenkins ran his nightstick over the cell bars, producing a machine-gun clatter. "Time to wrap it up in there," he said.

"We're not finished," Judith said.

"Hell, take five more minutes. Lover boy shouldn't need more than that for a little conjugal good-bye."

Judith watched Travis return to his office. "I don't like leaving you here with that man. You say he's threatened you?"

"Not in so many words. But that nightstick is never out of sight."

Judith fished out a pocket-size tape recorder and a roll of Scotch tape from her briefcase. "Where can we hide this recorder? If we get his threats on tape, the judge is sure to give you bail."

They both looked into the next cell. Samuel was staring at them vacantly.

Judith turned the back of the metal chair toward Samuel's cell and motioned to Owen to sit down.

Judith winked at Samuel and knelt in front of Owen. Then she began unzipping his fly.

"What the hell?" Owen said.

"Shh. This won't hurt a bit." She laid her head in his lap and fumbled under the chair.

Owen heard the soft snick of tape being torn from a dispenser. As Judith burrowed her face deeper into his lap, he felt the beginning of an erection.

She raised her head, smiled up at him, and moved her hands under the chair. He heard a click, and his own voice saying, "What the hell?" followed by Judith's admonition, "This won't hurt a bit." Then he heard a faint whirring noise as the recorder rewound.

Judith zipped up his fly, rose, and winked again at Samuel. Bending over Owen, she whispered, "Just keep it rewound. It's voice activated. It'll pick up anything said in this cell."

"Where'd you learn your audio/visual technique?" Owen asked hoarsely.

"I'm making it up as I go along," Judith's hair brushed Owen's cheek as she drew away.

"Well now, isn't that sweet," Travis's voice interrupted. "Is that some sort of privileged lawyer/client communication?"

Judith moved back and eyed Owen's chair. He couldn't tell whether she was examining his erection or trying to spot the tape recorder.

"I was just leaving," Judith said.

Travis unlocked the cell door and watched Judith depart. Twirling his nightstick on its leather strap, he said, "Next time she visits, stick to lawyer/client intercourse. Understood?"

The nightstick picked up speed and clanged off the metal chair. Owen's erection vanished, and he fought to keep his hands from groping under the chair to see if the tape recorder had been dislodged.

"Understood," Owen said.

OWEN MUSHED HIS microwaved dinner around with a plastic fork, wondering if he'd be able to keep it down. He could see that Samuel was having even more trouble with his dinner in the next cell. Each mouthful of gristly stew was followed by a loud sucking noise, as if extra hydraulic force was required to pass the concoction down his throat. Suddenly Samuel pitched forward, knocking over his tray and spewing vomit everywhere.

Owen yelled for help.

"Jesus Christ, Samuel," Travis shouted. "You're a disgrace to the troops."

Samuel scuttled backward on all fours.

Travis unrolled a hose from the end of the corridor and began sluicing the vomit toward the recessed drain in the middle of Samuel's cell. The hose splattered as much as it cleaned, and Travis stopped and turned off the water. "Shit. This isn't in my job description. You'll have to live with it until the deputies come for the late shift."

Samuel cowered in the corner.

"Bring me a mop and I'll clean it up," Owen said.

"Well now, why didn't I think of that," Travis said.

The sheriff wheeled a mop and janitor's bucket into Samuel's cell. After handcuffing Owen to the cell door, he lifted Samuel under the armpits and dragged him into Owen's cell. Then he released Owen's cuffs, led him into Samuel's cell, pointed to the mop and bucket, and said, "Be my guest."

Owen mopped up most of the mess, but the stench of vomit hung on.

"That's not half bad," Travis said, removing the mop and bucket. "Still smells a mite gamey, though." He locked the cell door behind him. "Tell you what, why don't you and Samuel swap cells for a while."

Owen felt a surge of panic. "I've got all those papers in my cell."

"That's easy to fix," Travis said. He gathered up an armful of manila folders from Owen's old cell and carried them into the cell Owen now occupied. Standing in the center of the cell, he opened his arms, said "Oops," and let the papers flutter down to the still-damp floor.

Owen knelt to pull the papers from the sticky floor while Travis let himself out. As he reset the lock, Travis said, "It just goes to show you that no good deed goes unpunished."

Samuel pulled the metal chair with the tape recorder over to the bars separating the two cells and dangled his hand through to Owen, saying, "Sorry, man."

Owen looked at the U.S. Marine Corps anchor tat-tooed on Samuel's forearm, reached out, and shook the extended hand. He thought about trying to retrieve the tape recorder from Samuel's chair, but decided against it. Unless Samuel knocked the chair over, no one was likely to find the recorder. Even if he did upend the chair, they could still recover so long as there were no deputies around. And anybody but Travis finding the recorder might blame Samuel anyhow. After all, it was in his cell.

Owen spread out the damp papers on his pallet, sorted them into chronological order, and tried to make sense out of the records. The credit card receipts, he realized, only showed that he'd spent time in coal country, and his visits to his mother explained that. The phone calls made from his office could be another matter. He started with the most recent records and found he recognized the numbers of roughly half of his long distance calls. Mary Beth's number, with its 304 area code, stood out because he'd memorized it and because it was easily the number he'd called most fre-quently. That was the point the feds were trying to make.

By the time he'd worked his way backward through a year's worth of records, Mary Beth's number was the only one he recognized. But he hadn't even known Mary Beth Hobbs a year ago. The phone records went with the office, and the office had belonged to Dwight Armitrage then. Owen had only occupied the cubicle for a few months, banished there so Walker Bashford could expand his own office. The year-old phone bills recorded calls made by Armitrage.

The feds had assumed Owen had always been in the of-fice Bashford roped off. It was exactly the mistake he hoped for if Judith's tape recorder were found in Samuel's new cell. Blame the person who touched it last. Guilt by association.

The feds had made the same mistake with the Billings-gate letterhead. Guilt by association. Maybe nobody planted the letterhead in his office. Maybe Armitrage had hidden it there before he died. Maybe Armitrage had set up Billings, Gates and Associates.

Owen flipped feverishly through the five years of phone records, circling the phone calls to Mary Beth. At least one a month, always a flurry near the end of the fiscal year. More to her than to any of the other properties Armitrage was auditing. Many more. Even more than Owen had been making to her. Something had been going on between Armitrage and Mary Beth. It was evidence all right, but not the kind he'd hoped to find. He needed to talk to Judith.

20

SUCH LITTLE THINGS

Mary Beth twisted the handkerchief she held in her lap and directed her words toward it. "Mr. Armitrage was on to us from the start."

Purvis Jenkins had seen his sister play this role many times before. The handkerchief twisting usually preceded an outrageous story that sent Purvis, sometimes justly, to the coal cellar for a tanning. He couldn't remember Mary Beth ever being taken to the coal cellar herself.

Purvis looked around the makeshift interrogation room Travis Jenkins had set up in his office. A U.S. attorney and a federal marshall sat at the desk opposite Mary Beth, pens poised over legal pads. A tape recorder was running on Travis's desk, and Travis and Judith Allison sat on either side of the office door, facing Mary Beth.

"Sis, maybe we ought to get you a lawyer here," Purvis said.

Mary Beth waved off her brother's suggestion and spoke to Judith. "I understand you're a lawyer. Maybe you could stop me if I seem to be getting myself into trouble."

"I'm afraid I can't do that," Judith said. "I already represent my ex-husband and I'm not sure your interests coincide with his."

"Oh, I'm sure they do." Unfazed, Mary Beth turned to the sheriff and said, "Travis, you understand these things better than I do. Will y'all promise to stop me if you see I'm doing more harm than good?"

Travis grunted and shifted in his chair.

"That's fine, then, just fine." Mary Beth glanced down at her handkerchief and addressed the U.S. attorney. "Armitage saw we were overcharging the government the minute he got Hollis's invoice. He showed up in my office one morning waving it and threatening to put us in jail for fraud."

"Your office," repeated the U.S. attorney. The attorney's name was Ed Williams and he reminded Purvis of a movie star, the guy who was in *The Hustler*. Not Paul Newman, but the other guy, the sharp shyster.

Williams turned to Purvis. "You know about any of this?"

"Not till now."

"I should have told you first thing, Purvis," Mary Beth said. "I know that now."

Purvis shrugged.

"Anyhow," Mary Beth continued, "he came after me. Maybe because I'd signed the invoice. Maybe because he thought a woman would be more vulnerable. I just don't know."

The federal marshal sitting beside Williams drummed

his fingers on his tablet. He was wearing an ill-fitting tweed jacket with a stain on the lapel; half a shirttail hung free under the jacket.

Mary Beth ignored the finger drumming. "After ranting and threatening, Armitage came up with a proposition. He'd sign off on our inflated invoice if we agreed to honor a contract with a bogus consulting firm for sixty-five thousand dollars a year."

"Billings, Gates and Associates," the finger-drumming marshal said.

"That's the one. Anyhow, what could I do? He sounded very convincing. And this was a way out."

"So you paid him off and he approved your invoices?" Williams asked.

Mary Beth nodded.

"But we got nothing at all out of this consulting firm?" Purvis asked.

"At first, he produced a few reports. Trivial stuff, mostly. Annual ridership summaries, things like that. He wanted to have something in the files in case they ever sent a real auditor. After a while, though, he didn't even bother with that."

"Pretty sweet setup," the marshal said. "What went sour?"

"Excuse me?" Mary Beth said.

"What went sour? Armitage is dead and your boondoggle is front-page news."

"Armitage wanted more money. He told me to double the size of his consulting contract."

"When was this?" her brother asked.

"Just before his last visit," Mary Beth told Purvis. "By that time you had parceled out all the subsidy in city services. I couldn't increase his contract without cutting something we needed. And risk having you figure everything out."

"I'd have slit his pecker sideways," Purvis said.

"Well, Armitrage came up with a plan. He drove down here to Contrary, inspected the system, and pretended to discover what he knew all along, that we were running two buses and charging for twenty."

"So his visit was a put-up job?" Purvis asked.

"I'm sorry, Purvis," Mary Beth said. "He said he'd confront you, let you stew a little, and then suggest we up the ante by billing for forty buses instead of twenty and splitting the difference with him. He thought you'd snap up the offer."

"Well, I didn't," Purvis said. "First off, I didn't trust the man. Wouldn't trust him as far as I can piss, and I always have to stand right over the urinal to keep my shoes dry."

"When you wouldn't bite, it all went bad."

"Didn't trust the man," Purvis repeated. "Any fool can see Contrary's not a forty-bus town. If it's gonna work, a lie has to fall somewhere near the truth."

"When Purvis turned him down, Armitrage started drinking," Mary Beth said. "Out there at Pokey Joe's. He just got drunker and angrier."

"Tried to rape Mary Beth in the parking lot," Purvis said. "Hollis and I put a stop to that quick enough."

The marshal drummed his fingers on his steno notebook. "What happened to Armitrage then?"

"Went on drinking, wound up at the bone pile."

The marshal flipped over a notebook page. "The bone pile?"

"Suffocated in sulphur fumes," Purvis said. "Not the first time we've lost a drunk out there. Won't be the last."

"Who signed the death warrant?"

"Doc Pritchard, I guess," Purvis said. "He does most of that."

"The same Doc Pritchard who's on your city payroll?"

"Don't see what that has to do with anything."

"I saw the body," Travis volunteered. "There was no question he'd suffocated."

"We're getting pretty far afield, here," Attorney Williams said, turning to Mary Beth. "Can you tell us any more about your dealings with Armitrage?"

"No. We sent him a check once a year, and he kept the city's subsidy money flowing. Everything went smoothly until he wanted a bigger cut."

"Bigger cut meant bigger risks," Purvis said. "Never smart to get too greedy. Skin a man more than once and you start to run out of hide."

"Any other kickbacks or payments involved?" the attorney asked.

"How do you mean?"

Williams stood up. "Was anybody else pocketing federal money?"

"Just the people on the town payroll," Mary Beth said. "But they worked for it."

Williams took a folder from Judith, pulled out a sheet of paper, and showed it to Mary Beth. "Is that your signature?"

Mary Beth glanced at the paper. "Yes, that's one of our Comet invoices."

Williams took another sheet from the folder. "What about this?"

Mary Beth glared at Judith. "Where did you get that?"

Purvis stepped between Williams and his sister. "What is it?"

"It's a copy of a signature card from a savings account," Williams said.

"A savings account where?" Purvis asked.

"The same bank where Armitrage did business under the name of Billings and Gates," Williams said. "He'd set up a separate account where he funneled ten percent of his take, regular as clockwork. He was the only one with access to the main account, but two names are on the signature card for the savings account."

"Let me see that." Purvis took the sheet from Williams. "The names here are D. W. Billings and Mary Gates."

Mary Beth looked down at her lap. "It's my signature."

"You better explain that to me," Purvis said.

Mary Beth twisted her handkerchief. "Armitrage said he'd put sixty-five hundred dollars a year away for me under the name Gates. I didn't know whether he did or not. I certainly never touched any of it. After Armitrage died, it was blood money."

The attorney exchanged glances with the federal marshal. "So you never touched the money?"

"Not even when I needed it for Stony."

Williams took the signature sheet back from Purvis. "You just embezzled instead."

"What's this about embezzlement?" Purvis asked.

"I'm sorry, Purvis." Mary Beth sighed. "I paid it all back before the auditor came."

Purvis held up both hands, palms outward. "I'm afraid that's all, gentlemen. I think my sister here definitely needs a lawyer."

Judith rose. "I hope that's not all. My client is in jail here because he's suspected of taking the funds that we just heard were embezzled by this man Armitrage."

"Your client has been jailed on a charge of double homicide," Williams said. "I don't see that one has anything to do with the other."

"My client was passed out at the bone pile," Judith said. "This man Armitrage died at the bone pile. They were both auditing a system that seems to be leaking money."

"That's just a coincidence," Travis Jenkins said.

"Coincidence or not, shouldn't somebody be investigating it?"

"Just like a lawyer," Travis said. "Blowing smoke at anything that moves."

Judith turned to Williams. "You argued at the bail hearing that the missing funds were my client's motive for murder. But he clearly had nothing to do with the missing money."

"That's so," Williams said. "Under the circumstances, I guess we can remove our objections to your client's release on bail."

"Why not drop the charges altogether?" Judith pressed.

"It's a double murder charge in a local jurisdiction. We don't have the authority to do that."

"When can I see the judge?"

"Judge is off fishing," Travis said. "Won't be back until the bail hearing."

"So my client has to stay in jail till then, even though the feds have dropped their objections to his release on bail?"

"Don't you worry," Travis said. "We'll take real good care of him."

"That's exactly what I'm afraid of." Judith turned to the federal attorney. "Please. Isn't there something we can do?"

"Not without the judge," Williams answered.

Purvis moved to stand behind Mary Beth. "What about my sister? Will you press charges?"

"That's up to the federal prosecutor," Williams said. "On the one hand, it's hard to see we've got anything to charge her with. She was coerced by Armitrage, and the money he set aside for her hasn't been touched." He paused and ran his finger over the folder he'd taken from Judith. "On the other hand, her signature is all over documents that were used to defraud the federal government."

"I ordered her to sign those invoices for the town," Purvis said. "And the federal government isn't coming after the town. In fact, our governor has found another tax pot to replace the bus payments."

Williams reached into the folder he was holding. "You didn't order her to sign this signature card."

"We only did such little things," Mary Beth said.

Purvis put his arm around his sister's shoulder.

"Such little things," she repeated, twisting her handkerchief in her lap.

Purvis tightened his grip on Mary Beth's shoulder. It wasn't clear that she could stay out of the coal cellar this time. It wasn't even clear to him that she deserved to.

21

THE DARKNESS WITHIN

STONY KNEW IT WAS A DREAM. The Dundee twins knelt in their combat fatigues on either side of him in a cavern that was much larger than any of those he'd crawled through in Vietnam. A searchlight rotated lazily behind them, throwing long shadows onto the forward cavern wall. That plinky Asian music started up and six Vietnamese children surrounded the searchlight, chanting and dancing in a circle. Stony recognized the shortest of the Vietnamese children, a young boy with coal black eyebrows and a scar that ran diagonally from above his left eye to his right earlobe. The boy wore shredded black pajamas, and his eyes never left Stony as he circled the searchlight.

The man who was Stony in the dream detached a hand grenade from his ammo belt. Stony knew what was coming, but was powerless to stop it. The Dundee twins knelt impassively beside the dream Stony as he pulled the pin, counted one-thousand-one, one-thousand-two, one-thousand-three, and rolled the grenade toward the search-light. The boy in shredded black pajamas broke ranks with the other children, watched the grenade as it wobbled toward him, and soccer kicked it back toward Stony.

Stony sucked in his breath as the grenade approached. For some reason he'd continued counting, one-thousand-six, one-thousand-seven, one-thousand-eight, but he couldn't move, couldn't shout, couldn't even exhale. The grenade bounced in front of him and kicked sideways, rolling to a stop against the cavern wall. Still unable to ex-hale, his mental count continued: one-thousand-nine, one-thousand-ten . . .

Stony woke up drenched in sweat, gasping to clear his clogged throat. He rolled to the side of his cot, grabbed his chamber pot, and spat a mixture of blood and phlegm into the porcelain container. Then he lay back on the cot and inhaled. He hadn't actually seen the boy's face, hadn't known it was a boy, until his grenade was well on its way. He was sure of that. As sure as he was of anything. But his dreams kept changing the timing, rearranging the perspec-tive, shifting the blame.

The cough was always worse in the morning, so he stayed close to the chamber pot as he pulled on his flannel workshirt and jeans. He checked the refrigerator and found two six-packs of Strohs and a dozen sticks of dyna-mite. He admired the symmetry of it. Twelve beers, twelve sticks of dynamite. It was all he'd need for the day. He opened a bottle of Strohs and swigged it as he carried a six-pack to the cooler in his truck. The beer soothed and calmed his throat. Best cough medicine in the world, he thought. He'd load the rest later, after he'd run his errands.

★ ★ ★

HE PARKED HIS truck in Mary Beth's driveway just as she was leaving for work. "Stuart's been coming around the mine a lot lately," he said through the window of her Chevy Nova.

"Stuart's at school already."

"I don't want him out at the mine. Don't want him mining."

"He just wants to be with you."

"Best he doesn't follow me to the mine. I don't want him mining."

"Is that beer on your breath? Stony, it's early in the morning."

Stony tried to suppress a cough, failed, and spat in the driveway. "I know what time it is, Goddamm it."

He wiped his mouth on the cuff of his flannel shirt and steadied himself against the side of the Nova. "Reckon you'll be taking up with that man Allison?"

"He's in jail."

"Don't expect him to be there much longer."

"I don't see it's any of your business who I take up with." She leaned forward to turn the key in the ignition.

Stony reached through the car window and grabbed Mary Beth's wrist. "That fellow you said tried to rape you. What was his name? I suppose that was none of my business either."

"Armitrage. His name was Armitrage. I was afraid . . ."

"So it's only my business when you're afraid?"

"That wasn't what I meant."

Stony released her wrist. "Jeb Stuart's always my business."

"Of course."

"Give me your word you won't let him go on mining."

"How can I do that?"

Stony started to reply, but found he didn't have the breath for it. Seized by a coughing spasm, he bent over the hood of Mary Beth's Nova. When he was finally able to breathe freely, he straightened himself and pounded a fist on the car roof. "I'm sorry. I'm not angry with you. It's this damn cough."

Mary Beth shifted into reverse. "See Doc Pritchard. Take care of it."

"I intend to take care of it," Stony said as Mary Beth backed out of the driveway. "I surely do."

TRAVIS JENKINS CONFISCATED Stony's bottle opener, pocket knife, and truck keys. "Not used to seeing you here as a visitor," the sheriff said.

"Just doing my civic duty."

"Well, don't plan on doing any more than ten minutes of it. I'll come get you when your time's up." He turned the key to let Stony into the cell. "You got another visitor," he told Owen.

Stony strode into the cell and held out his hand. "We met out to Pokey Joe's. Before that we met at the state baseball championships. But that was a while back."

"I know who you are," Owen said.

"You pitched for Barkley against us. We were expecting some big fireballer, but you came in and cut us down with junky stuff."

"The fireballer wrapped his motorcycle around a tree."

"That's what we heard." Stony straddled the dented metal chair. "Point is, you came in as a last-minute substitute and did just fine."

"You didn't come here to talk baseball."

"Nope, sure didn't." Stony looked around the bare cell. "This place smells."

Owen pointed his thumb at the next cell where Samuel was snoring. "Samuel there had a vomiting spell. We're not quite free of it yet."

"I've shared cells with Samuel before."

"Just why did you come?" Owen asked.

Stony scraped his chair closer to Owen and said in a low voice, "I know who killed Hatfield McCoy."

"Then we should get the sheriff."

Stony grabbed Owen's arm. "I'm not ready to talk to the sheriff just yet. You got to let me do this my way. I'll get you out of here, but you got to let me do it my way."

"How long is your way going to take?"

"You'll be out tonight. Tomorrow at the latest." Stony tipped forward on the metal chair. "But I need for you to promise you'll do something for me in return."

"Promise? Promise what?"

"You know my son Stuart?"

Owen nodded.

"I want you to promise me you'll take him away from coal country."

"Take him away . . . ?"

"Boy wants to be a miner. Hell, there aren't any miners anymore. Mining killed off the last three generations of Hobbses. Each one younger than the last."

"But how can I take him away?"

"I don't mean for you to kidnap him. Just take him away for a while. Take him back to D.C. with you. Show him there's other things to do besides picking coal. Help him find a little out-of-state college that needs a good catcher."

"Why don't you do this yourself?"

"Don't you think I would if I could?" Stony fought off a coughing spell and sucked in his breath. "I can't, that's all. Look at me. By the time I got out of here and saw there was something different, I was married and tied to mining. And what I saw in 'Nam made mining look awful good by comparison. I don't want that to happen to Stuart."

"What about Stuart's mom?"

"You want to take Mary Beth away, too, that's between you and her. You should know, though, Mary Beth will do whatever suits her best, regardless of Stuart."

"That's not what I meant."

"What did you mean?"

"Stuart lives with Mary Beth. She's his mother. She has to have a say in this."

"I think I can convince her. What'll it take to convince you?"

"I don't know. It sounds so crazy. Out of the blue."

Stony coughed into his handkerchief. "Look here. I've never had to ask nothing from nobody. I guess I'm not much good at it. But I'm asking you as best I can to take care of the one thing in the world that's dearest to me."

"Why me?"

"Because Jeb Stuart likes you. Because folks say you're straight. Because you're the only person I know with roots both inside and outside this county. Because if I get you out of this cell, you'll owe me. And because, God help me, I've flat run out of time to think of a better way."

"And you're sure you can get me out of here?"

"Sure as sunset. But I won't be around for Stuart after that."

"Then I'd be honored to look after Stuart."

Stony held out his hand. " 'Preciate it."

Owen took the hand. "Sorry I gave you grief about it at first."

"Don't see it matters much. There's enough grief in here to go around." Stony went to the cell door and called for the sheriff.

"Stuart's a good boy," Stony said as he waited.

"I know that."

Stony was silent as Travis let him out of the cell. After the door clanged shut, Stony grabbed a cell bar as if he wanted to reopen it. "The two of you'll do fine," he said through the bars.

"I know that, too," Owen said.

Travis yanked Stony's arm. "That's enough between the two of you."

Owen raised his hand and said, "Good luck."

Stony raised his hand in return and followed the sheriff down the corridor.

STONY SAT IN the cab of his truck with a lined yellow tablet on his lap, trying to get the facts straight in his mind. He was sure of most of them, but some still mixed with his nightmares in an uncertain brew. He took a long pull from the bottle of Strohs, licked the tip of his ballpoint pen, and began to write.

To Sheriff Jenkins and Judge Brown:

Owen Allison is innocent of the crimes he is charged with. I know because I killed Snooker Hatfield. The night it happened, I'd been watching my ex-wife's house and followed Allison in my truck when he left. I saw Hatfield McCoy and his cousin ambush him at the bone pile and stopped to help out. By the time I got there, Allison was out cold and Snooker had dragged him halfway down to the creek. I went after Snooker and we went at it. It took me some time to put Snooker down, and in the process I stove in his skull with a piece of shale.

When Snooker went down, Hatfield McCoy leveled a shotgun on me from the top of the bone pile. That's when Hollis Atkins hit McCoy's wheelchair from behind and knocked him down the slope. Hollis had spotted my truck and stopped to see what was going on. He is not to blame for what happened. He was only trying to save my life.

With my record, I thought it would go hard with me, so I took Snooker's body to the sinkhole and hid it. Hatfield McCoy's shotgun is in the creek below the sinkhole. Hollis Atkins will attest to the truth of this, but he is not to blame.

Stony read what he had written. It all seemed clear and right. He wasn't so sure of the rest of it. He'd been pretty drunk and pretty mad. But he wanted to get all of it down. He took another pull on the Strohs and continued.

I had been watching Mary Beth's house off and on ever since I caught the federal man Armitrage trying to rape her. I pulled him off her and hit him till he dropped. Then I hit him some more. I guess I didn't stop soon enough.

I'm sorry for the grief I caused, and for Mr. Allison being in jail. But I never took on anybody that didn't have it coming.

I swear this is all true.

(Signed) Stonewall Jackson Hobbs

It was true. He'd never taken on anybody that wasn't looking for trouble. Except for that Vietnamese boy in the tunnel. But what was he doing in the tunnel anyhow? What were either of us doing in the tunnel?

Stony folded the yellow sheets of paper and stuffed them into an envelope. How was he going to deliver it? Nobody had found the note he'd left in his mining shed when he was afraid he might not return from his throat operation. He had to make sure this letter found its way into the right hands. If he handed it to Travis now, though, the sheriff might arrest him before he finished what he had to do. He could mail the letter, but that would leave Owen Allison in jail at least two extra days while the post office fussed with it. Hollis was his best bet. He could trust Hollis to deliver the letter without looking at its contents. He could take a letter to Mary Beth, too.

"FIGURED YOU'D BE coming around," Hollis said when Stony walked into his office at the bus barn.

The aroma of wet pine from the creek bed outside mingled with the smell of axle grease and diesel fuel from the Quonset hut.

"There's a man in jail for what we did," Stony said.

"That's why I figured you'd be coming around."

"I'm fixing to get him out." Stony handed Hollis the

envelope with the letter he'd just written. "Anything happens to me, I want you to deliver this to the sheriff right away."

"Something likely to happen to you?"

"Never can tell. Life don't come with no guarantees." He pulled a second envelope from his jeans. "I've got one here for Mary Beth, too."

Hollis weighed the envelopes in the palm of his hand and laid them on his desk. "Never known you to write much."

"I wanted to get it right. The letter to Travis lays it all out, just the way it went down. Leaves you free and clear."

"Hatfield was drawing a bead on you. I didn't mean to kill him."

"You may have to come forward and testify. Don't worry about it. Just tell the truth. You'll be okay. I'm the one with the history of violence. I'm the one that hid Snooker's body. All you did was save my ass and pull Owen Allison out of the bone pile."

"If that guy with the flashlight hadn't showed up, we could have hid Hatfield, too. Maybe avoided all this."

"No need to tell anybody that. Just stick to what happened."

"That's likely to be hard on you," Hollis said.

"Believe me, Hollis, that's the least of my worries. Just see those letters get delivered if I'm not around."

"You can count on me."

"I know I can," Stony said. He held out his hand. "You've been a good friend, Hollis. I count myself lucky to have known you."

The extended hand seemed to startle Hollis. He stood

up, shook it, and said, "How about we go out to Pokey Joe's, down a few?"

"Can't. Got things to do."

"Hell, so do I," Hollis said. "Let's go anyhow. What's important in life?"

"Things I've got to do won't keep. You go, have one for me."

STONY LOADED THE dynamite and blasting caps into the rail cart and began shouldering it uphill toward the mine. He stopped on a level spot just short of the mine entrance and opened the last of the Strohs. The first gulp cooled his throat, and he let a little of the beer trickle under his sweaty collar. He fished a crumpled pack of Camels from his shirt pocket, struck a kitchen match on the side of the rail cart, lit the cigarette, and inhaled deeply. He followed the cigarette with a quick swig of beer to suppress the cough he felt welling up from his lungs.

The beer soothed his throat. Stony was surprised at how calm he felt. In Vietnam, he'd always been on edge. It was not knowing that brought the edginess. Not knowing what he might find in the next tunnel. Maybe he wouldn't be quiet enough. Or quick enough. Maybe they were already waiting for him. He peered through a puff of smoke at his blue dump truck and the gravel road that wound its way down to the creek bed. He'd run out of maybes. He knew what waited inside, and the knowledge calmed him.

He raised the beer bottle to his lips like a bugle and let the last of the liquid flow down his throat. Then he balanced the empty bottle carefully on the rail tie and dropped his cigarette down its neck. There was a faint hiss, and a thin wisp of smoke left the bottle and lost itself in the clear afternoon air.

Stony wedged his back against the cart and strained to move it uphill into the mine. The wheels creaked and the vibrations shook the bottle of Strohs off its rail perch. Stony paused and watched the bottle bump and roll downhill toward his dump truck. His back ached from the uphill push. Soon, he knew, the slope would crest and he could ride the cart downhill for a short stretch before he had to shove it deeper into the darkness.

22

THE TIE THAT BINDS

Owen awoke in his darkened cell to find Sheriff Travis Jenkins poking him in the ribs with a nightstick.

"Get up," the sheriff said. "You're free to go."

"What's going on?"

"Shh," the sheriff said. "No need to wake Samuel."

Deep, bone-rattling snores came from the next cell. Owen struggled to focus his eyes in the darkness and saw that his cell door was open. "What's going on?" he asked again.

"Stony Hobbs blew himself up this afternoon," the sheriff said. "He left a note saying he killed McCoy and his cousin. You're free to go."

"Where's Judith?"

"In her motel, I reckon. You want, I'll drive you over there."

"What time is it?"

"A little after ten. Most likely, she's still up."

Owen pulled his pants off the metal chair, which wobbled and scraped on the concrete floor.

"I told you to try not to wake Samuel," the sheriff rasped.

"Sorry. It's hard to see."

"You'll get used to it."

Owen struggled into his pants and shirt, then picked up the file folders. "I hope you've got my bill ready. I forgot to ask for a late checkout."

The sheriff took Owen's dress-up suit and tie and stood aside to let him lead the way out of the cell. "It's all taken care of."

IN THE OUTER office, a single hooded lamp was lit on a bare desk. Owen stopped at the waist-high gate separating the deputies' work stations from the public waiting room.

"There's a buzzer under the counter," the sheriff said. "On your left. It opens the gate."

Owen groped under the ledge without finding the buzzer. He set his papers on the counter and searched for the button with both hands.

"Let me get it," the sheriff said, moving up behind Owen.

As Owen stepped aside, the sheriff looped the white and yellow necktie over his head and twisted it tight around his windpipe.

Owen braced his feet against the locked gate and pushed off against the sheriff, who staggered backward, dragging Owen with him. The two men stumbled into

Owen's cell and fell hard, with Owen's skull cracking against the sheriff's jaw. Owen tore loose from the necktie and rolled free.

The sheriff rose to block the cell door. He unholstered his gun and flicked the necktie at Owen. "You're about to hang yourself."

"Why?"

"Remorse."

"If Hobbs confessed, why am I remorseful?"

The sheriff leveled his gun on Owen. "Nobody's ever going to read Hobbs's letter. I burned it."

Owen looked at the gun barrel. "Why?"

"Simple son of a bitch couldn't leave well enough alone. He confessed to killing your man Armitrage, too."

Owen retreated to the far corner of the cell. "My God."

"Trouble was, he said he beat Armitrage to death. Caught him with Mary Beth. Clobbered him pretty good."

Owen remembered the tape recorder in the next cell. "What's wrong with that?"

"Armitrage didn't die from Stony's beating. Stony was too drunk himself to do any lasting damage."

"Then how did he die?"

"He suffocated at the bone pile. Doc Pritchard signed off on it. So did I."

"But why burn the letter?"

"A drunk wandering into the bone pile's one thing. A beaten man being dragged there's another. It's a can of worms I don't want opened."

"You dragged him there. That's why you burned the letter. You took Armitrage to the bone pile."

"The sorry shit had been in Mary Beth's pants for years. He didn't deserve to live." The sheriff pointed his gun at Owen's crotch. "You've been humping her, too."

"Killing me won't give you a clear shot at Mary Beth. You've known her since you were kids and it hasn't done you any good."

The gun wavered in the sheriff's hand. "There was always Stony. Then that guy from D.C. showed up after the divorce. Now there's you." The sheriff steadied the gun and fixed it on Owen. "You should have gotten out when you found that coal in your car."

"You won't shoot me. It'll blow your suicide story."

"Don't be too sure I won't shoot. Maybe I caught you trying to escape."

"Maybe we need a witness to my escape." Owen kicked the metal chair sideways. As it clanged against the bars separating the cells, he yelled, "Wake up, Samuel!"

The gun barked. Concrete chipped at Owen's feet. "You'll be sorry you woke Samuel."

The smell of gunpowder filled the cell. "I thought we could use a witness."

"Samuel will say what I want him to say. Or he won't say anything."

"Hear that, Samuel?" Owen said, without taking his eyes off the sheriff. "He'll shoot you, too."

The sheriff holstered his gun. "Nobody's going to shoot anybody." He knotted Owen's necktie and stretched it taut. "We're just going to have a little hanging."

Travis shut the cell door. "Long as there's no note, Mary Beth stands to collect Stony's accidental death policy. Don't you want to help Mary Beth?"

Owen charged Travis, ramming him back against the

bars of Samuel's cell. Samuel's tattooed arm circled the sheriff's neck, while his free hand clamped the lawman's left wrist through the bars. Travis kicked out at Owen with his leather boots, but Samuel held him imprisoned against the bars.

Owen lifted the sheriff's gun, handcuffs, and keys from his belt and cuffed the lawman's flailing right wrist to the cell bars.

Owen used Travis's keys to unlock Samuel's cell door. "You got a place to go?"

"Away," Samuel said.

"Sounds like a solid plan. The quicker the better."

Samuel turned in the doorway, clicked his bare heels together, saluted the thrashing sheriff, and raced out.

The sheriff yanked at his handcuffs, rattling them up and down the restraining bar. "You're a dead man, motherfucker," he told Owen.

"Eventually. But not now. And not with my own necktie."

"You'll be back in this cell before morning."

"Not after I tell the feds what really happened at the bone pile. They're likely to be interested in how Armitrage got there, too."

Travis's handcuffs squealed up and down, leaving a silvery trail on the black cell bar. "I burned Hobbs's letter. It's my word against yours."

Owen turned over the metal chair in Samuel's cell and tore Judith's tape recorder free. "Not quite. It's your word against mine and Panasonic's."

"YOU GOT IT all on tape?" Judith asked. She sat on the edge of the rumpled motel bed wearing blue jeans and the extra-large T-shirt she'd been sleeping in when Owen pounded on her door.

"I haven't had time to check." Owen set the tiny recorder on the nightstand squeezed between the twin beds, rewound a short length of tape, and pushed the *play* button.

Samuel's snores came out loud and clear.

"At least we know the voice-activated feature works," Judith said.

"Shit," Owen said. "All we got were random cell noises."

"Let it run," Judith said. "Maybe you got something later."

"We don't have time to let it run. The sheriff will come here as soon as someone finds him."

"We'll deal with that when it happens. Let's see whether you recorded anything besides snores."

On the tape, a cell door creaked. The muted voice of the sheriff said, "Get up."

Owen turned up the volume. The sheriff's voice said, more clearly, "You're free to go."

Owen's voice answered, "What's going on?"

"Shh," the sheriff said. "No need to wake Samuel." Snores filled the background. Then the recorder clicked off.

"Out of tape," Owen said. "We ran out of tape."

"You got a little bit of the sheriff."

"Nothing incriminating."

"Enough to show he let you go."

"He'll try to get me back as soon as he gets loose. He's got it in his head I'm all that stands between him and Mary Beth. I think I should take your car and head out of these hills."

Judith took her car keys from her purse. Instead of giving them to Owen, she held them in a tight fist. "It's too risky. If Travis catches you out there, he'll shoot first and claim you were an armed fugitive."

"He'll do the same if he catches me here, and this is the first place he'll look."

"He won't shoot you if you're in federal custody."

"Oh, sure. The feds have been a big help so far. If it weren't for them I'd be out on bail."

"I think we should take them this tape and tell them your story."

"What if they turn me over to Travis?"

"I don't see how they can do that."

"It's his jurisdiction."

"You wait here. I'll take the tape and try to cut a deal. Williams's room is just down the hall."

"Williams is their attorney?"

"The one who looks like George C. Scott. He's not a bad guy."

"What if they won't deal?"

"Then we've lost five minutes." Judith pulled a blue crew-neck sweater over her T-shirt. "Got a better idea?"

"Leave me your car keys."

She took his wrist and placed the keys in his hand. "It's the rented white Camaro in the side lot." Still holding his wrist, she said, "Promise me you won't leave until I've talked to Williams."

Owen opened the curtains. "I'll wait in the car and watch this window. If you cut a deal, close these curtains and I'll come in. If the light comes on and the curtains don't close, I'm gone."

★   ★   ★

THE CAMARO SMELLED of stale cigarette smoke. The dashboard clock read ten minutes to eleven. Ten minutes until the night shift came on at the jail. An early arrival might have found Travis already. Judith's motel would be the first place they'd come. They wouldn't know which car was hers, but her room would be the first place they'd look. Her window was still dark.

Owen shifted in the driver's seat. The gun he'd taken from the sheriff chafed the small of his back. He felt his edge slipping away. He could have been on the road to D.C., Barkley, California, anywhere. But Judith was right; if that badged maniac caught up with him on the road, he'd shoot to kill. Still, the sheriff couldn't operate outside the county. Owen fingered the key in the ignition. Hell, why wouldn't Travis cross the county line? There was no jurisdiction on a bullet.

Judith's window was still dark. A loaded coal train rumbled along the riverbank. Owen knew from the eastbound direction and the sonorous roar that the hoppers were full. He could catch up with the train and ride the cars to Hampton Roads. Travis wouldn't check the coal train. Owen remembered riding it as a kid. Well, starting to, anyhow. He'd gotten off at the first water stop, while Wes Whitfield rode all the way to Norfolk.

Eight minutes to eleven. How long would it take to get Travis free of his handcuffs? Most likely, there was an extra key somewhere. He listened for the sound of sirens.

The light went on in Judith's window. Owen turned the key in the ignition. Then the curtains closed and he killed the motor.

★ ★ ★

"IS THAT ALL you've got?" Williams, the federal attorney, nodded toward the tape recorder on the motel room table. He was wearing navy blue suitpants and red plaid suspenders over a starched white T-shirt.

"That, my word, and my bruises," Owen said. He lifted his chin to show the skin rubbed raw by the makeshift noose.

Williams reached out and traced the bruises on Owen's neck with his thumb. "What kept him from killing you?"

"He got too close to the prisoner in the next cell, a Vietnam vet named Samuel. Samuel held Travis while I let us both out."

Williams picked up the tape recorder. "There's not enough here for a conviction."

"Travis doesn't know that," Owen said. "He almost tore the bars down when he saw I had a tape recorder in the cell."

"You're suggesting we try to bluff him?"

"Why not? You kept me in jail with less evidence than I've got on that tape."

One of the federal marshals who had arrested Owen came through the door wearing a shoulder holster over blue striped pajamas. When he saw Owen, he reached for his gun.

Williams stopped him by raising his hand, palm outward. "It's all right, Stephens. Mr. Allison here may not be the bad guy after all."

"That's for the judge to decide," Stephens said.

Owen edged toward the door. "I'm not going back to that man's jail."

"Technically, we're in his jurisdiction," Williams said.

Judith stepped between Owen and the marshal's gun. "Don't renege on me here," she told Williams. "You agreed to protect Owen."

"Best way to do that is to get him out of the county."

Sirens wailed. "Too late for that," Stephens said.

Three squad cars sprayed gravel as they squealed into the parking lot.

"They outnumber us," Stephens said.

"We could be better off that way," Williams said. "Travis won't try anything in front of lots of deputies. If he comes up alone, though, we could all be in trouble." Williams took Owen's arm and gestured toward the bathroom. "Probably best if you're out of sight."

"What about Judith?"

"She'd better wait with us. There's safety in numbers. If she's alone, Travis might be tempted to manhandle her to locate you."

Owen had just closed the bathroom door when he heard a fist pounding on the outer door and Travis shouting, "Open up, it's the sheriff."

Travis's voice, louder now, bellowed, "Keep your hands away from that holster, mister."

Then Williams's voice, "There's no need to wave those guns around."

"I'm looking for this lawyer lady's ex," Travis said. "I'm asking you, lawman to lawman, if you've seen him."

"I'm not answering so long as you're pointing guns at us."

"He won't get away. My boys have the motel surrounded and we've blocked off every route out of town."

The bathroom door was hinged to open inward, hiding the shower fixture. Owen stepped into the shower.

"He's been here, hasn't he?" Travis said. "That's why the three of you are having this pajama party."

Owen took the sheriff's gun from under his shirt and hefted it, wondering if it had a safety.

"Shit, he must still be here."

Owen's hand closed around the pistol. If it had a safety, he hoped it was off.

"You there in the bathroom, Allison? You in there, you're dead meat."

The bathroom door slammed open. Travis came through sideways, one pistol pointing back at the federal marshal, the other leveled at the toilet.

Owen stepped out from behind the door and aimed his pistol at the sheriff's navel. "Drop both those guns, Travis, or there'll be more dead meat here than you expected."

Travis hesitated.

"Drop them," Owen repeated.

The pistols clattered on the floor.

"You won't get anywhere," the sheriff said. "My boys have the motel surrounded."

"That doesn't matter," Williams said. "This man surrendered voluntarily to me. He's in federal custody."

"You feds have funny ideas about custody. Looks to me like he's got a gun in his hand."

Owen handed the pistol to Williams, who kept it trained on Travis Jenkins.

"That man's my prisoner," Travis said. "He escaped from my jail. This is my jurisdiction."

"He says you set him free. Says you tried to strangle him."

"Bullshit. Him and Samuel got the drop on me. I roughed

him up a little trying to keep him in his cell, but the two of them were too much for me."

"So you didn't unlock his cell door and tell him he was free to go?"

"Do I look like the Prisoner's Aid Society to you?"

"Maybe we ought to play him the tape." Owen placed the recorder on the nightstand and pushed the *play* button.

The sound of Samuel's snores filled the room, followed by Travis's voice saying, "Get up. You're free to go."

Travis lunged for the recorder.

Owen snatched up the recorder and shut it off. "The rest of this tape is likely to embarrass you, Sheriff. Maybe you'd rather talk to Williams here, lawman to lawman."

"You son of a bitch," Travis said. "He raped Mary Beth."

"This man raped someone?" Williams asked.

"No, the other federal son of a bitch. The one in the bone pile."

Owen flipped the tape recorder to Williams. "Get him to tell you about the bone pile. Lawman to lawman." He took Judith's arm and started to leave the room.

"You can't let him go," Travis said. "He's in custody."

"According to the tape, you already let him go," Williams said. "Looks to me like you're the one in custody now."

23

THE FACTS OF LIFE
(AND DEATH)

Owen and Judith watched from her motel window as the sheriff's squad cars left the parking lot.

"There goes Travis, back to his own jail," Judith said.

"Can't think of a better place for him."

"That's for sure." Judith closed the curtains as the sound of sirens faded into the night. "They ought to clear out a cell for your girlfriend, too."

"Mary Beth? Why would she go to jail?"

"She told her violent ex-husband and a psychotic cop with the hots for her that Armitrage tried to rape her. You think she didn't know what would happen?"

"He did try to rape her. Purvis said so."

"She probably staged it. After all, she was sleeping with Armitrage."

"He forced her to."

"For four years? Face it, Owen, your little friend's about as exclusive as the IRS. And just as greedy."

"Why greedy?"

"Think, Owen. Who was the only person besides Armitage who stood to profit from any of this?"

"Mary Beth never touched a cent of that money."

"That's because things got out of hand and escalated to murder. You can bet she would have drained those accounts once the statute of limitations ran out."

"You don't know that."

"You're right, I don't."

"Even if what you say is true, she hasn't done anything indictable."

"How about conspiracy to defraud the government?"

"You said it was Armitage's idea. And Purvis runs the Contrary Comet. Nobody's going after Mary Beth."

"You could be right about that. Armitage took the money and he's dead. It all ties up neatly for the feds. They may still decide to prosecute, though. After all, your little friend was the Gates in 'Billings and Gates.' "

"Next you'll be telling me she hired Hatfield to assault me, told Travis to strangle me, and faked her orgasms."

"I can't speak for her orgasms, but you were always a sucker for a couple of quick moans and a long sigh." Judith made a kissing noise with her lips. "As for Hatfield and Travis, they probably acted on their own. There was no reason for Mary Beth to want you dead. You were no threat to her. But there's no question she got Travis to burn Stony's letter."

"What makes you think that?"

"Travis told you about Stony's insurance. He wouldn't

have known about that unless he'd talked to Mary Beth. She's smart enough to know she couldn't collect accidental death insurance with a suicide note floating around."

"Anybody else figure in your conspiracy theory? The CIA? Martians?"

"I just don't want to see you hurt."

"That's a new concern for you."

"I don't deserve that."

"You're right. I'm sorry. You've been great through all of this." He reached to touch her but she slapped his hand away.

"No kidding," Owen said. "You handled the law, planted the tape recorder, and stood up to Travis and his guns."

"You're right. I'm really pretty terrific."

Owen joined her on the bed. "I'm glad we got that settled."

"You know, there was a conspiracy of sorts against you. Williams told me your boss was manufacturing evidence to use against you. Most of it was so flimsy Williams wouldn't touch it. We could go after your boss if you want."

"Go after Bashford? In court, you mean?"

"That's what I do. In this case it'd be a real pleasure."

"I've had enough of courts and Bashford to last me a lifetime. I hope I never see either one again."

"You mean you're not going back to work for the feds?"

"Not now. Not ever."

"What'll you do?"

"Move back to California. Maybe try to build a consulting firm again."

"It might work this time. You seem to be a little less rigid."

"Less rigid?"

"The Owen I used to know would never have signed that Contrary invoice."

"Look where it got me."

"It worked out all right in the end."

"It hasn't ended. Stony Hobbs asked me to take his son away from here. That's why he blew up the mine. He wasn't after insurance. He just didn't want his boy to grow up working underground."

"That's a pretty drastic solution."

"I got the impression he never did anything easy in his life."

"Will you do it? Take the boy, I mean."

"If he'll come. If Mary Beth will let him go."

"It's not a package deal? The mother doesn't come with the son?"

"Stony didn't seem to think so."

"What do you think?"

"I think Stony was probably right."

"He chose well. You'd make a good father."

"You didn't always think so."

"I was wrong about a lot of things. I hadn't seen you face down a gun-toting sheriff."

"I was trembling in the bathroom while he was waving his guns at you. I still don't know if my safety was on or off."

"You looked as if you knew what you were doing. You bluffed him with the recorder, too."

"You're the one that planted the recorder in the first place. I've still got lipstick on my fly."

"We had to make it look good for Samuel. And Travis, too, if he was watching."

Owen slumped down on the bed and lay back on a pillow. "You know, I've got no place to go tonight."

"Think they won't hold your cell at the jail?"

"I imagine they've already released it to our friend Travis."

Judith stretched out beside him. "What did you have in mind?"

"How about a little game of 'Hide the Recorder'?"

"I left the recorder with Williams."

"Couldn't we just, you know, go through the motions without it?"

"You mean, like, practice?"

"Just in case we ever have to hide one again."

Judith traced the line of his chin with her finger. "You've had a hard day. Are you sure you're up for it?"

Owen captured her finger and kissed it. "Maybe not. You just said you thought I was less rigid then I used to be."

She unbuttoned the top button of his shirt. "I've been wrong about a lot of things lately."

PURVIS JENKINS AND Hollis Atkins were sitting on the front stoop of Mary Beth's house when Owen arrived to attend Stony Hobbs's wake. Both men were nursing clear drinks and sweating in the late afternoon heat.

Hollis kneaded the knuckles of his calloused hands. "I should of seen it coming. I should have stopped him."

"No way you could of seen it," Purvis said.

"Man gives me two letters to deliver if something happens to him. Don't tell me I shouldn't of seen it coming."

"Nothing you could have done. A man like Stony

who's really set on blowing himself up will do it with a soggy firecracker if he has to."

Hollis cracked a knuckle. "Should of seen it coming."

"Did you say Stony gave you two letters to deliver?" Owen asked.

"Two letters," Hollis bowed his head. "One to the sheriff, one to Mary Beth."

"Things haven't been easy for Mary Beth since this thing broke," Purvis said. "Seems like the whole town's against her. She's trying to make amends by holding Stony's wake."

"Why's the whole town against her?" Owen asked.

"Her being in bed with Armitrage, for one thing."

"Seems like the town's known about that for some time," Owen said. "Everyone but me, in fact."

"A divorcée sleeping with a man on the sly just makes for good gossip," Purvis said. "Sleeping with him for money, though, especially when it's the town's money, now that's a horse of a different hue."

Owen saw Mary Beth through the window, serving coffee to a squat, balding man he didn't recognize. Her blond hair was drawn back tightly in a French twist, and she wore a severe black pantsuit. If she saw him, she gave no sign.

Owen patted Hollis on the shoulder and walked up the steps between the two men. "Purvis is right, Hollis. You couldn't have done anything."

INSIDE, WOMEN CLUSTERED around the dining room table, occasionally breaking free to carry coffee or beer to men in ill-fitting dark suits who conversed in low tones in the corners of rooms. Owen saw that the couch on which he'd first made love to Mary Beth had been removed. In its place was a closed oak coffin set on two sawhorses covered with black crepe paper. A framed photograph of a young Stony wearing a cloth army cap smiled out at mourners from atop the coffin. A purple sash holding a large gold medal was draped over the photo.

"My God," Owen said. "That's the Congressional Medal of Honor."

Mary Beth came up behind him. "A lot of good it did him."

"I didn't know."

"He didn't broadcast it."

"Can we talk somewhere? In private?"

Mary Beth took his hand and led him past the accusing eyes of the women in the dining room into a small laundry room off the kitchen.

"I'm sorry about Stony," Owen began.

"Thank you."

"He came to see me the day he died."

"I know."

"He asked me to see that Stuart doesn't stay in Contrary."

"I know. He left me a letter."

"I thought Stuart might visit me this summer. After school's out."

"In Washington?"

"Actually, I'm thinking of moving to California. I won't take him if you don't agree."

"It's what Stony wanted."

"Then it's all right with you?"

"I think so, for the summer. After that, we'll see. My future's none too certain, as I'm sure you know." She started to open the laundry room door, then turned to ask, "Did Stony leave you a note?"

"A note?"

"Asking you to take Stuart?"

"No. He just visited my cell."

"That's good. Notes make it look like he committed suicide."

"But he did commit suicide."

"No, it was a mining accident. Otherwise there's no insurance. There's an insurance investigator nosing around outside. It's best if you don't tell *anyone* about Stony's visit."

"You're asking me to lie for you?"

"You shouldn't have to lie. Just don't volunteer any information about Stony's visit. And it's not only for me, it's for Stuart as well."

"How is it for Stuart?"

"The money will send him to college. And you want me to approve his stay with you."

"Are you saying his coming to California hinges on what I tell the insurance investigator?"

Mary Beth grasped Owen's wrist. "Let me just say it again." Her eyes froze and hardened like blue agates. "It's best if you don't tell *anyone* about Stony's visit."

"Not even Stuart?"

"Especially not Stuart."

"I ought to talk to him about California." Owen pulled his wrist free of Mary Beth's grasp. "If that's all right with you."

"He's out on the back porch. Just remember our little talk."

★   ★   ★

STUART SAT ALONE on the back steps thumping a scuffed baseball into his catcher's mitt. He barely looked up when Owen sat down beside him.

"I'm sorry about your dad," Owen said.

Stuart squeezed the mitt hard around the scuffed ball. "I didn't catch the way he wanted me to."

Owen put his arm around Stuart's shoulder.

"I would have tried it his way," Stuart said. "There just wasn't time."

"Your dad was proud of your catching. He told me so."

"You talked to him?"

"A few days . . . no, some time ago. He said he hoped you'd go on catching in college."

"He never went to college."

"He went to war instead."

"You see his medal?"

"It's quite a medal. The best there is."

"Bet your ass," Stuart said.

Beyond the hollow the pointed tips of birch trees sawed at the edge of the setting sun. A few lightning bugs dotted the heavy grass between the back porch and the garage. Crickets chirped in the creek below the garage.

"I'm going back to California soon," Owen said. "How'd you like to come along and spend the summer with me?"

"Would Mom come?"

"No," Owen said quickly. "She might visit. Mostly, though, it'd be just you and me."

"I don't know. All my friends are here."

"They'll still be here when you get back."

"Where in California?"

"San Francisco. We could watch the Giants. And the A's, too."

"Is Disneyland near there?"

"No. But we could drive down to Disneyland if we wanted."

Stuart thumped the ball into his catcher's mitt. "What would I do?"

Owen squeezed Stuart's shoulder. "I'm not even sure what I'm going to do. We could find out together."

"What'd my mom say?"

"She said it's up to you."

The ball thumped into the mitt.

"Your dad said he thought it would be a good idea if you got away from these hills for a while."

"You and dad talked about me?"

"He didn't want to talk about much else. He loved you."

"He tell you that?"

"He didn't have to."

Stuart wiped his nose with the wristband of his catcher's mitt. "I never told him that."

"You didn't have to."

Stuart shrugged off Owen's arm and stood up. Keeping his back to Owen, he asked, "You say he wanted me to go? To California, I mean?"

"That's what he said."

"Then I'll do it." Stuart walked a few steps to the garage and laid his glove and ball carefully inside the door. Without looking back, he stuck his hands in his pockets and walked down the slope toward the creek.

★   ★   ★

As SOON AS Stuart disappeared, Mary Beth joined Owen on the back porch. She was carrying a handful of crumpled napkins.

"Stuart says he'll come to California," Owen said. "For the summer."

"It's what Stony wanted." Mary Beth sat down on the step above Owen's. "I understand you're back with your ex-wife."

"Who told you that?"

She smoothed the crumpled napkins on her lap. "Sheriff Jenkins."

"Have you seen him since they locked him up?"

"Certainly not."

"Then you talked to him before. You talked to him about Stony's letter, didn't you?"

"I only asked him not to make the letter public. The same as I asked you not to tell about Stony's talk. For the insurance."

"Mary Beth. That letter had information clearing me. Travis burned it."

"I'm sorry, Owen. I surely didn't know everything that was in the letter. I hope you don't think . . ."

"You knew Travis killed Armitrage."

"I knew no such thing."

"You knew Stony had beaten him senseless."

"Stony caught him trying to rape me."

"This was after he'd tried to rape you in Pokey Joe's parking lot?"

"After I'd gone home."

"He tried to rape you twice in one day?"

Mary Beth twisted the top napkin. "I hope you don't think I led him on."

"I think you led him just far enough to get him into the sights of Stony and the sheriff."

"I had no control over the sheriff. Or Stony either, for that matter."

"I think you counted on them to scare Armitrage off. The same way you're counting on me to lie to the insurance investigator."

"It's not the same thing at all. I had no idea Travis would kill Armitrage."

"You underestimated his obsession. He didn't stop there. He tried to kill me because of you."

"I had nothing to do with that."

"Maybe not. But he sure cut a bloody path through your suitors."

Mary Beth stood to go back inside. "I thought we had something special."

Owen squinted into the setting sun. "So did I. We were both wrong."

ON HIS WAY out Owen stopped in front of Stony's coffin.

"Friend of the deceased?" a voice asked.

"Only met him once or twice."

"Damn shame. Young feller like that, blowing himself to bits."

Owen turned to see the squat balding man he'd watched earlier taking coffee from Mary Beth.

"Doug Taylor, Providential Insurance."

"Investigator?"

The man pursed his lips and nodded.

"A little out of place here, aren't you?" Owen asked.

"Just trying to get things squared away as soon as possible. You see the deceased recently?"

Owen saw Mary Beth watching him. "The day he died."

"He seem despondent to you? Like he'd have any reason to take his own life?"

The sun's glare obscured the picture of Stony and made a fiery circle of the medal on the coffin.

Owen ignored the question and told the truth as he knew it. "Stony Hobbs? Stony Hobbs was a hero. A certified local hero."

OWEN WATCHED AS the two-engine turbo prop approached the Huntington airport. When he had been in high school, the entire Marshall College football team had died when their plane had failed to make the runway on a rainy return from a road game. Ever since then, flying into the airport made Owen nervous. On the other hand, flying out never bothered him.

"Is that our plane?" Stuart asked. "It looks pretty small."

"It'll get us to Cincinnati," Owen said. "We'll take a bigger plane out of there into San Francisco."

"Will it be a bumpy ride?"

Owen looked up into the cloudless blue sky. "Not enough to notice."

Stuart hoisted his duffel bag onto his shoulder. STONEWALL JACKSON HOBBS, US ARMY was stenciled in fading letters on the side of the bag.

"You'll write now, won't you, honey?" Mary Beth said.

"We'll call as soon as we arrive," Owen said.

"Don't worry, Mom," Stuart said. "Know what?"

"What?" Mary Beth nearly shouted to make herself heard over the plane's engine.

"When I get to California, I think I'll use my whole name."

"Stony would like that," Mary Beth said.

"He always called me Jeb Stuart."

"Jeb Stuart Hobbs," Owen said. "It's a good name."

The plane taxied up to the fence where the passengers waited.

Stuart shifted his duffel bag and hugged his mother awkwardly.

"You take good care of him, you hear?" she said to Owen.

"Don't worry about us," Owen said.

The ground attendant opened the fence gate and Owen led Stuart toward the plane. When they reached the roll-out steps, he stepped aside, "After you, Jeb Stuart."

The boy clambered up the four steps, stopped at the cabin entrance, lowered his duffel bag, waved over Owen's shoulder to his mother, and ducked inside.

Owen could feel Mary Beth's eyes on him as he followed her son up the roll-out steps. He lowered his head to clear the cabin threshold and entered the plane without looking back.

John Billheimer, a native of West Virginia, lives in Portola Valley, California. This is his first novel.